4.19 R

CELG

JH

JUN -- 2017

The
Amish Heart
of ICE MOUNTAIN

Center Point
Large Print

The
Amish Heart
of ICE MOUNTAIN

Kelly Long

CENTER POINT LARGE PRINT
THORNDIKE, MAINE

This Center Point Large Print edition is published
in the year 2017 by arrangement with
Kensington Publishing Corp.

The text of this Large Print edition is unabridged.
In other aspects, this book may vary
from the original edition.
Printed in the United States of America
on permanent paper.
Set in 16-point Times New Roman type.

ISBN: 978-1-68324-347-2

Library of Congress Cataloging-in-Publication Data

Names: Long, Kelly, author.
Title: The Amish heart of Ice Mountain / Kelly Long.
Description: Center Point Large Print edition. | Thorndike, Maine :
Center Point Large Print, 2017.
Identifiers: LCCN 2016059553 | ISBN 9781683243472
    (hardcover : alk. paper)
Subjects: LCSH: Amish—Fiction. | Large type books. | GSAFD: Love
stories. | Christian fiction.
Classification: LCC PS3612.O497 A827 2016 | DDC 813/.6—dc23
LC record available at https://lccn.loc.gov/2016059553

The
Amish Heart
of ICE MOUNTAIN

Prologue

Ice Mountain, Coudersport, PA
Thirteen Years Ago

He was fascinated by the work his *grossdaudi* did deep in the woods, all of the mixing and heat and bubbling. But when he reached out to touch the copper tubing, his grandfather gave him a slap in the mouth that sent him reeling across the forest floor. He slowly got to his feet, looking up at his *grossdaudi* as he wiped the blood from his mouth. For a moment something wavered in the *auld* man's eyes that he didn't understand, but then his grandfather bent over the spout and poured a fair portion of clear liquid into a Mason jar and handed it to him.

"Drink it," the old man commanded.

He drank. The stuff burned the back of his throat like fire and he choked and coughed. His *grossdaudi* laughed. "You'll soon get used to it, *buwe*."

And he did. He found, at eight years of age, that the liquid calmed him after the burn, made him feel warm and tight in his belly, in the place in his heart where he missed his dead *mamm* the most. But it was his and *grossdaudi*'s secret—that clear liquid fire. . . . Not for any on Ice Mountain to know. And he drank . . .

7

Chapter One

Ice Mountain, Coudersport, PA
The Present Day

The late-day summer storm came up fast and furious, splattering twenty-one-year-old *Amisch* Edward King with leaves and small branches as he dragged his tall frame from the damp pine needle floor of the forest. He rubbed his hands over his eyes, gave up his hat for lost, and decided he'd better seek shelter as soon as possible.

Then he remembered . . . His *aulder bruder*, Joseph, had essentially kicked him out of the *haus* that afternoon for drinking and other things he'd prefer not to think on.

"*Gott*," he muttered, pushing through the whipping trees in the general direction of *Grossmuder* May's cabin. The *auld* woman had been a healer to the *Amisch* community, and Edward had the idle thought that her recent passing was a sad loss, but right now all he wanted was the dryness of her temporarily empty cabin.

He staggered on, his white shirt and black pants clinging to him as he swiped the rain from his mouth and hitched up a suspender. It was rough going in the pelting storm, but he walked on, used to the feeling of getting through life half blind. He sighed to himself as lightning formed an angry zigzag in the distance, casting an almost greenish glow over everything that cowered beneath the rain.

Finally he gained the cabin and clambered up the front porch steps to open the unlocked door and collapsed in a heap on the hard wood kitchen floor.

"I'll find the bed later," he muttered aloud to himself, then gave in to the blissful pull of drunken sleep.

Sarah Mast, the new young healer of Ice Mountain, pushed the bedstead back against the wall of the cabin's bedroom and heard a loud thump. She shivered a bit, still not used to living in *Grossmuder* May's *auld* home even after two days, and decided that a limb had probably struck the front of the cabin. She dusted her hands on her white apron, then walked into the kitchen, only to stop dead still at the sight of the man lying in a growing puddle upon the floor.

He groaned and turned his face slightly and she drew in a sharp breath. She recognized the dark blond hair, handsome face, and lithe body only too well. *Edward King . . . There was a time, not too long ago, when I would have done anything he asked of me, when I kissed his mouth with hot ease, when I let him* . . . She drew her thoughts up sharply. Of course, she'd never let him trespass on her virtue . . . *but maybe I wanted him to.* . . . She banished the thought; that was all before he'd left the mountain to work on the Marcellus Shale gas rigs. *He left to make money so we could wed sooner . . . well, that's all turned out beautifully.* She smiled wryly, then sat down at the table to eat a makeshift supper of fresh bread and apple butter. She eyed Edward's inert figure impassively, then rose to wash her dishes, not bothering to be especially quiet in the process. Then she retook her seat at the table with a cup of licorice tea.

He stirred soon, as she'd expected he would, clutching his head, then raising himself up on his elbows. "*Ach*, my head," he moaned.

"Fresh ginger root, lemon juice, honey, and a bit of potassium," Sarah recited from memory.

"What?" He frowned.

"The cure for what ails you," she said succinctly. "You look terrible."

"*Danki*, Sarah. . . . So are you gonna get that stuff for me or what?"

"*Nee.*" She tapped a foot while she sipped a bit of tea. "I think the headache will do you *gut.*" She ignored the impulse of her fingers to bring him immediate relief and tried to remember how he'd been treating her lately.

He raised a soaked arm and she had to look

10

away from the play of well-defined muscles beneath his plastered white shirt. "Joseph threw me out."

"As well he might."

"Yeah, but this cabin was supposed to be deserted for a bit." He dragged himself to a sitting position and looked up at her, owl-eyed. "Why are you here, sweet?"

She ignored the endearment. "I'm the new healer, remember?"

He almost scowled. "How can I forget? I'm surprised your *fater* is actually going to let you live here alone. *Gott* knows he would have killed me had he figured out we were . . ."

She straightened her back. *We were . . . past tense. Well, he's finally* kumme *out and said it at least . . . even though I was the one who told him it was over. . . . Has it only been a day since that conversation?*

She'd stood tense and trying to be resolute in one of her *fater*'s smaller barns while Edward had slipped inside their place of many meetings. She'd taken in his tall frame, lithe grace, and handsome half smile and told herself that she was being a fool. She knew that his drinking was probably more than occasional and he'd been avoiding her like the plague lately, not even so much as helping her down from a high step at Ben Kauffman's store. *I deserve better,* she'd told herself as he sauntered close. But, unfortunately,

11

there was none better than Edward King on the mountain, and the man knew it. She'd pursed her lips. *Better to court some ugly man with a good heart than to be dragged about by my feelings* . . . But when Edward reached out a hand to lazily run his finger down the length of her arm, she knew she'd never be content with anyone but him. She'd steeled her senses and swallowed.

"I've been wanting to talk with you," he'd whispered huskily.

"I find that hard to believe," she'd snapped, ignoring the fact that he'd circled behind her to press close against her skirts, his hands now on her shoulders.

She shivered, knowing it would be so easy to melt back against him and let him touch and feel and . . . "I want to break our courtship."

She felt the sudden tension in his body as his hands slipped from her and he came back around to look down at her.

"What did you say?"

She wet her lips. "You—you heard me."

"Why?"

She wanted to curse; he actually sounded curious.

"Because you've wanted to break it, too, Edward King. You've barely looked at me since you got back from the rigs, and I know that you've been drinking and—I—I want it over, that's all."

He smiled, a wolfish look that made her shiver with suppressed excitement, and bent closer to her.

"I wrote a letter," he murmured.

"What?" she asked in confusion, knowing she had seen no missive from him nor was it his habit to write love letters; still, the idea intrigued her despite her assertion that she wanted to end their relationship. "What letter?"

"A letter to someone higher up who works at the Marcellus Shale; you know, the gas find? Well, one of their drilling companies—I've invited them to Ice Mountain." He thumbed his way around her throat and she blinked, then parted her lips in surprised anger.

"What are you talking about, Edward? Do you know what it would mean if geologists found gas here and then . . ."

"Sarah? Be you in there?" Her *fater*'s voice penetrated the peg-and-groove wood of the door, and she stared at Edward in rising panic.

But he'd merely shrugged and slipped behind a high pile of hay, leaving her to face her father's curiosity alone.

"I'm sorry," he said roughly, and she jumped, coming back to the present. She couldn't control the physical response she had to the deep timbre of his voice. It was as though someone had run a warm finger down her spine, and she shifted a bit on the hard-backed chair.

"What for?" she asked dryly. "Us? Or the fact that you invited Marcellus Shale to Ice Mountain?"

Edward's frown deepened. "I wasn't thinking when I wrote to the gas company."

"*Nee*, and you were probably drinking," she pointed out, ignoring the inner voice that told her she was being truthful yet cruel.

"Well," he sighed. "You're probably right at that. I'd better get going." He started to haul himself to his feet, then paused to cover his mouth as he sneezed.

She listened for a moment to the heavy rain on the cabin roof and drew a deep breath. "You'll catch pneumonia, Edward. Stay here and dry your shirt and go when the storm passes."

He stood up and met her eyes with his piercing blue gaze. "You sure, Sarah?"

She nodded. *But I'm not sure at all,* she thought wildly when he eased his suspenders down and began to pull pins from his shirtfront with long fingers.

She got up and turned to the refuge of the huge cupboard *Grossmuder* May had left behind, willing to Sarah a wealth of cures and comforts. She tried to focus on some of the bottles of rarer herbs, but he sneezed again. She grabbed a ginger root and had begun to grate it when a loud knock sounded on the front door.

"Sarah!" a voice boomed, louder than the thunder, and she turned to look at the barechested

14

Edward in slow, dawning horror. It was her *fater*. . . .

Life and protocol for the Mountain *Amisch* was far behind modern times. There was a rigid code of honor that existed among his people and he knew that being in a state of undress with an unmarried girl was simply not acceptable. Edward shuddered, knowing that Mahlon Mast was enough of a bully to force a marriage out of such circumstances, and he longed for the *auld* pegged wooden floor to open up and swallow him whole. But no such thing happened, and the front door opened to reveal not only Mahlon Mast but Bishop Umble as well.

Edward muttered a curse under his breath as the two older men stared at him in mute fascination and dawning disapproval, while he stood, shivering, in the sudden influx of cool air from the rain outside. *Great . . . This looks great . . .*

He glanced at Sarah, who appeared frozen with a ginger root in her hand, her gray eyes wide and scared. *Damn her* fater *anyway. The girl is our healer—it should be perfectly fine if I have my shirt off. She shouldn't have to be frightened. . . .*

He straightened his bare shoulders and turned to face the other men.

"You!" Mahlon Mast sputtered, lifting a meaty hand to point a finger as thick as a sausage at him.

Bishop Umble frowned, obviously catching the drift of Sarah's *fater*'s thoughts. "Now, Mahlon . . ."

"I got caught in the storm. Sarah was kind enough to offer me shelter and is preparing a warm drink for me while my shirt dries. That's all." Edward kept his voice calm and level, though the back of his head was starting to pound.

"*Nee*," Mahlon growled. "I've seen you before, sneakin' about our *haus*, always makin' some excuse. . . . You tell me, Edward King, that you've not been courtin' my *dochder*."

Edward drew in a harsh breath and glanced again at Sarah. *What am I supposed to say when it's the absolute truth and Sarah's not about to lie?*

"Well?" Mahlon demanded.

"Now, now," Bishop Umble murmured. "You know, Mahlon, that all of our young folks' courting is done in secret at *nacht*. There's nothing wrong with that."

"*Jah*," Mahlon retorted. "But here he's astandin' in broad daylight, half naked, and I tell you that it's my girl and it's dishonor."

"And is she going to marry every man she sees with his shirt off and still be the healer for Ice Mountain?" Edward snapped.

Mahlon looked like his eyes were about to bug out of his head and he took an aggressive step closer. "She ain't healin' you, *buwe*. You got

16

nuthin' much wrong with you but your ways and your drinkin' and lyin' and—"

"And that makes me the perfect husband for someone like Sarah, right?"

Mahlon's thick finger traced an invisible rifle scope up and down Edward's bare chest. "You'll do right by her and you'll learn to be the man she deserves, or else . . ."

"*Fater, sei se gut*," Sarah began.

"Enough," Mahlon gritted out. "I ought to beat him senseless for this presuming on your honor. But there's no help for it. . . . Bishop, marry them."

"*Fater*, I don't want to marry him," Sarah said calmly, but Edward heard the desperation in her voice and he couldn't deny that it hurt somewhere deep inside. She had told him that she never wanted to see him again only yesterday, and she'd probably kill him if she knew how much he drank and about the girls he'd seen while he was away and about his anger and hopelessness and . . .

"I'm sorry, Sarah," Bishop Umble said finally, stroking his long gray beard. "I believe your *fater* is right and Edward will become the man you deserve and you a fitting wife for him. We must not allow dalliance among our young people, especially with you in such a position of service to the community. I will marry you, and I believe that *Derr Herr* will make things right between you both."

17

Then, as if from a long distance away, Edward heard the fall of the ginger root as it hit the hardwood floor—a dull thump, like the one in his head, like a single beat of his terrified heart.

Chapter Two

It was not the wedding any girl would have wanted. Sarah had absolutely no desire to marry Edward King, even though it had been what she'd been dreaming of for the past year. . . . But that had been when she'd thought he'd wanted her, when she believed in his schemes, and hadn't seen him drunk. Now she could barely bring herself to change into the blue dress her *fater* insisted upon—blue for marrying. She paused in adjusting her *kapp* and listened in surreal fascination to the rain still beating mercilessly against the cabin. *Getting married . . . while Mamm and Clara and Ernest and Samuel sit unsuspecting at home. . . . Perhaps* Fater *will relent and allow time for the rest of the family to come. . . . But no, he believed that a sin should be made right as soon as possible . . . no matter anyone's feelings.* Ach, *how I miss* Grossmuder May—she *would have helped somehow, but there's no sense longing for someone gone from here, like a red leaf in a fast-moving stream. . . . But at least I have her journal. . . .*

Sarah glanced at the old heavy book on her bedside table and on impulse went quickly to open it. So far, she'd savored each early entry, reading of May's girlhood far from Ice Mountain. But now Sarah turned with furtive fingertips to the penciled page she'd only glanced at marked MY WEDDING DAY and began to read almost in desperation. She knew it might be wiser to seek counsel from *Gott*'s Word, but she needed the touch of a woman friend now. And, as she lifted the book to the rain-washed window, time stood still, then fell away in the gentle loops and lines of *Grossmuder*'s writing.

October 13, 1940

I saw to our three milch cows before dawn and I believe that *Fater* intends to give us Rosie, my favorite cow, as a wedding gift. I hope that Elias will be pleased—it is so hard to tell what his thoughts are at times. But perhaps I am nervous over being a wife after being the baby of my family for so long. And fifteen is a *gut* age for marrying, or so my mamm says. . . . Still, I will miss my room and sleeping with Esther, but I won't miss her cold feet! There, my sisters *kumme* now to braid my hair up and I will not write again until I am Frau Stolfus. *Gott* bless our union!

May G. Miller

Sarah let the pages rifle closed between her fingers and put the book back on her table. *Fifteen . . . If* Grossmuder *could marry at fifteen, then surely I can at nineteen. . . .* She squared her shoulders and pushed aside the long curtain that separated the bedroom from the kitchen, prepared to face her future with as much confidence as her shaking hands would allow.

The three men stood in silence when she reentered the room. Edward had loosely pinned his soaking shirt on, but the strong cords of his throat were still visible and his suspenders still hung down about his lean waist. He was visibly shivering and she bit back a protest at making him put on his wet clothes again, knowing that would only condemn him further in her *fater*'s eyes. *I might as well do what I can to see that they get along, considering this marriage is supposed to last forever. . . .* She blinked. *Forever . . .*

Edward sneezed, and it seemed to galvanize Bishop Umble into action. "It is unusual, I admit to you all, for me to both perform the marriage and stand as a witness at the same time. . . ."

Her *fater* gave a low growl of acknowledgment and the bishop stroked his gray beard. "Still," he cleared his throat, "I suppose we must proceed . . . though I'm beginning to think that this is the only way couples seem to get married anymore on Ice Mountain—irate *faters* and all."

Sarah knew that the bishop was referring to Edward's own sister, Mary, who had been forced to wed after being caught in a passionate embrace with an *Englischer*. Yet Mary and Jude certainly seemed now to be deeply in love and made one of the most striking couples on the mountain.

She sighed, then came back to the moment with a heart thump as she heard Bishop Umble speak the High German words of the wedding ceremony. She was aware of Edward's tall presence beside her and the faint smell of moonshine mixed with his own scent of pine and woods and sultry sun. She longed to close her eyes against memories of stolen kisses and fervent embraces and tried to remember that he wanted her like this no more than she wanted him.

Somehow, then, the ceremony was over. She saw her *fater* visibly relax, a bit of the angry redness leaving his face, and the bishop put his hands behind his back. Sarah knew Bishop Umble's posture; it was a stance of exhortation or encouragement, as he often stood during church service. *Here comes the lecture . . . I'm so tired all of a sudden. I don't think I can stand it. . . .* But she assumed a properly interested expression, ignoring for the moment the fact that Edward had begun to cough. She simply wanted everyone to be gone.

But Bishop Umble pursed his lips and spoke.

"I have one suggestion for your marriage. It's an abbreviated statement from Sir Winston Churchill. . . ."

Ach, buwe. Sarah flicked back one of her *kapp* strings and sensed Edward shift his weight on the *auld* floorboards.

" 'Never give up,' " the bishop pronounced with singular solemnity, then clapped his hat back on his head. "*Kumme*, Mahlon, we'll leave this husband and wife in peace."

Sarah watched her *fater* bluster, then grab Edward by his loose shirt collar. "If you ever hurt her, I'll . . ."

"Mahlon!" Bishop Umble snapped. "Remember yourself."

Her *fater* grunted and released Edward, and Sarah let out the breath she realized she'd been holding. Then both older men went out into the rain and the door closed with a definitive thump, her *fater* not even bidding her farewell.

She closed her eyes on tears at the abrupt dismissal, not that she'd come to expect anything more from her *daed*—he was far from affectionate and remote as the moon at times. She swallowed, longing for comfort of some kind, and looked askance at her new husband.

Mahlon Mast fisted his hands deep into his pockets as he parted from the bishop and began on the path toward home. Anne would be waiting supper and wondering what kept him. He scowled as he kicked a stray rock out of his way and again felt a deep urge to lay hands on Edward King. It seemed unfathomable to him that Sarah now belonged to the insufferable *buwe*, and that it had been at his own insistence. *But what else was I to do . . .*

"Hi, there."

Mahlon came to a dead stop, so involved in his own thoughts that he'd nearly run full tilt into Jude Lyons.

"*Ach* . . . hiya."

Mahlon had a cautious friendship with the younger man who'd only recently joined the Ice Mountain *Amisch* community.

"Is something wrong?" Jude asked, adjusting his spectacles.

"Wrong? *Jah* . . . and you can ask yer *bruder*-in-law what."

Jude frowned. "You mean Edward?"

"Sure I do. He jest married my Sarah."

"Why now? Although I know they've been courting."

Mahlon snorted. "Am I the last on this mountain to know such things for certain?"

"Oh, I bet I'll be the last one to fathom it when Rose starts to court." Jude spoke of his new baby daughter with obvious pride.

"I've got to get on," Mahlon said, knowing he was being abrupt.

"Sure. I'll see you soon, and don't worry about Edward—he'll turn out all right. Remember, you didn't like me so much when we first met. Maybe Edward deserves a chance, too."

Mahlon shrugged. "I don't think I got it in me to give it to him."

"You might be surprised." Jude smiled.

"I don't think so."

"I need a drink," Edward said, reaching a hand behind his neck as if to ease an ache.

"*Nee*, you don't," Sarah cried and he half smiled.

"I'd wager you need one yourself, Sarah, after that fiasco." He coughed and started to ease back out of his shirt. "When everybody's settled down, we'll get an annulment or something."

"What?" Her voice seemed shrill and hurt his head.

"Sarah, sweet . . . please . . . why not let me lie down for a few hours . . . shake off this cold." He brushed past her, patting her shoulder absently, and made for the bed in the other room.

"Are you *narrisch*?" she asked, following him.

"Crazy?" He tugged off a boot. "*Nee*, but I am probably still a little drunk."

"And married," she pointed out.

"And married," he agreed with a yawn, slipping off his pants.

He felt her frustration, but it seemed muted

somehow, cocooned away from him as he lifted the quilts and slid into the warm bed with an audible sigh. "You'll see, Sarah," he slurred. "Everything will be all right."

He thought he was dreaming. The wind had picked up until it seemed to shake the very foundation of the old cabin, and there was an ominous glow to the light outside the bedroom window. The sound of limbs breaking like the crack of gunfire penetrated the storm and he sighed, rolling to his back and stretching out his right arm to a more comfortable position. When the ancient oak toppled and fell through the roof of the cabin, he came awake long enough to feel a brutal crushing weight, a red haze of pain, and then, mercifully, darkness.

Chapter Three

"Mrs. King?"

Sarah looked up from her folded hands as the surgeon spoke her new name from the doorway of the crowded waiting room. She got to her feet in a daze, aware of friends and family in vinyl chairs behind her, but her eyes focused oddly on the single drop of blood on the doctor's scrubs.

Her steps were halting and the older doctor reached out a hand to her, guiding her gently by the elbow into the quiet hall of the large hospital where Edward had been flown.

"Mrs. King, your husband is stable. We were able to stop the bleeding, but he did lose his right eye and, despite our best efforts, will have some pretty severe scarring on the right side of his face."

Sarah nodded, steepled her hands together, then pressed her fingers to her lips. "But he will live?" she asked.

"Yes," the doctor answered gently. "Would you like to see him? He's fairly well sedated, but he might be able to hear you if you talk to him."

Sarah dropped her hands to her sides. "Yes . . . please."

She followed the doctor through a myriad of doors, moving deeper into the recesses of the building, until the rooms became smaller, quieter, and a feeling of sober vigil hung in the air.

"In here." The doctor gestured, and she went inside the open door. A nurse was pressing buttons on a computer but paused to smile kindly in her direction, then slipped away, leaving Sarah to approach the bed alone.

Edward's head was swathed in bandages, and the right side of his face as well. Tubes and machines surrounded his bed like alien sentinels and she longed to care for him in the simplicity of home. She forgot, for the moment, his slurred promise of an annulment, and all of her that thanked *Gott* for the gift of healing she carried wanted to help him now.

She glanced into the hallway, then got as close to his left side as possible, bending to stroke the back of his strong hand, which looked strangely out of place against the crisp white sheet. She whispered in his ear.

"Edward, it's Sarah." *Your wife* . . . "You're in a big hospital—they had to helicopter you from Coudersport. But you're going to be all right . . ." *But, dear* Gott, *is he? Losing his eye and having his handsome face scarred will surely affect him emotionally. . . .*

He stirred and moaned faintly and she spoke a bit louder.

"I'm going to stay with you, Edward. Don't be afraid." She looked up when the nurse reentered.

"I'm sorry, ma'am, I'll have to ask you to go back to the waiting room. He needs to sleep. The doctor said you can come back in a few hours and stay longer."

Sarah nodded, then impulsively bent and kissed Edward's cheek, wondering if he'd accept such an action if he was fully awake. And then she followed the nurse out of the room.

It was dark except for the muted glow and beep of strange machines when Edward woke to feel with tentative fingers at the mass of bandages on his face and head. He tried to remember how he'd come to the hospital room, but all he could seem to recall was standing in front of Bishop Umble and Mahlon Mast and marrying Sarah. *Marrying Sarah . . . but she'd made it clear that she didn't want to have anything to do with him. . . .*

"Edward?"

He turned his head in the direction of Sarah's gentle voice as a soft overhead light came on, and he thought he must be in a dream.

"Edward, you're in the hospital. A tree fell on *Grossmuder* May's cabin and you were badly hurt."

"What's wrong with my head?" His voice sounded strange to his own ears and his throat hurt.

There was an infinitesimal pause, and then she moved into his line of vision. Her gray eyes were wide, searching, but he saw a calmness there that made him relax for a moment. "Edward, the doctors couldn't save your right eye."

He tried to process her words and reached his fingers once more to the wad of bandages over the side of his face. "What?"

He saw the concern in her stare but no pity, and he thought that perhaps he had heard wrong.

"Your right eye is gone," she said slowly.

He nodded, thinking of the only trip his family had ever taken away from Ice Mountain, when his mother was still alive. A trip to Cape May—to the seaside. Where he'd seen a one-eyed man begging for money along the boardwalk. The man's empty eye socket had been uncovered and had gleamed with sullen red scarring in a way that had seemed both fascinating and horrifying.

Now Edward knew a fear in his soul, that he would be monstrous, despite Sarah's level gaze. He shuddered and would have turned away had her voice not stopped him.

"You're alive, Edward King. Alive," she said firmly. "And you can still see—it would have been so different had that tree fallen a few inches further. *Derr Herr* had His Hand on you."

Edward couldn't stop the bitter laugh that escaped his lips. "*Jah*, right. Next you'll be telling me that *Gott* has a plan for my life in being like this. Leave me be."

"I can't simply leave you, Edward . . . you're my husband." Her half whisper was urgent.

He swallowed hard. "If you think I'll let you stick to this marriage out of pity, you've got it all wrong, sweet. . . . I remember now, you told me you never wanted to see me again, and your damn *fater* bullied you into . . ."

"Edward," she hissed. "Don't swear."

"I'll do a helluva lot more than swear if you don't get out. Now."

He watched her stand still as a statue and he drew a deep breath. "Get out!"

A nurse came hurrying into the room as bells went off. Edward didn't care, nor did he want to think about the stricken look on Sarah's face. He wanted to be left alone.

A long time after he sensed that Sarah was gone, he allowed bitter, silent tears to slip from his now single eye and cursed God for letting him live.

"I have a role in the community," Sarah whispered to her new sister-in-law, Mary Lyons. They sat in the hospital's cafeteria, quietly talking in the small hours of the morning.

"And Edward doesn't," Mary said. "Though my *bruder* is *gut* at growing things."

Sarah looked at her, surprised. "Is he? We never—I guess we never got around to talk about that because we were too busy—well, never mind."

Mary smiled faintly and squeezed her hand. "I understand. Jude and I had a lot of—um, never mind—time together."

"*Jah*, but Jude loves you, and you have a wonderful baby and your life is *gut*."

"And you don't think Edward loves you? Or maybe you don't love him?"

Sarah shook her head. "I love him; I don't like him much of late, though. I actually told him I didn't want to see him anymore, and then he showed up at the cabin . . . and then my *fater* and the bishop came. . . . *Ach*, Mary, I know he's your *bruder*, but I don't know who I'm married to."

"*Gott* will work it out, Sarah. You will see."

"I know *Derr Herr*'s power, but I also know your *bruder*'s strong will. He . . . well, his response to all of this will either destroy him or build him as a man."

"Then we must pray for the building," Mary said simply.

Sarah nodded, wondering how much Edward's younger sister knew about his drinking. Then she smiled and crushed the plastic sandwich wrapper she held. "I'd better go back up now. Perhaps he'll feel more like seeing—I mean, being with me. . . ."

Mary smiled. "*Jah*. Of course he will."

"I don't want to talk to you," Edward said sullenly, avoiding his big *bruder*'s gaze. "And why in the hell are you here anyway? You threw me out."

"Watch your tongue," Joseph answered in a mild tone. "You deserved to be thrown out and, obviously, it was *Derr Herr*'s will that you marry Sarah and . . ."

Edward sneered. "What's the matter, Joseph? Can't bring that handsome mouth of yours to say that it was *Gott*'s will that I'm half blind? You're worthless . . ."

He watched his *bruder* bend his dark head and regretted his words for a brief moment, but then Joseph looked him straight in the eye.

"And you're angry, like you have been for

quite some time. At least all of these machines keep you from drinking. That's one thing to be thankful for in this."

"Yeah," Edward choked. "It's a great way to dry out ... . not that I wouldn't like to crawl out of my skin."

"Tell the doctor," Joseph urged. "Maybe he can give you something to help you relax."

Edward closed his eye. "Shut up, Joe."

"I see his temper hasn't improved."

Sarah's soft voice penetrated Edward's senses, making him even more furious, but he drew a deep breath, determined not to let her see how much she affected him—more than he'd ever remembered when he'd been away.

He opened his eye. "What do you want, my sweet frau? *Kumme* to gawk at the deformed penitent?"

"I came to check on you because I care, Edward. The doctor is coming in to do his rounds; I saw him in the hall. He says they'll take the bandages off in a few days and then you can go home."

"And where exactly is home?" Edward asked wearily, unable to keep the edge from his voice.

Joseph sighed aloud, but Sarah spoke with audible confidence. "Home with me, your wife, Edward."

"Uh, maybe I'd better go out," Joseph interjected.

"Yeah, go and take her with you."

"Sarah can *kumme* and go as she pleases," Joseph said in a level warning at his rudeness; then Edward heard him stalk away, his work boots heavy on the tile flooring.

When she said nothing after a few long minutes, he turned his head and glared at her, not expecting to see the dark circles beneath her gray eyes or the faint wisps of brown hair that escaped her *kapp*. *She's tired, and I'm acting like an idiot . . . but there is no way I'm going to let her do her* Amisch *duty and stay married to a freak. . . .*

"Why don't you go get some rest, Sarah?" he said finally, opting for level politeness instead of anger. *Maybe she'll listen to pure reason . . .*

"I'm fine. I'm used to being up at all hours with *Grossmuder*—I mean, I was." She broke off abruptly, and it occurred to him how close she must have grown to the old healer before her death.

"Well, you miss her—that's normal." *Unlike me—I am far from normal.*

"You shouldn't feel sorry for yourself," she chided, and he stared at her until his eye ached, wondering at her odd perception. *I guess she's not so normal either.* The thought provoked him and he felt his anger rise once more.

"I can feel what I want," he snapped. "And I don't feel like having you as a wife. I'm not

33

going to accept your sense of duty—which I know is stronger than a goat's grip. So, seriously, give this up."

She silently shook her head back and forth and he slapped the mattress. *I could hurt her, tell her that she means nothing . . .* but the idea brought on a distant feeling of disquiet that soured his stomach. . . . And, he knew her—she'd probably simply absorb the hurt of his words and go on with the marriage.

"All right, sweet," he drawled, trying to subdue his frustration. "If you are so intent on a marriage you told me you didn't want, then a wedding in name only is exactly what you'll get. I will not touch you, not even a fingertip—so that when you finally tire of living with me, you'll be able to seek an honest annulment—if the bishop will somehow allow it."

She stared at him. "You mean—we won't, you won't . . ."

"Right. But no one will ever know. To the godforsaken world of Ice Mountain, we'll settle down to wedded bliss, but your life will be far from it."

"I'm used to that . . . you know my *fater*," she said quietly, and he suddenly wished he could find his way back to the time and place before he left for the rigs; it had been so easy and graceful with her then. *And I was so much less of a mess . . .*

34

"All right, Sarah, you've got what you wanted or more than you bargained for—you can sit by my bedside and dab at your eyes, though we both know where your heart truly lies."

He wanted to look away from her faint smile of denial, the gentle revelation of her pearly teeth—it was enough to make him feel aroused, which made him feel alive, and he wasn't quite ready to live yet.

"I'm tired," he said honestly, and he watched as she turned to go—his would-be savior, his new wife—whom he swore he'd never touch. . . . It was more than enough for one bedside visit.

Chapter Four

He awoke to a gentle touch on his arm and peered sleepily at the old man who stood beside his bed.

"You want anything, son?"

Yeah, my right eye . . . and a smooth drink of shine. . . .

"I got candy bars, magazines, some peanuts, too."

"No, thanks." Edward slumped down, hoping the guy would go away.

"I'm a volunteer. Been one for a few years now."

Edward heard him slide a chair across the floor

with a slight screech and suppressed an irritated groan.

"Yep, had to find something to do after my wife died."

And here we go . . . more good news. But Edward was too well brought up in the ways of his people, trained that elders should be respected, for him to dismiss the other man.

"I get to meet all kinds of folks here—some sicker than others."

"Yeah," Edward muttered glumly. "I bet."

"How sick are you, son?"

Edward swung his head, glaring at the old man with as much intensity as he could muster with his single line of vision. "I lost my right eye."

The old man nodded. "I see your face is bandaged."

"Scarred too."

"I suppose there's all kinds of scars—some that we see, some we don't. Take me, for instance—used to be a real heavy drinker in my time."

"How'd you give it up?" Edward asked idly. *Not that I plan on it . . .*

"I found something I loved more."

"Yeah? Well, you know drinking is a disease, a sickness. Some people can't help it."

The old man nodded. "True. I was only telling you my experience."

Edward exhaled and closed his eye briefly. It seemed that only a moment had passed, but he realized he must have fallen asleep. When he opened his eye, the old man was gone and a young nurse was by his side, adjusting some tubing.

"That old guy can sure talk," he commented with a stretch.

"What old guy is that?" She smiled at him, blinking wide blue eyes.

"The old man—the volunteer. He was here a bit ago."

She shook her head and he felt like an idiot.

"I don't know who you mean, but volunteers come and go," she said.

"Yeah," Edward muttered, confused. "I bet they do."

He pushed the old man's words out of his mind and drifted back to a fitful sleep.

Sarah wanted to be there when they took the bandages off, even though he'd ranted and thrown his water pitcher against the wall. But studying under *Grossmuder* May had taught Sarah many things—not the least of which was patience.

"Your wounds make no difference to me," she'd assured him, ignoring the now familiar ringing of bells at his escapade.

"And why not?" he'd asked sarcastically. "Because you're the healer now and you're above all those superficial things like looks?

Because I remember fine how you used to touch my face, run your pretty tongue up my throat, and tell me you couldn't wait to be married. . . . Well, here we are, so don't have the temerity to tell me that it doesn't matter."

She sniffed, realizing that any way she answered would only condemn her further in his sight. She was glad when the doctor had *kumme* in, whistling and brisk.

"All right, Mr. King, enough with upsetting the nurses and your young wife. We'll have those bandages off and see what's what." The doctor ignored his own crude pun and lowered the bed, leaving Sarah to step aside.

The physician pulled out a pair of blunt-tipped scissors and began to work while Sarah prayed. When the clutter was cleared away, the doctor lifted a mirror from a tray and held it out to Edward.

"Now remember, it may be possible to give you a prosthetic eye. I think we've done the best we can with the scarring, though certainly plastic surgery may be an option. . . . Mrs. King, if you'd like to step closer."

The doctor moved and Sarah stepped back to the bed, watching the back of the mirror as Edward lifted it toward himself for a brief moment. She jumped when the mirror was cast to the floor to shatter heavily.

"I'll get somebody to clean that up," the doctor

murmured. "It's a normal reaction." He patted Sarah's shoulder. "And I'll leave this eye patch to use for a time as you adjust your balance and peripheral sight. A good day, Mr. King, Mrs. King."

Sarah had watched him go, then turned back to face her husband. The empty eye socket was healing over well as far as she could tell, and even the puckered scars on his high cheekbone looked pink and healthy.

She stepped as quietly as she could over the glass crunching beneath her sensible shoes and picked up the eye patch from his lap, playing absently with its black elastic band while she struggled to find something to say. How could she tell him that he still looked impossibly handsome and, with the patch, he'd make a rakish pirate of an *Amisch* man?

"I don't want your pity," he'd gritted out into the silence, and she lifted her head, his gaze slamming into her.

"I'm not offering it." Her toes curled inside her black shoes. *And I'm really not . . . Why should he be pitied? He is young, still attractive, healthy . . . there are many who could say far less.*

"Well, don't ever offer it, Sarah King, or I'll chew your little rump. Understand?" His blue eye bored into her.

She'd nodded, both annoyed and fascinated by his words, and pleased at the fight in them. . . .

•••

Mahlon Mast nodded to his wife as he came into the family kitchen before dawn.

"Don't forget your work gloves," Anne said softly.

"*Nee*, I won't. I expect cutting that tree up will be a job. It was probably over two hundred years old." He took the cup of coffee she offered and drank it in one gulp.

"I—I can't help but wonder how the *buwe* is, and Sarah. Perhaps we should have gone to the hospital with them."

"Ye've the other *kinner* to tend. We'll hear word soon enough."

"I prayed for him last *nacht*—Edward King," Anne said, taking back his cup. "Did you?"

Mahlon frowned. "A man's prayers are his own."

"*Ach*, I know, but . . ."

"I best be going." He turned and drew his hat from a peg near the door.

"*Jah*, Mahlon. I'll see you there later, when I help the women with the food."

He gave a brief nod and left the cabin for the inky darkness of the day.

Chapter Five

"This whole thing sucks," Edward muttered, relishing the guttural *Englisch* slang he'd learned on the gas rigs.

The majority of the mountain community was putting the final touches on the cabin, having done the bulk of the repairs while he'd been in the hospital. The tree that had taken his sight had been chopped into neatly stacked firewood and he knew he'd be grimly reminded of his injury every time he sought to warm himself that winter. *How like the* Amisch . . . *to be so practical, turning brutal fate into provision. . . . Though I suppose I could warm myself up with my wife . . . if she'd stop looking like a poker was up her back . . . and, if I hadn't sworn not to touch her. . . .*

He glanced at Sarah, still unused to the claustrophobic feeling of the eye patch. Then a sudden, contrary image came to mind—a girl who'd visited a bar near the rig in West Virginia—blond-haired, blue-eyed, and so willing to pull him outside. He'd let himself kiss her, thinking it meant nothing . . . letting himself forget Sarah waiting back on Ice Mountain. He'd even confessed to Joseph, though that hadn't made him feel any better, and now, sitting in front of the cabin, with Sarah standing beside him, he felt worse than ever about it.

"Do you want something to drink?" Sarah's soft voice broke into his thoughts and he startled guiltily.

"I'm not an invalid," he snapped, regretting his tone immediately when he saw her flinch from the periphery of his left eye.

"I thought you might be thirsty," she said tightly. "That's all."

He sighed. "*Nee*, nothing to drink." *Nothing to drink . . . No more moonshine—tell me I don't need it.*

"I know what you're thinking," she murmured.

"What?" he ground out, not exactly doubting her assertion.

"That you want to be able to help—that it's a man's job to build his own home."

"Yeah . . . that's right."

"Are you being sarcastic?"

Oddly, he wanted to laugh. "No, sweet. I'm never that."

"All right. I've had enough. I'm going to help the women with the food. Here comes Joseph; he can bear your wit for a while."

He turned to watch her walk away, then glanced back at his *bruder*. "Go away."

Joseph stood directly in front of him. "*Kumme* on. Get out of that chair. I want to show you something out back."

"Why don't you see how your pretty pregnant wife is doing?" Edward suggested, gesturing to his redheaded sister-in-law, Priscilla, as she passed, carrying some clean sheets over her arm. She smiled in their direction but kept moving across the hilly lawn.

"She's more than fine," Joseph said in an appreciative tone, and Edward gritted his teeth at his brother's smitten ways with his wife.

"You've got the perfect life now—haven't you, Joe?"

"*Ach*, you know better than that. . . . Now *kumme* or I'll escort you myself."

Edward scowled but obeyed, knowing his big *bruder* too well to doubt his polite threat. He walked slowly over the uneven ground, ignoring Joseph's obvious arm, extended for support. Edward felt oddly off-balance, as he'd been warned he would in the hospital, but he'd been told that things would right themselves in a few weeks. For now, he wanted to growl at the myriad of *kinner* running about, making him feel even more uncertain of his footsteps.

Then a child ran full tilt into his right leg, and he would have stumbled had Joseph not caught him in time. He shook off Joe's hand and glared down at the towheaded *buwe*, recognizing Sarah's younger *bruder*, Samuel.

"Watch where you're running," Edward snapped with a dark frown, meant to discourage the child.

But Samuel smiled up at him with a gap-toothed grin. "Sorry, *Bruder* Edward."

Edward chafed under the name brother, having no desire to be reminded that Mahlon Mast's family was now close kin.

"You look like a pirate," Samuel pointed out in the ensuing silence, his small head tilted as he stared upward. "You need a sword."

"*Jah*, and I'd use the broad side of it to swat your behind."

The *buwe* giggled, obviously not put off, and slipped his small hand into Edward's with casual ease. Edward was shaken by the child's touch, all warmth and trust, and he reluctantly let his fingers settle around the tender bones, ignoring Joe's stare.

"All right," Edward grumbled. "Before we get run into again, what is it that you want to show me?"

They rounded the cabin and Joe pointed to the large, sprawling patch of tilled earth, set in a fertile dip in the ground. "There." Joe pointed, indicating some youths, whitewashing wood frames near the ground.

"Cold frames." Edward couldn't contain the note of interest that rang in his voice as he moved closer. "Made from the blasted tree, no doubt?"

"Yep." Joseph smiled.

But Edward didn't care. . . . Here was something that intrigued him—cold-climate gardening and extending the growing season. The cold frames were like flat, square greenhouses, their wood bases set in the ground and topped with large panes of old framed window glass. Usually, the cold frames were set level with the ground, allowing about eight inches between glass and earth for winter plantings to grow. But these frames were angled into the hillside, which would permit even taller growth at the back end of the frame.

"You've angled them," Edward noticed, nodding to the *aulder buwes*.

"The better to catch the sun's warmth back here," Joseph agreed. "And there's about six inches of mulch insulation beneath each frame to prevent any frost from creeping in."

"*Gut* idea." Edward found himself smiling, much to his surprise. He'd experimented with heirloom seeds and cold frames for years, up until the last winter, which he'd spent secretly meeting Sarah and dreaming of getting away from the mountain to work on the rigs. Now all of his natural interest in planting and the earth came rushing back with vital intensity.

"I know *Grossmuder* May taught Sarah to dry herbs," Joseph said. "But I figured you might know some that you could keep growing fresh."

Edward released Samuel's hand to hunker down next to one of the cold frames. He lifted the handle on the glass frame and breathed in the scent of freshly turned earth. "Sure—there's chives, lemon balm, feverfew—a whole bunch of things."

"*Gut.* Then you ought to be a great help to your wife."

His *bruder*'s words registered and Edward slowly closed the glass lid and rose to his feet.

"Look, Joe, I appreciate the cold frames, but don't assume that my job in life is simply to help my wife."

"Don't you wanna help Sarah?" Samuel piped up, and Edward's flash of frustration grew. He had no desire to sound unkind about Sarah, but he couldn't help the feeling of being lost when it came to her all-important role as healer for the community. He knew his attitude was probably unfair, but he felt too overwhelmed to work it out at the present moment.

"Of course I want to help Sarah," he bit out with reluctance, looking down at Samuel and wondering how a seven-year-old's expression could be both so doubtful and so optimistic at the same time.

"*Jah*, that's *gut*," the child pronounced finally.

"You better watch out, Edward." Joseph laughed in an undertone. "This little one might be giving you the broad side of a sword if you don't take care of his sister."

"Yeah, *danki*, Joe. I didn't quite pick up on that. . . ." Edward's smile was sour and his momentary joy in the cold frames was gone, but he told himself that he couldn't expect much more, given the way his life was going lately.

Sarah walked with brisk intent across the grass. She wanted to leave Edward and his bad attitude far behind. She wondered vaguely if his moods would always be so unpredictable and knew he created more stress in her mind since his accident than she'd felt even at her first midwifery experience. She blinked when she heard a woman cry her name.

"Sarah! Come quickly. Charlotte's gotten into a wasps' nest."

Sarah recognized Letty Zook's anxious call and took off at a run, knowing that four-year-old Charlotte Zook had been born blind and had probably gotten into the nest by accident.

"Where's the sting?" Sarah asked, putting her arm around the sobbing black-haired little girl while her *mamm* circled anxiously.

"Above her eye, I think. *Ach*, maybe in her eye, too." Letty pointed to the rising welts between her daughter's dark blue left eye and black brow.

Sarah grabbed a glass of water from a nearby table and emptied it onto the well-trod ground. She pulled Charlotte down close to her and worked the water into the ground with her fingertips, then took the mud and quickly dabbed it onto the child's eyelid and brow. Then she automatically began to pray.

Chapter Six

The slender white feathers were speckled with blood, proof that one of the barn cats had had a go at the dove but had lost a meal. Still, the bird hobbled, off center, with pathetic flaps of its useless wing, and Mahlon watched his dochder, twelve-year-old Sarah, instinctively catch up the bird, hold it close, and feel the certain frantic pulse of its heart with her fingertips.

"Best wring its neck, Sarah." Mahlon sighed, shaking his head. "There's no fixin' that wing. It's sure to be broken."

He ignored the look of shock in her gray eyes and busied himself with some loose harness. He was surprised when he heard her burst out with a sharp cry. "Nee . . . I won't. She's still alive."

He turned in shock at her open defiance, but then his gaze was caught by the sudden fervor in her eyes, in the repeated movement of her fingers. An odd feeling chased down the back of his spine as he watched her small hand caress the dove's feathers. He took a step closer to her, feeling afraid but unsure of the reason.

"Sarah?" The sound of his own voice, hollow and uncertain, frightened him.

She didn't look up but peered closer at the bird as she ran her hand along the broken wing, *again and again. And then the dove struggled in her grasp. She loosened her hold and the bird flew free, high up into the blue of the sky, silhouetted against the light.*

Mahlon shuddered and couldn't move. Like now; like then . . .

Mahlon realized he'd broken out into a cold sweat as Letty's shrill voice penetrated the fog in his mind.

"Sarah! Is Charlotte all right?"

Mahlon caught his hand on the table's edge and stared over his daughter's shoulder at the mud that smudged the little girl's eyelid. Sarah moved her fingertips and looked into the blue iris, and he feared, *Gott* forgive him, he feared, even before Charlotte blinked, that sight had been given to the child in her previously blind eye.

The grapevine of the small *Amisch* community had tendrils in every corner, and Ice Mountain knew about Charlotte Zook's wasp mishap with a rapidity that defied explanation. Of course Letty's loud praise of the new healer helped, but when Edward came into the cabin to find Sarah, he saw his wife slumped at the kitchen table while her *fater* whispered frantic words over her, his breath coming in audible gasps.

"How could ya try to do it, Sarah? Here . . . today . . . with everyone about. They'll think you a hex and you know it, and then . . ."

49

"And then what?" Edward asked, trying to keep a rein on the inexplicable anger he felt at seeing Sarah berated.

Mahlon Mast rounded the table's edge and thrust his face close to Edward's. "You shut up . . . you got no call to be speaking here. You think you can understand when I've been prayin' fer her near to ten years?"

"I think if you're worried that your daughter will be thought a witch that you might not have been praying hard enough."

"Edward, don't . . ." Sarah spoke tiredly.

"Don't what? You think I'm going to let him behave like this in your—our *haus*? A hex? Ha . . . Next he'll be expecting that the neighbors will be taking up pitchforks against you."

Mahlon gnashed his teeth and inched closer. "All right, then, Edward King. You whose wife she be—explain it to me. Explain how she can . . ." His voice dropped to a whisper. "Explain how she can do some—things, and tell me you haven't found it strange yerself."

"I haven't found it strange at all, and all she did was remove a stinger. You'd think she made Charlotte Zook see or something. . . ." But here he broke off as his eye met Mahlon's, and a strange fissure of sensation rushed through his consciousness. *What if she could really heal the blind?* He blinked and Mahlon snorted.

"Uh-huh."

"Look, Sarah healed my *fater*—you know that," Edward said, low. "Without her, he'd likely be dead now." Edward couldn't control his words or the pulse of memory they produced in his mind.

He didn't want to remember . . . because it was one of the oddest things he'd ever experienced in his life. But still, he saw himself and Joseph as they watched helplessly while their *daed* had struggled for breath, knowing for certain he surely would die. But then Sarah had come and run calming hands down his *dat*'s arms and across his cancer-shrunken chest.

"It's not the cancer. I think he's had a heart attack," she'd said softly, almost to herself.

"A heart attack?" Edward had groaned aloud.

But Sarah had continued to work quietly, slipping herbs beneath his *fater*'s tongue and speaking to him softly.

And that had been all. Edward had held his breath and watched, amazed, as his *fater*'s face was suddenly suffused with color as he drew a deep, full breath. He opened his eyes and reached up to stroke his beard. Then he looked at Sarah. "*Danki*," he'd whispered.

Edward had watched her nod with a humble bow. "*Gott* be praised," she'd said. "Now give him something to eat and drink and let him be still for today."

She'd gotten up, nodded to Edward, and slipped from their midst.

Even now, Edward couldn't recall the moments without a distinct chill running down his spine. *Sarah . . . my Sarah . . . a healer. And it wasn't only my* daed*'s heart—the cancer went into full remission that day, too. . . . So strange . . . Gott, Mahlon's right. . . . I don't understand.*

Edward inched past his father-in-law's bulk and went to Sarah. He had to restrain himself from putting his hand on her fine-boned shoulder. Instead, he stood rigid and tall. "We'd like to be alone now."

Mahlon jammed on his hat. "*Jah*, I bet you would. . . . I'll be takin' the children and yer *mamm* home, girl. Jest think on what I said. . . ."

Edward sighed when the cabin door closed. "What did he say, Sarah?"

Chapter Seven

Sarah wished she could turn into the comfort of Edward's shirt and burrow like some small prey animal, but she sat still as a field mouse in the open, staring at the knotholes in the kitchen table, very conscious of his lean hip near her shoulder.

"It doesn't matter what he said," she whispered.

"Why?"

"Because he's said it all before . . . I—I try not to listen." *There, that was an admission I shouldn't have made to him. It does no gut to appear weak as water when he's sworn never to touch me.* . . .

But suddenly, he stooped down next to her chair and her breath caught in her throat. She half-turned to look at his handsome profile, made more intriguing by the black eye patch against his sun-drenched hair.

"I promised not to touch you," he whispered.

"I know."

"And I won't." His voice was tight, and something in her responded with heat low in her belly.

She nodded, confused by his nearness, the sunshine and male scent of him—earthy but like the mountains. He drew closer to her, facing her fully.

"I won't touch you with my hands, Sarah, or with my body. But I never said my breath or my words were off limits, did I?"

"*Ne—nee,*" she stuttered.

"*Gut* . . . because I want to say things to you to make you forget your *fater*'s words. I want you to gasp and hurt with wanting and to feel the thick hardness of the chair beneath your bottom. Can you feel it?"

She half-shook her head, mesmerized by his voice, entranced by his language and the slow pull of syllables. "I—*jah.*"

"Mmm—*gut.* Very *gut.* And now I want you to think about the rigid oaken chair and to imagine that you're sitting on it in the pulsing coolness of the creek. But . . ." He smiled, a wolfish flash of white teeth. "You've forgotten your clothes, sweet. . . . Can you see yourself?"

"I—can't. . . ." she managed.

"Shh," he soothed. "You've lost your clothes and you're all alone; no one can see—I promise. And the hard chair sits steady on the creek bottom while the water tickles your toes and licks at you, laps you with a silken rush."

This must be a sin, she thought wildly, her fingertips pressing into the wood of the table, but she could see it in her mind, see herself as he so languorously described.

"So," he murmured and leaned to blow softly against her exposed throat. "The water is so much more than wet; it's slick and the air is hot. You bend over and trail your hair in the wetness. Do you feel it, sweet?"

She drew a deep, trembling breath. She couldn't let him do this to her, no matter his motives. "Edward," she gasped and rose in abrupt haste. "I—*danki*—but I—I've forgotten about my *fater*'s words."

She stared at his boots, unable to look him in the face, then turned and fled to the relative seclusion of the bedroom.

Edward blew out a harsh breath and rubbed his head against the side of the chair. *I hurt, dammit, and it's my own stupid fault. . . .*

He eased himself to his feet, feeling dizzy, and

54

had the overwhelming urge to drink. It seemed a natural solution to the faint pain in his head and the deep ache elsewhere. His gaze fell on the crock jug that protruded slightly from the curtain at the bottom of Sarah's herbal cabinet, which had been strangely preserved from the tree damage.

He took a step closer. His fingertips itched. Of course Sarah used whiskey or bourbon to mix her tinctures and such. He swallowed hard. *One drink. I should be able to have one drink and stop . . . but what if I can't?* He thrust the intrusive thought away and shot a furtive glance at the closed bedroom curtain, then bent to swing up the jug with familiar ease. He uncorked it and drew a deep, stabilizing breath of the alcohol. *Whiskey . . . pure and simple.* He took a quick swallow, enjoying the burn, then closed his eye and drank deep.

Sarah put a hand to her chest to try to still the rampant throb of her heart, but it seemed a fruitless task. Edward had gotten her so riled up inside that she didn't know what to do with herself, and even the spacious, bright new bedroom did little to distract her until her gaze fell on the bed.

She'd noticed Joseph carving the headboard from the abundance of wood of the old tree, but now she paused with a smile to run her fingers down the stripped oak with its natural knots highlighted by a thin sheen of varnish. She trailed her hand to the expanse of quilt and the blue and yellow Double Wedding Ring pattern, its gentle loops and vivid intertwining of fabric unfamiliar to her from what she remembered of *Grossmuder* May's cupboards. It must be a gift from the women of the community, she thought, her mouth softening in tenderness. Kind hands must have made up the bed while she was treating Charlotte outside . . . *a new quilt for a new bed for a new marriage. . . .* She flushed at the train of her thoughts, recalling exactly why she'd escaped to the bedroom. Still, she couldn't help but suck in a deep breath of air and close her lashes for a brief prayer.

O Gott, *let it be a new marriage in truth. Help us to work together through both hard times and* gut *and give me wisdom to see my husband's true heart. . . .*

She opened her eyes and glanced at *Grossmuder* May's journal, which she'd placed in a prominent spot on a hand-carved tabletop near a Mason jar of late summer flowers. Sarah crossed the hardwood floor and found herself paging for the entry that followed her mentor's wedding. She longed for a simplistic and easy explanation of life, but as she read, the breath caught in her throat as the words seemed to leap up at her from the aged page.

October 16, 1940

Elias broke my arm yesterday, but I set it straight and told his *mamm* that I'd fallen from the barn loft when she stopped over. It hurt something awful last *nacht*. . . . I must be more careful of his temper and remember how he likes his ham steak. I did burn it. I'm grateful it wasn't the arm or hand I write with or my strongest milking arm. I best see about lunch.

May Stolfus

Sarah felt tears fill her eyes as she reread the brief entry. *October 16—three days—only three days after their wedding . . . Yet* Grossmuder *May had seemed so indomitable, such a strong and true one to seek counsel from . . . How could she not simply go home and tell her* fater? Then Sarah lifted her head—would she herself tell her *daed* such a thing? Give up on her marriage?

Her conscience provoked her, and for some reason she wanted to see Edward and talk with him, maybe apologize for running away from his wanton but well-meant words. The journal entry reminded her confusedly that she was blessed with a gracious husband. Then she half-smiled. . . . *Gracious? No. Grumpy and irritable and delicious? Yes* . . . She closed the journal and put it down, then moved to slide aside the curtain that separated her from her husband.

• • •

"Edward!"

He choked as he stared in frustration at his wife's outraged face.

"I came out to apologize," Sarah cried.

"What the devil for?" he snapped, letting the jug slide down to his hip as he swiped his mouth with the back of his hand.

"For—for—*ach*, I don't know, but drinking *Grossmuder* May's medicinal jug is . . ."

"Medicinal?" He laughed harshly. "Well, maybe it is medicinal for me at that."

She marched her small frame over to snatch the jug from his hand. He let it go easily and watched her step back, the container hugged to her abdomen.

She'd look pretty pregnant. . . . He scowled at his wayward thought and thrust it aside. "Tell me, sweet, what exactly is the difference between you using whiskey as a base for your tinctures and me drinking it straight? All you're doing is mixing in a few herbs and . . ."

"You don't understand the first thing about what I mix or how much. I don't even think you want to know what I do, but *jah*, I use the whiskey—you abuse it. That's the difference."

He was a bit taken aback by her level and factual statement and it irritated him beyond measure, especially when he realized yet again that he couldn't kiss her quiet.

"What now, sweet," he snapped instead, "do you judge others' motives as well as healing the sick?"

Her bottom lip quivered like a hurt child's, and he could have kicked himself. *Spineless fool . . .*

"That wasn't fair," she whispered finally and he nodded.

"You're right, my frau, but neither is life. You'd best hide that jug where I can't find it again." He brushed past her and made for the front door, slamming it behind him. Then he leaned against the wood, wanting to go back in and comfort her but unable to bring himself to do so.

He stepped unsteadily off the porch and started a careful climb away from the cabin, glad that his stomach roiled with so much whiskey after a dry spell. *If I throw up, it'll be exactly what I deserve. . . .*

He swallowed and took a misstep, carefully righting himself, then wishing it might be as easy to be better in life . . . *but I don't know how . . . I don't even know what better looks like. I only know what my grandfather did and that is pain, plain and simple. And Sarah deserves so much more as a wife . . . so much more than I can give. . . .*

He kept moving forward, putting one foot in front of the other, knowing that going back was simply not an option.

Chapter Eight

Sarah swiped at her eyes with the backs of her hands as a brisk knock sounded on the cabin door. She frowned. *I don't care if he's out there on his knees, I'll still . . .* She flung the door open and blinked in surprise at Martha Umble, the bishop's gray-haired, dark-eyed frau.

"Frau . . . Umble," Sarah stuttered.

Martha Umble was insightful but usually dour, and Sarah wasn't sure she was ready for any pious wisdom at the moment. She bit her lip at the irreverent thought, but then her face cleared; perhaps the older woman merely needed her services as a healer.

Sarah widened the door. *"Sei se gut, kumme* in."

Martha grunted and entered, then proceeded to make herself comfortable at the kitchen table, placing the typical hand-sewn blue bag the *Amisch* women often carried in lieu of a purse on the wood in front of her. Sarah quickly took a chair opposite her.

"Is there—something I can do for you?" Sarah asked.

"Tea. Rose tea. But *nee*, there's nothing you can do for me, though I think there's much that can do for you."

"Ookaay." Sarah smiled in a vague manner and

60

got up to set the rose petals brewing, then took her chair again.

Frau Umble leaned forward. "It's like this—you lost May—your teacher but also your friend, right?"

Sarah nodded, wondering where the conversation was headed as the other woman continued.

"And I lost—though we talk through our letters—my friend, Mary Malizza, 'cause she went back to run her inn."

Sarah recalled the flamboyant Mary Malizza, whom Edward had brought to the mountain earlier that summer for a visit. Mary and Martha Umble had become, oddly, strange and fast friends until Mary had to go back to West Virginia to run her inn for the rig workers.

"Well—" Martha slapped her aged hands down on the tabletop and Sarah jumped. "That's it then, child. I've *kumme* to be your friend, if you'll have me."

Sarah had to laugh with pleasure. Only among her people could one perceive a need and be so calm in offering to fulfill it. She didn't know Martha Umble any more than the man in the *munn*, but she had a *gut* inkling that there was much more beneath the surface than met the eye. She leaned across the table with both hands extended.

"I accept with pleasure, Martha . . . *danki*."

Martha squeezed her hands with a half-toothed

smile. "*Gut!*" Her voice dropped to a conspiratorial whisper. "Now let's talk about that one-eyed wild husband of yours."

Sarah dropped her gaze and wondered what she'd gotten herself into. . . .

Edward picked his way down to the main path that led past Ben Kauffman's store and decided abruptly that he'd rather not meet anyone from the community at the moment. Instead, he turned onto a side trail that wound into the forest and nearly stumbled over an exposed root. Clearly, being half drunk and half blind was not a particularly *gut* combination, and he pulled a long stick for support from the heavy brush with reluctance.

He'd only gone about ten feet when he nearly bumped into an *Englischer* dressed in khakis, a flannel shirt, and a hard hat.

Edward scowled. It was not always unusual to find an outsider on the mountain, but the man's dress of a rig engineer set off all kinds of alarms in his head.

"Hiya," the man said, shifting the backpack he carried to extend a hand. "I'm Jim Hanson with R and D Incorporated."

Edward didn't return the handshake, and the other man smiled a bit nervously. "I'm an engineer working for a company on the Marcellus Shale find—do you—know about it?"

No, I'm a dumb Amischer *who never hears*

news beyond the latest cow's birthing. . . . "I know about it."

The man broke into a smile. "Great! Well, R and D has done some initial testing and it looks like it might be possible to put a well up around these parts."

"A well and then a rig?" Edward asked, clearly surprising the engineer with his question.

"You know the difference? I didn't think the Amish concerned themselves with things like that, but then again, I heard it was an Amish man who wrote to our company, suggesting we take a look."

Edward squeezed the stick he held hard, longing to take a swing at the guy for his obvious ignorance and then wanting to knock himself flat, too, for being the writer of the now deeply regretted letter.

"Look, why don't you forget about wells and rigs?" Edward said finally. "These mountains can be dangerous for someone who doesn't know his way around. I'd go back where I came from if I were you."

The engineer's face cleared and he laughed a bit and shrugged. "Sorry, but I've got a job to do. I came to find an Edward King—he's Amish. Any idea which direction I should take?"

A starling darted overhead, drawing out the moment with its shrill cry, and Edward shook his head, then extended his hand.

"Edward King. Not exactly happy to meet you."

• • •

Mahlon moved his milking stool to the next cow and tried not to think about the strange ache in his heart. He was willing to acknowledge to himself that he missed Sarah, but it was something more. *Fear* . . . The word drifted across his consciousness with a sinister power, and he immediately tried to ignore it, muttering part of a Bible verse aloud and startling *auld* Bessy so that she kicked.

Truth be told, he'd been afraid for as long as he could remember . . . of his *fater*, of knives, of guns, of women, of his own children. He grimaced as he recalled the time *Grossmuder* May had come to this very barn to make her case for Sarah studying to become a healer for the community.

He'd heard the tap of her cane first against the wooden floor and had peered blankly up at her from his milking stool. The *auld* healer had no call to visit his barn—he was as healthy as a horse.

"You'd get a fair sight more milk, Mahlon Mast, if you wouldn't pull so hard on that left teat." *Grossmuder* May gave him a toothless smile and he'd felt himself flush.

"I've been milkin' since I was a *buwe*," he'd retorted, but there was no true strength to his words; May had always made him nervous.

"We all have somethin' to learn, no matter how long we've been doin' a familiar thing."

He'd felt like there was more to her words than just teats and milk and he'd let his hands drop to rest on his thighs. "What can I do for you, *Grossmuder* May?"

She'd sniffed. "*Ach*, somethin' ye won't be wantin' ta do, I wager. But I'll ask it jest the same—I'm not long fer this world, Mahlon, and Ice Mountain needs a healer. I feel yer *dochder*, Sarah, has the right spirit fer doin' the job."

He'd swallowed at her words, heard the cow shift restlessly in the dry straw, then felt a shiver go through him as he thought of the mysteries of healing. . . . *Sarah . . . my Sarah . . .*

"*Ach*, don't give in to the fear that haunts ye— give the child a chance fer a different sort of life." *Grossmuder* May had nudged him with the tip of her cane and he'd nearly jumped.

"I ain't afraid."

The *auld* woman had cackled out a laugh, but then he'd seen her wrinkled face soften in the dim shadows of the barn. "*Ach*, but ye are—and one day, ye'll face those fears. But fer now, we talk of Sarah. What do ye say to me teachin' her how to serve our people?"

I'll face those fears, he thought, hearing the words echo again and again in his mind. But when it came to Sarah, and the way May put it, he knew in his heart that he had no choice.

"*Jah*," he'd muttered. "*Jah*, she may serve."

Chapter Nine

Edward found his way back to his new home before dark; the whiskey had long before lost its glow in light of the appearance of the engineer. He sighed as he eased open the front door, hoping Sarah would be asleep. Instead, she was reclining in a high-backed brass tub. She'd moved the kitchen table and chairs to the side to make room for her bath. His gaze was transfixed as the water formed rivulets of steam around her surprised face.

He almost backed out of the room; it could fast turn into a torture chamber, he realized painfully. But he steeled his resolve, closed the door behind him, and pulled the latch tight. He turned to face her, fighting to keep his gaze above her shoulders, then dropped his leg over a turned hard-backed chair. He pillowed his chin on his fist, watching her.

She pulled her slender knees up to her chest and hugged her arms about herself, but there was no mistaking the gentle and enticing curves of her body as the water caught the kerosene lamplight and glistened on her skin.

"Get out," she finally managed, the shock still on her face.

Yet he couldn't leave. He'd never seen how long

her hair was before, but now, piled in a haphazard mass atop her head, a few honeyed brown strands fell loose to touch the floor, while a few more lay against the slender curve of her neck.

"*Nee*," he whispered, mesmerized. "I've been out all afternoon and done my penance for stealing your drink. Now I'm thinking that a husband's right to watch his wife bathe may be a gift—one I'd not thought of before."

She arched a dark brow. "I would have supposed you'd thought of everything before."

"In regard to physical pleasure?" He lowered his gaze. "Why, thank you, I think."

His lone eye didn't miss the rosy flush coloring her cheeks as she glared at him before looking away. He ignored the fact that his knuckles were white where he clenched them beneath his chin and wondered exactly what she imagined he knew . . . the ideas were as tantalizing as she was, sitting there.

"I wish you'd give me some privacy."

"I wasn't aware that was part of our agreement." He was teasing her, and working himself up at the same time. "I'm pretty comfortable right here." *Liar.*

She shook her head, the loose, damp strands sticking to her shoulders. "If the situation were reversed, I'd let you take your bath in peace."

"I'd rather you wouldn't." He continued to look at her, this time meeting her eyes. Keeping his gaze on her face gave him a little relief. He didn't want to take the teasing too far.

But if she only knew what she was doing to him simply by sitting in a tub of bathwater . . .

She tried to finish her bath as demurely as she could, making sure to keep herself as covered as possible with her arms. After a few minutes, he saw her shiver. He immediately rose and moved near the tub while she floundered, sloshing water over the sides, still trying to cover herself from his view.

"*Kumme.* Enough of this foolishness." He picked up a towel from the pile on the floor and opened it wide. "You'll catch a chill if you sit there much longer, and I'll not be responsible for the healer becoming ill."

She stared at the outstretched towel with a doubtful look. "Close your eye," she demanded.

He obliged with a smile, but not before taking a quick peek as she hoisted herself from the water to her feet.

Rosy breasts, the curve of her hip and bottom, and long, long legs all caught in a flash in his mind, forcing him to grip the edges of the towel hard as she stepped into its embrace. He swore he could sense the warmth of her freshly bathed skin through the towel between them. Unconsciously, he inched the fabric closer to him so that she nearly stumbled to reach for it as she stepped on the floor.

He caught her close, breathing in the heady

scent of citrus and rain, all of which struck him with painful familiarity. It was her own beautiful scent, one that reminded him of deep kisses and stolen touches. He dipped his head toward her neck so that he might breathe more deeply of her; then he opened his eye.

"Edward," she squeaked, her small hands against his chest, burning like twin brands. "You said no touching—remember?"

Sarah felt herself grow both more aroused and frustrated. He thought this was a game, one that she didn't necessarily want to play on his terms. She looked up into his face and saw the faintly teasing glint in his eye. She realized with vague intuition that he probably enjoyed playing with her as much as a cat did a mouse. But he was crossing a line—one he had drawn himself.

He smiled down at her lazily. "I'm not touching you," he said, holding up the towel a bit and forcing her nearer his tall frame. "At least not now."

She gasped as she was caught by the rapidly dampening cotton against her back and the press of his body at her front. She shifted nervously, inadvertently rubbing her hip against his waist.

He winced, and she felt him. He was more affected than he was letting on—just as she was.

She looked up to see his blue eye flash with pain and passion, mingling in a simmering heat that brought her restless hands to a stop as she grasped his blue shirtfront.

But then he drew the towel across her shoulders and purposefully stepped away. "Go to bed," he growled with abrupt hoarseness.

But she couldn't move, not even when his gaze raked her bare front from head to toe. She was being bold. Brazen, even. Yet a part of her somehow realized she wanted him to look. She wanted him to see her.

"Sarah." His tone held warning and want.

She bit her bottom lip, watching his reaction, still not making a move to cover herself.

He muttered a curse and snatched up a second towel, tossing it over her. "For *Gott*'s sake, Sarah, I'm not a saint." He turned his back to her, raking his hand through his hair. "I'll sleep out here by the fire tonight."

A sudden flush of shame came over her as she grasped the towels to her body. His words released her from the enchantment that had thrilled and confused her at the same time. But now embarrassment drove her from him. She wanted to get away from him as soon as she could. She hurried to the bedroom, pulling the curtain closed behind her, wondering what she'd done.

Sarah squirmed on the hard church service bench, trying to discipline her thoughts into some semblance of worship. But even the usual hymns, sung low and without music, did little to soothe her when she thought of her husband's body so close to hers after last night's bath.

I'm wanton . . . I confess that I'm wanton for desiring my husband's touch, Derr Herr . . .

An abrupt poke in her ribs brought her crashing back to the present as Martha Umble gave her a smile.

"Thought you were drifting off," the older woman whispered.

Sarah flushed and shook her head.

Though she tried to keep her attention on the bishop, her gaze wandered until she saw Edward's bright blond head. He was sitting next to Joseph, both *bruders* head and shoulders above those men nearest them. She had to control her rampant thoughts once more until Bishop Umble rose to preach, and soon she was caught up as usual in the *auld* leader's odd but provoking manner of speaking.

"The most difficult type of forgiveness is often that of forgiving ourselves." The bishop's voice echoed in the Zooks' biggest barn, startling a stray pigeon and breaking the fragrant silence of the somnolent summer day.

Sarah watched as he paced before the community, his hands behind his back, his wrinkled face introspective and lifted to the sunshine that made its way through stray cracks in the weathered wood.

"If we are to 'love our neighbor as our self,' then it follows that we are to love ourselves. Yet many of us carry *auld* wounds, *auld* guilt—and we stay—unforgiven inside."

Sarah sucked in a breath as she thought of her own *fater*, and her gaze darted to where the gray-beards sat together. *Surely he carries the mystery of some wound inside of him. . . . Ach, Derr Herr, let him somehow be healed and learn to forgive himself. . . .* Then her thoughts caught and held as her soul prayed of its own volition. *And let Edward be healed as well . . .*

Even when he'd been fully sighted, Edward had hated the milling about that normally took place after the bimonthly church service. But now he felt positively trapped behind his eye patch by the general babble and blur of faces and found himself searching for his wife's trim frame in the press of the community.

Joseph nudged him gently. "She's over there, to the right, by the barn door."

"Is it so obvious what I'm thinking?" Edward asked sourly even while he managed a polite nod at Ben Kauffman, the general store owner.

"Probably only to me—and your frau of course."

"Yeah . . . right."

"You don't think Sarah knows you?" Joseph asked mildly as he shouldered a way for them through the crowd.

"*Nee*," Edward returned, then felt himself broadsided by a female form. He half-turned, putting up a hand instinctively so he wouldn't fall, and came in contact with a full breast. He jerked his hand away as Deborah Zook, the eldest of the Zook girls at twenty-two, cooed softly at him and then burst into a sultry giggle. He felt himself flush at his lack of coordination.

"Why, Edward King, and just out of service, too . . . whatever will my *fater* say?"

"My apologies, Deborah," he muttered stiffly. "But I'd wager your *fater* would remember that I'm newly married."

"I know, and lucky girl, too but I'd like to think that a man like you is wasted on someone as sedate as the new healer."

Edward felt an unexpected surge of anger at hearing his wife maligned and would have said more if Joseph hadn't obviously taken the situation in at a glance.

"Won't your *mamm* be expecting your help with the food, Deborah?" His voice was cold, level, and Edward appreciated the interruption for once.

The girl flounced away without another word and Edward exhaled slowly.

"Forget her," Joseph said, "though she looks at you like something she could eat with a spoon."

"*Danki* you lout." Both *bruders* laughed low together as they cleared the barn doors and stepped into the late summer sunshine.

Edward moved away from Joseph to make his way to Sarah, but his steps slowed as he realized she was surrounded by her entire family—including her *fater*.

Great . . . Edward sighed to himself, then decided he might as well get things over with and started to walk forward to greet his new in-laws.

Then an odd sound cut through the air. The pervading noise came from overhead, and Edward felt the press of those gathered as they exited the barn to stare into the sky. A helicopter broke the nearby line of trees and flew almost directly overhead. A long rope and a bright red satchel hung from the base of the aircraft, then was detached as the copter roared away.

Edward heard the questions swirling around him and knew he was the only one who was seemingly unmoved by the appearance of an aircraft so close to the mountain. He . . . and Sarah. He watched her separate herself from her family and walk toward him, her gray eyes wide and set.

"Edward, what have you done?" she asked above the concerned murmurings around them.

"Only what I've already confessed, sweet. Are you surprised?"

She took a step closer to him. "You know as well as I do that the helicopter was carrying surveillance equipment—for Marcellus Shale.

They're surveying to see if the gas find runs under Ice Mountain."

Edward squinted at the blue sky, then looked back to her. "How do you know that? And what if it does? It could mean a lot of money and a change of life for our people."

"An end of life for our people, you mean." She hugged her arms about herself. "We have to tell the bishop."

He caught her elbow. "No need, sweet. I imagine our resident engineer is about to do that for us."

Edward turned her to face the tree line as Jim Hanson, the engineer he'd met in the woods, started toward the gathered group. He walked with easy strides, carrying a roll of maps in one hand.

"Who is that?" Sarah asked softly, and Edward steeled himself against the pain of her question.

"Destiny calling," he answered, then moved to introduce the engineer to the community.

Chapter Ten

Mahlon caught his wife's arm and automatically pulled her behind him as Jim Hanson approached. Edward moved to greet the man with obvious familiarity. "Stay here with the *kinner*," Mahlon commanded. "I must see what this is all about."

He inched through the still crowd, unable to hear the words Edward exchanged with the *Englischer*. But then, his new son-in-law seemed to welcome the bishop's approaching presence and, after a moment, they all three turned to face the community that stood waiting with dignified reserve.

"Folks, I'd like to introduce to you Jim Hanson—an engineer," Bishop Umble said loud enough for everyone to hear. He turned to the *Englischer*. "What brings you to Ice Mountain, Jim?"

"One of your own Amish folks gave us an invitation to come and explore this area." The engineer grinned as he spoke in a patronizing tone. He pulled out a piece of paper from the pocket of his tan pants, then held it up. "Edward King here seems to know a lot about the gas rigs. Going on the information he gave us, our company, R and D, believes we will find that the Marcellus Shale, and its deep gas reserves, run under this mountain. If we do, you folks stand to make a lot of money." He looked around at the crowd, still smiling, as if full of confidence and pride. "Although we're pretty sure we'll find the gas, we need to do a bit more exploration. The helicopter that just flew over is dropping off research equipment for our company."

Mahlon shifted his weight and tried to ignore the quiet murmurings around him as his own anger rose within him. *My own son-in-law invited* Englischers *to invade the mountain. . . .*

Bishop Umble put his hands behind his back and cleared his throat. His expression, as usual, was inscrutable. "Are you staying hereabouts, Jim?"

"In one of the little cabins on the other side of the mountain." The engineer continued to smile, as if his grin was all he needed to pacify the crowd. "Any of you are welcome to come over to see me. We can talk and share a cup of coffee whenever you'd like."

The bishop nodded. "*Danki*—er, thank you, Jim. We'll do that." He turned to his fellow *Amisch*. "But for now, I'd like everyone to return to their homes for prayer about this . . . situation." He cleared his throat again. "The men will meet and talk tonight at my barn. Seven o'clock sharp."

Mahlon caught the brief hesitation in the bishop's stance before he turned and extended a hand to the engineer, who shook it gladly. Then the *Englischer* turned and walked off.

Mahlon glared as he saw Edward King do the same, leaving Sarah behind. *The audacity. Dear* Gott*, he'll be shunned for writing that letter. . . .* Mahlon's hands fisted at his sides as the crowd quietly dispersed, following the bishop's command to go home and pray . . . leaving Mahlon no choice but to do the same.

Edward walked numbly on the faint forest trail, his gait uneven because of his eyesight. Then he turned with abrupt surety into a thick patch of mountain laurel and stopped. Before him stood his most recent still. He breathed out a| sigh of relief.

He'd halfheartedly promised himself that he wouldn't come back to this hidden place after his accident. But after the meeting, the urge to drink had clawed at him, the call too great to ignore. He bent to flip up a small dirt-covered trapdoor in the forest floor. He stared down at the carefully lined up Mason jars sitting in the cool earthen dugout and mentally made a count. Twenty-three. *Enough to drink . . . enough to sell to* Englischers *off the mountain . . . and so easy to make more.*

He pulled up one jar of the clear liquid, his mouth already watering at the idea of the relief the shine would bring. No, not relief. Release, from the pain that squeezed his chest so tight he found it difficult to draw a deep breath. From that moment when he'd looked at Sarah's face as Jim Hanson spoke, and his heart started to crack. Gott, *who needs a wife if it means seeing a woman in pain,* nee, *anguish. . . .*

He carefully lowered the trapdoor, kicked some pine straw over it, then unscrewed the lid of the Mason jar. He drew in a deep breath and put the glass to his lips as the first drops hit the back of his throat like the spatter of a dream.

"I'd have a word with you, *sohn*. If you've the time."

Edward choked and spun to see Bishop Umble standing calmly by the still. The *auld* man casually fingered a coil of cool copper while Edward blinked at him like he was an apparition. The moonshine sloshed over his hand as he took an unsteady side step, then straightened in bewilderment. "How did you find me?"

The bishop smiled easily. "You forget that I've been bishop on this mountain since long before you were born . . . ran it when your *grossdaudi* was still young, in fact."

"Yeah," Edward muttered, pushing aside the onslaught of emotions the mention of his grandfather produced.

The bishop's smile disappeared. He sighed and gestured to some nearby stumps. "Would you care to sit and talk?"

Nee . . . *not for a second, because you're probably going to tell me I'm shunned or doomed. What would happen to Sarah then?* He swallowed and nodded. "Sure." He couldn't steady his hands as he tried to screw the lid back on the jar. He gave up and let it sit askew as he carried it with him to sit down near the mountain's spiritual leader.

79

"Fall's coming," the bishop declared, leaning back a bit and staring up at the sky.

Edward wished the old man would get to the point. He watched him and clutched the damp jar between his hands like a glistening charm.

Bishop Umble dropped his head, then slanted him a glance. "What were your reasons for writing that letter, *sohn*?"

Edward wet his lips. *Because I wanted out . . . because this place, this damn perfect place needs to be modernized, because I suck at being* Amisch *. . . and because I was drunk.*

"Make something up," the bishop suggested, eyeing him with a mild smile.

Edward bowed his head and rubbed hard at the jar. "I—I don't know what to say. I guess I wanted to make things better for our people, give them the chance to choose an improved life. I mean, the money could—"

"*Ach, jah*, the money . . . what men won't do for money in the world." He turned a knowing gaze on Edward. "Yet, Edward King, I somehow don't think money matters much to you."

Edward paused. "It doesn't." *There, that was the truth.*

The bishop slapped his thighs, then rose to his feet. "All right, then. I expect there'll be plenty of questions tonight at the barn, but I'll answer them the best I can. All you need to do is show up."

Edward stared up at him. "That's—that's it? You're not—I mean, I thought . . ."

Bishop Umble walked toward him and passed a light hand over Edward's head. "Do you understand grace, *sohn*? The infinite mysterious love that knows no bounds, that gives without asking what there is in return?"

"*Nee*," Edward whispered, feeling trapped and miserable and half-reduced to tears by the *auld* man's gentle words. He'd heard about grace all his life. But until that moment, it had only been a word, something thrown around as a concept but rarely put into practice. He'd never understood what it meant . . . and now he suspected he'd caught a small glimpse of the power both the word and the act contained.

"You will understand one day, Edward King." The bishop glanced at the still again. "If you'd lengthen the distillate of copper on your still, you'd get better than one hundred thirty proof on your second run."

Edward's eye widened as the old man disappeared behind the tangle of laurel. He'd not only been spared a lecture and a shunning, he'd also been given a tip to make his moonshine better. What had just happened here?

He stared down at the jar in his hands and for a long moment wrestled harder than ever not to give in to the pull of the drink. Then he shook himself, remembered who and what he was, and unscrewed the lid. "Grace," he muttered aloud, swallowing a thick mouthful. "Ha!"

Sarah refused her family's offer to take her back to her *auld* home to spend the afternoon in prayer after Edward had left the service without her. Instead, she stalked away from the murmurs of the other women and headed to her cabin, flinging open the door, prepared for battle. But, of course, Edward wasn't there.

She groaned aloud in frustration and hastily grabbed a decades-old gathering basket from a hook on the wall and marched back outside. Though any kind of work was frowned upon on Sundays, she rationalized that gathering herbs to help the sick would surely be acceptable to *Gott*.

She walked in the thick woods, her anger slowly dissipating as she found herself listening to the striking call of a blue jay and catching the scent of late summer wild roses. She found what looked like a deer trail and began to follow it, pausing to stop and gather some wild mint, which made a good cure for stomach upset.

A man's whistling caused her to straighten in surprise, and she was amazed to see Bishop Umble walking toward her along the path. Usually the poor man did not stray beyond the center of the community with his duties as bishop.

"*Ach*, Sarah King, a fine day, *jah*?"

"*Ja-ah*," she stuttered. *If you didn't count the letter her own husband had written and the appearance of the helicopter and . . .*

"Do you know, I believe I saw some more mint up ahead and off to the left of the trail—right by the stand of laurel." He gave her a benign smile and she stared after him for a moment as he moved past her and began to whistle once more. Then she shrugged and made her way to the mountain laurel, looking carefully for the additional mint.

She searched for the plant but didn't see a trace of it. "He must have been mistaken," she muttered and started to back out of the bushes when the distinct sound of a man's singing made her freeze to the spot.

"Alas my love, you do me wrong
To cast me off discourteously;
And I have loved you oh so long
Delighting in your company . . ."

There was no mistaking the rich timbre of the voice, though she'd only heard him sing church hymns. But the choice of his song today had little to do with community meetings and the words irked her. She pushed through the laurel, not yet wanting to reveal herself.

Then she saw the still and the Mason jar in his big hand. She stumbled over a root, nearly dropping her basket, but managed to keep on her feet as she walked into the small clearing. The singing stopped.

He stared at her as if she was an apparition. She put a hand up to straighten her *kapp*, then jerked her fingers down again. *How can he make me feel self-conscious, like I'm intruding on some intimacy in his life, when he's the one who's doing wrong?*

She bit her lip as he continued to stare at her and it hit her hard . . . *because I am intruding. He loves to drink . . . alcohol is the thing he lets in the closest . . . not me.* The thought filled her with anger and fury and she stamped a small foot in frustration. "Why are you doing this?" she demanded.

He shrugged and gave her a surly half smile. "Since when has the location of my still become a public stopping point?"

"The bishop told me there was some mint here and . . ." She trailed off. Had Bishop Umble seen the still? Surely not, because Edward continued to drink.

He raised the jar to his mouth and took a long swig. She advanced three steps closer to him, longing to knock the liquid from his hand. But there was something powerful and dangerous about him sitting there, something that made her want to both touch him and run away.

He got to his feet with easy grace, and she noted

that his white shirt had pulled loose from one side of his waistband. He looked like what he was—dissolute and rakish—and yet, *Gott* help her, she wanted him with her body and heart.

She decided to back away when he lazily stepped toward her, but his laughter halted her steps and she felt herself press back against a giant tree. She clutched her gathering basket almost defensively in front of her and waited while loud heartbeats echoed in her ears to see what he'd do next.

He moved across the forest floor until he stood before her, the jar in one hand while he reached out with his other to casually run his fingertips down the curve of her left breast. She caught her breath and pressed harder against the tree, thankful for its steadiness.

"You always wear gray," he mused, continuing the slow exploration of her breast until she shivered as he brushed the tight centered bud. "Why?"

She shook her head, her words feeling thick and caught at the back of her throat. "I—I don't know."

"Because you want to hide, to blend in, to be the perfect, unseen *Amisch* woman. . . ." He took another swallow from the jar and leaned near enough so that his breath brushed her cheek and she could almost taste the smell of the alcohol on him.

She sucked in a staggered breath when he shifted the jar and transferred his attentions to her right breast. "I—I don't want to be perfect."

Something changed in the lines of his handsome face at her words and he bent into her, forcing her to arch her back. "Like hell you don't," he breathed.

Then a thought triggered mercifully in her brain. "You're touching me," she cried, almost in desperation against her own traitorous body. "You're breaking your word."

He squeezed her breast and laughed softly. "Damn right, sweet, and it's my word to break. Besides, I'm a little drunk, and maybe I won't remember . . . or else I'll never forget."

He moved so fast that she couldn't catch her breath. He flung the glass jar from him and she heard it shatter against a rock. Then he grabbed her basket and tossed it aside, too. She was about to protest when he slammed his mouth into hers, catching her small hands in each of his own and raising them above her head.

He pressed her hard against the thick tree, ignoring her tight, breathy cries as he worked his tongue against her lips, demanding entry until she yielded and he drove deep into her soft mouth. She whimpered, but he pressed on, wanting something and nothing and everything from her. She tasted like honey and spring, and he swayed a bit on his feet, shaken by how much he wanted her as his wife in truth. And it would be so simple—*right here. . . .* But something in his spirit compelled him beyond the demands of his body, and he tore himself away from her with a savage cry, letting her hands drop and bending over to put his hands on his knees, like a runner after a marathon, trying to catch his breath.

Then he felt the air from the rush of her skirt and straightened in time to see her run off into the laurel as if the devil himself was at her heels. . . .

Chapter Eleven

"I was shunned for far less than that *buwe*'s letter." Mahlon spoke in gruff tones as he tipped in the aged bentwood rocker. He sat on his front porch next to Anne in the waning light of day as Ernest and Samuel lugged milk pails back from the nearest barn.

"Perhaps," Anne said softly. "But Bishop Umble is a just man, while Bishop Loftus was . . . not."

"Just? *Jah* . . . I guess. But what does justice have to do with mercy?" Mahlon swallowed hard as his mind telescoped far into his own past. . . .

He'd been eighteen the summer after he'd joined the church. There had been no opportunity for *Rumspringa* under Bishop Loftus's rule. Either a youth joined the church or left the community—not that he hadn't wanted to leave. He'd wanted to go when he'd been nine, since the first time he saw his *fater* strike his *mamm*. But that was kept in silence, along with so many of the altercations that took place during his growing-up years—an adolescence full of secrets and lies and darkness. . . .

Then that summer day came—a picnic after a church meeting and moments that seemed highlighted in his consciousness, frozen like tender apple blossoms caught in a cruel ice storm. His mother had tripped and spilled the bowl of fragrant potato salad down his *fater*'s shirtfront.

Mahlon had held his breath, sudden alarm and unexpected rage coursing through him. If they were at home, he knew the abuse his mother would have suffered for such an infraction. And for a moment he'd forgotten where they were. Blinded by the urge to protect her, he'd grabbed his *mamm*, pulling her instinctively behind him, then turned to face his *fater*, who'd risen to his full height, a good head taller than Mahlon. Anger flashed in the man's eyes, so quickly only Mahlon saw it. But it hadn't mattered; nothing had existed except the fact that he needed to keep his mother safe. For once, he needed to take a stand. He swung and struck his father full in his long-bearded face.

The blow made an echoing sound that broke into his mind, and he suddenly became aware of the people gathered around him, staring at him in horror. He'd struck his father, dishonored him before all. The clumps of potato salad on the other man's white shirt began to dance in sick drips before Mahlon's eyes as Bishop Loftus walked slowly toward them.

Mahlon straightened his spine before meeting his father's gaze. He didn't know what to expect, but he hadn't been prepared for the sinister glare that pierced him like the blade of a knife, making him nearly back away out of fear. Then the look was gone and his *fater* stood, bowing his head and appearing entirely grief-stricken that his son would shame him in front of his people.

Mahlon had been confused, shaken, as his *mamm* had left him, ignoring him completely as she hurried to his *fater*. She didn't look at Mahlon as she laid her small hand on his *fater*'s arm. Taking his side, the way she always had.

"Mahlon Mast." Bishop Loftus's voice was low but still loud enough to carry to the ears of every single witness. "What have you done?"

A different kind of fear traveled up his spine. *What did I do? Dear* Gott, *what did I do?*

"Mahlon?"

He jerked at the sound of Anne's soft voice. Blindly, he tipped forward in his chair, trying to span the chasm between the past and the present. He slowly turned to look at her. "*Jah*?"

"Be you well? You seem far away."

He got to his feet and shook his head. "I'm fine. I'll head over to the bishop's barn now and we will see. . . ." He swallowed, the images of that day finally fading into the recesses of his memory. "We will see what our new *sohn*-in-law has wrought."

He ignored his wife's worried gaze and stepped off the porch into the coolness of the evening.

Sarah ran all the way home after her encounter with her husband in the woods. She gained the cabin and slammed the door behind her, gulping in air, only to be startled out of breath again when a peal of feminine laughter caused her heart to miss a beat.

Sarah peered into the relative dimness of the cabin's kitchen and saw Deborah Zook, a girl near her own age, rise from a chair with sultry grace.

"*Ach*, so the healer returns. It seems that *Grossmuder* May was a lot easier to get hold of, but of course she never looked like she could run around the mountain with her hair half down."

Sarah swallowed and resisted the urge to straighten her *kapp* and hair. She squared her shoulders instead, assuming the calm poise and confidence she used when treating members of the community.

"Are you ill, Deborah? What can I do for you?"

The dark-haired girl stepped closer, and Sarah could see the mix of mischief and curiosity in her eyes. Deborah lowered her voice, the tone more than a bit inappropriate. "I took a peek into your new bedroom."

Sarah frowned. "Why would you do that?"

"To see if that man of yours was home." She smirked. "Too bad he wasn't."

Sarah blew out a breath of exasperation, ignoring the rising anger she felt, not only at the girl's nerve but that she would dare to violate Sarah's privacy. Yet as a healer, she had a responsibility not to judge those who sought her out. Though it didn't mean she had to be overly nice, either. "What do you need, Deborah? I'm a little busy right now."

Deborah dropped the smirk, her wide eyes suddenly blinking with uncertainty as she leaned closer to Sarah. "Be it true that anything I tell you here is private like—just between us?"

Sarah hesitated. *Grossmuder* May had taught her that visits and ailments were to be kept confidential as much as possible, but something about Deborah's question made her feel leery. Yet Sarah had an obligation to help . . . *probably it's only some female problem or question. . . .* "*Jah*," she said. "Whatever we discuss is to be kept private."

"*Gut.*" Deborah smiled faintly. "You see, it's

like this—me and Isaiah Smucker have been, well, we've been doin' it lately."

" 'Doin' it'?"

Deborah rolled her eyes. "You know what I mean. Having a little fun . . . and a few other things." She grinned, as if reliving a pleasant memory. Then she looked at Sarah again. "But I don't want to get caught pregnant. Do you have some herbal mixture that can help?"

Sarah stood stunned. She understood Deborah's meaning completely and worked to hide her shock. Birth control was not permitted by her people unless the pregnancy would be a danger to the mother. Instead, women usually accepted children as they came along, each child normally seen as a blessing from *Derr Herr*. To want to prevent pregnancy simply to enjoy premarital sex was unheard of . . . yet not unthought of.

Sarah's mind mentally paged through *Grossmuder* May's book of recipes to the concoction used to prevent pregnancy. She struggled desperately in her mind and heart for a few moments— Who was she to judge what Deborah was doing when she herself might have been in the same situation with Edward had *Gott* not intervened? And which was worse—having premarital sex or having a baby born out of wedlock? Could she even answer that question?

She wet her lips. "You and Isaiah plan to marry?"

Deborah shrugged. "Maybe. Or maybe I'll marry Ezra Pine—me and him have done it a few times, too."

Sarah swallowed, appalled at the other girl's casual admitting to promiscuous behavior, yet outwardly remaining calm. "Deborah—have you thought—well, maybe of waiting until you marry to . . ."

Deborah gave a husky laugh and stepped forward to flick at Sarah's *kapp* string. "What? Like you—*gut* little girl? I heard the bishop had to force your marriage because he caught Edward naked with you."

"That's not true," Sarah protested hotly.

"Uh-huh. Well, it's not like I can't understand it—I mean, a man like Edward has needs. Probably more than the average male around here." She looked at Sarah, the derisive smirk reappearing. "Though what he saw in you, I'll never—"

"I think you can leave now, Deborah," Sarah said, crossing her arms over her chest. "I'm afraid I can't help you."

The other girl curled a sneering lip at her. "That's what I thought you'd say, Sarah King. I can tell by the way you're lookin' at me that you think you're better. More pure." Her eyes narrowed. "One thing's for sure—you ain't no *Grossmuder* May."

And with that final parting shot, Deborah

93

pushed past her to leave with an echoing slam of the cabin door.

Sarah drew a deep breath and felt her eyes well with tears. *I'm not* Grossmuder *May.* She dropped her head in her hands. *Despite how I feel, I shouldn't have made a decision out of anger. I should have prayed. I should have prayed with her. . . .*

A loud knock sounded on the door, causing her to spin around. She went quickly to fling open the wood. "*Ach*, Deborah, I . . ." She stopped and stared blankly at Mary Lyons, Edward's sister, who held her baby, Rose, in her arms.

"Deborah?" Mary asked in her sweet voice. "*Ach*, were you expecting someone? I could *kumme* back later."

"*Nee*," Sarah assured her sister-in-law hastily. "What is it?"

"I know I'm probably being silly because Rose is still so young, but I wondered if she might be teething? She seems fretful."

Sarah almost sighed with relief. *Teething . . . at least I can handle that.* And she urged Mary inside.

The bishop's barn was lit by a myriad of kerosene lanterns that attracted small white moths and gave the place an almost festive air that grated on Edward's senses and made him straighten his eye patch with uneasy fingers. He'd waited until nearly the hour of the appointed meeting to slip inside with his hat pulled low, not expecting Joseph to step from the long shadow of the barn door and touch his arm.

"*Daed* and I are up front. We've saved you a seat," Joseph murmured; then his tone changed abruptly. "Have you been drinking?"

"Only a little," Edward muttered, not wanting to think about the two Mason jars he'd drained after Sarah had run away. His behavior with her had been hazardous and unforgivable. Drinking deeply had seemed like the most logical thing to do to assuage his guilt. But now his head was pounding and he didn't want to hear it from his big *bruder*.

Yet Joseph dropped the matter and turned when Bishop Umble rose to stand before the men of the community.

"*Kumme*," Joseph whispered, and Edward followed with reluctance, aware that all eyes were focused on him.

He slid onto the long bench next to his father and *bruder*-in-law, Jude. Edward's *daed* appeared anxious and gave him a wan smile. Edward had barely had the chance to speak with his *fater* since the accident and now felt shame that the *auld* man appeared so visibly distressed. But Jude nodded with encouragement and Joseph pressed shoulder to shoulder against his right side, and he felt somewhat comforted for a moment. Then Bishop Umble began to speak.

"At times, *Derr Herr* brings things into our lives that we do not expect, that we have not asked for nor do we appear to want. I believe young Edward King's letter and its results may be exactly such a thing—given from the Hand of *Gott* to judge our response. Now, I will hear your questions and concerns."

Edward felt everything drift strangely away from him in that moment; the bishop's words were not what he expected despite their odd conversation at the still. Somehow or other, Bishop Umble made it appear as though what he'd done was working into *Gott*'s plan, and he heard the *auld* leader's question once more in his mind: *Do you understand grace?*

A cranky old voice broke through his reverie and Edward recognized Amos Smucker as he raised the question that surely must be on everyone's mind.

"Are you going to shun Edward King or not?"

Edward waited, his heart beating hard in his ears in the suddenly palpable silence.

Bishop Umble peered out at the crowd as he stroked his long white beard. "Not," he declared emphatically. "Now, next question."

Chapter Twelve

December 12, 1940

I had an early miscarriage two days ago and almost bled to death. Elias would not send for the midwife until the very last moment because he said I was "a poor breeder—better off dead." But Frau Zug came and packed the bleeding and somehow got hold of an orange to make me fresh juice. It tasted so *gut* to my dry throat. I don't mind overmuch about the miscarriage—may *Gott* forgive me— because I know Elias will turn any children against me—a long life to *kumme* of hate and sorrow. . . . Frau Zug spoke to me quietly when he left the room. She whispered to me the ingredients for a potion that will prevent future pregnancies. Again, I must beg *Derr Herr*'s forgiveness, but I cannot risk my life again, she says . . . and I will not.

May

Sarah shivered in the candlelight, her body tense beneath the bedcovers as she read the shocking entry in the journal. She longed to reach back through time and put her arms around the young May, who'd somehow taken on the strength of the *auld* healer she'd known and loved.

Sarah leaned back against the full feather pillows and twined a piece of her hair around her finger as Deborah Zook's words from that afternoon came back to her. . . . *I am no* Grossmuder *May. . . . Perhaps she was refined by pain and somehow became stronger because of it . . . perhaps Edward is my refining fire, though in no way is he cruel as Elias was. . . .*

"What are you reading?"

Sarah jumped at the husky sound of her husband's voice. She glanced over to see him lounging in the doorway, suspenders loose about his lean waist, his shirt undone, with one arm raised against the wood so that the lamplight caught on the golden thatch at the juncture of his underarm. She quickly closed the journal.

"An *auld* book, that's all. How was the meeting?"

He half smiled. "If you're asking whether I'm shunned, the answer is *nee*, though it was by sheer will of the *gut* bishop that it didn't happen. . . . Are you disappointed, my sweet?"

"What? *Nee*, of course not." She frowned, confused by his question and by the provoking guilt it aroused inside her. *Of course I didn't want to see him shunned, but maybe if someone would speak to him about his behavior, then . . .* She drew rein on the thought. *Then what? Then I wouldn't have to try to manage him?*

She watched as he moved from the doorway with lazy ease, his eye patch very black against the sun-streaked blond of his overly long hair. She moistened her lips as she recalled his burning kiss in the woods and wondered what he was about. . . . Up until now he'd slept before the fire embers, but tonight he seemed moody and purposeful.

She set the journal on her bedside table and lay her hands on the light summer quilt that was drawn over her lap. He rounded the bed and sat down, his back to her. Then he took his shirt off.

"Edward, what are you doing?" She knew that her voice came out a bit high, but she had only to stretch out a hand and she would be able to touch the whipcord strength of his back.

He sighed aloud. "Undressing."

"Why?" she squeaked, and he turned to toss her a grin over his shoulder.

"Nervous?"

"*N—ee*," she stuttered.

He laughed softly. "Don't worry, Sarah King, I already tasted your responsiveness earlier in the woods. I could have had you then, standing up, against that old oak." He rose and slid off his black pants, and she averted her gaze, longing for a place to hide from both his words and his actions. "Not that standing would have been the most comfortable position for a virgin's delicacy . . ." He slid under the quilt and top sheet, and his big body immediately radiated a warmth of its own, coming to her like a blatant caress. He propped himself up on one elbow and faced her, reaching to play with a strand of her hair, while she sat as still as a baby hare.

"*Nee*," he said softly. "Not standing up the first time. When I take you, I want you to *kumme* willingly, to beg me to—"

"Stop!" Childlike, she flung her hands over her ears, unable to tolerate his words or the suggestive images he conjured up. She felt the heat of her cheeks beneath the bottom of the palms of her hands and only reluctantly let her hands drop when he gave her right arm a pull.

He smiled at her wolfishly. "Go to sleep, *boppli*. I mean what I say, and despite the fact that I broke my word earlier about touching you, I now give you my pledge that I will not . . . make love to you . . . until you . . . ask me to."

"Which will never happen," she burst out, half in relief, half in turmoil.

He arched a dark brow at her over his blue tiger's eye. "Never is a very long time. . . . *Gut nacht.*"

And then he rolled over on his side, leaving only the thin quilt tangled on his hip, and she turned out the lamp when she caught a glimpse of the tight, rounded curve of his buttock. She shuffled beneath her half of the quilt and turned on her side, gripping the edge of the bed so as not to touch him in any way, and fell into a dreamless sleep.

● ● ●

Edward gently closed the glass lid on the cold frame after sowing a *gut* handful of carrots and some salad greens. The early morning air brought proof that fall was near as yellowed leaves spun like dancers to settle upon the ground at his feet. He emptied a packet of radish seed into the palm of his hand and was moving on to the next frame when the morning air was cut by the whinnied scream of a horse.

Edward looked up and saw Ben Kauffman and Joseph trying to gain control of a big black gelding. Neither man was apparently having any luck. He pocketed the seed, then hurried as quickly as his eye would allow down the hill to the main track.

The horse reared as he approached, but Edward caught the reins easily, stepping without concern between the slashing front hooves. Immediately, the beast calmed, sensing the lack of fear, and Joseph blew out a harsh breath.

"Edward," he gasped. "You always did have a way with animals."

"*Ach*, and he's a big fine lad. Where's he from?" Edward asked softly, then blew just as gently into the flaring nostrils of the horse.

Ben Kauffman pulled out a red hankie and wiped his brow. "Auction, gosh darn it! I paid for him at auction down Lancaster way and had him brought up here . . . thought he would be a *gut* buggy and sleigh horse for the missus, but as soon as I tried to hitch him up, he went wild. *Narrisch* horse!"

Edward ran an admiring hand down the corded strength of the animal's fine neck. "What are you going to do with him?"

"Why, sell him back or shoot him," Ben growled in frustration.

Edward thought fast, then spoke. "Suppose you let me train him to the buggy for a short time and then we'll see?"

Ben rubbed a meaty hand across the back of his neck in thought. "Well, what'll you charge?"

"Nothing." Edward smiled. "But you pay for his feed. What's his name?"

Ben scowled. "Sunny."

Edward hid another smile and Ben nodded wearily. "You've got yourself a deal. I'll have the *buwes* bring over his tack and feed. Let me know when you need more."

Edward shook Ben's hand, then watched as the older man stomped away.

"Are you *narrisch* yourself?" Joseph asked when Ben was out of earshot.

"What?" Edward asked, raising a brow.

"What's Sarah going to say about having this brute in the barn with *auld* Mollie? That mare won't put up with any baloney."

"This horse is as gentle as a kitten," Edward praised, running his fingers down the black shock of Sunny's mane.

Joseph raised a tentative hand to do the same and the horse began to prance away; he let his hand drop back to his side. "Right. A kitten."

But Edward laughed out loud, feeling right as rain for the first time in a long while.

Sarah awoke to find herself alone in the bed, then glanced at the windup alarm clock and sat bolt upright. Eight a.m. She'd never slept so late in her life, and years of long training drove her to frantically jump from the bed and run into the kitchen, appalled that Edward would have had to get his own breakfast. *Not that it would hurt him one bit . . .* But when she looked around, there was no sign of any cooking or any fresh dishes in the drain. Then she heard an exultant whoop from outside the window and peered out in time to see Edward thunder past the cabin on the back of a big black horse, a welter of colorful leaves flying in the animal's wake.

Sarah felt a clutch of fear in her heart. She didn't recognize the horse, but she knew recklessness when she saw it, and she realized that she couldn't stand the thought of Edward's big, beautiful body lying broken at the bottom of the hill. She ran outdoors, careless of her nightdress and bare feet, and tried to chase after her *narrisch* husband, flailing her arms in their wide billowing sleeves.

She gave up after stubbing her toe and watched him tear around the cabin again to bring the horse to a breakneck stop beside her, frightening her with the proximity of the huge gelding.

"*Gut* morning, sweet." Edward laughed, leaning down to pat the lathered side of the horse.

"What are you doing?" she yelled, hopping on one foot, nursing her sore toe.

He grinned, a flash of white teeth, and slid down from the saddle. "Are you all right, Sarah?"

"*Jah*," she snapped, stopping her hopping and trying to look dignified, despite her wind-whipped hair.

He held the bridle of the horse easily and she started to fume at his scaring her so.

"Edward King, I asked what are you doing?"

"With your permission, my sweet, allow me to introduce the latest temporary member of the family—Sunny. Ben Kauffman came round this morning and gave me a chance at training him to a buggy, and I couldn't pass up the opportunity to work with such fine horseflesh."

She put her hands on her hips. "You do not have my permission and . . ." She broke off when she saw that Edward's gaze had dropped lower on her person, and she realized that she was standing in the sunlight with nothing but her nightgown on. "Oooh, you," she exclaimed, crossing her arms in front of her chest.

He gave her a wicked laugh, then reached

out and caught her about the waist, pulling her inexorably toward him. She felt a quiver of fear go through her at the nearness of the huge horse and winced away from its inquisitive nose as it nudged at her hair.

"See, Sunny likes you," Edward said, bending to nuzzle at her neck with a too-comfortable air. She tried to pull back but sensed that her stiff movements agitated the horse. She stood still instead, unable to ignore the enticing scent of Edward's skin: part sunshine, part sweat, and all male.

"Please, Sarah . . . say yes to the horse," he murmured, moving his mouth to the curve of her ear. "When I'm riding, I forget about my eye."

The words she might have spoken froze on her lips. He'd just confessed a vulnerability, and the acknowledgment almost shocked her.

"You—never talk about your eye," she whispered.

He shrugged against her, and she longed to slip her arms around him, but the horse kept her still.

"All right," she said after a moment. "Keep him for a time."

She felt rather than heard his sigh of relief, but when he lifted his head, his blue eye glinted with passion and power, and she wondered if she'd imagined the crack in his proverbial armor.

"*Danki*, Sarah."

She nodded, glad when he slid his arm from

around her waist, but the horse suddenly pranced and Edward loosened his hold on the reins, making soothing sounds from the back of his throat. Sarah stepped backward and cried out with abrupt pain. The horse tossed its head and Edward glanced down at her.

"Are you all right?" he asked quietly.

Sarah hobbled to the grass and plopped her bottom down on the side of the path. She turned her foot over and grimaced.

"It's a cocklebur," she muttered and began to try to pull the rounded burr from her foot.

"Wait here," Edward said, and she had the vague sense of him moving away with the horse.

He was back in a few moments and she gritted her teeth, working over the two remaining needle-like burrs.

Edward knelt down in front of her and gently took her foot into his big hands. "Let me," he said.

She would have protested, but the briars hurt and she fell back on her elbows, closing her eyes against the glare of the sun. Then she heard the click of a pocketknife and her eyes flew open. "What are you doing? I've got tweezers up at the cabin."

"Do you really think I'd hurt you?" he soothed. "Just relax. I'm going to use the back of the blade and catch the briar between my thumb and the knife."

"Well, then, you'll hurt yourself." She wriggled in objection but stilled as she felt his hands moving with both care and competence.

She felt the relief after a brief time and glanced down to see her husband putting away his knife. She made to rise, but he forestalled any movement on her part by turning her foot and pressing his lips against the inner curve of her ankle.

She watched, lips parted, mesmerized, as if she was outside herself, while he continued to kiss her where she'd never dreamed of being kissed.

Chapter Thirteen

Edward put his mouth against the fine bones of her pale ankle and felt himself shudder with passion. Although Mountain *Amisch* women usually went barefoot, he'd never seen Sarah do so, and he had the thought that he was revealing a secret part of her, exposing more of the woman she really was, instead of the removed girl she pretended to be. He ran his tongue upward, along her calf, and she squeaked and tried to squirm away.

He couldn't help but laugh and looked up to see her gray eyes wide with shock, but he also recognized a shimmer of pleasure. It was enough to move him up the grass, next to her, on his belly. He flung an arm over her hips to keep her still and balanced on his elbow, leaning over to gently kiss a freckle on her pert nose.

"Edward, let me up. Anyone could *kumme* along." She tried to move, and he caught a handful of her nightgown.

"Be still or I pull, sweet," he said, smiling and giving a slight tug to the cotton fabric. She stopped moving instantly, allowing him to study her face at his leisure. She really was beautiful. . . . The thought shook him. . . .

"Don't stare at me so," she complained.

"Why? You must know you're lovely," he said almost stiffly.

She closed her eyes, her dark lashes resting on the cream of her skin, and shook her head. "*Nee*," she whispered.

He frowned. "Look at me, Sarah King."

She did so hesitantly, staring up at him, biting her lips with white teeth.

"You, my sweet, are beautiful, like the rush of spring water and the play of sunshine, and I don't want you to ever forget it."

He watched her struggle with his pronouncement, disbelief and joy mingling in the twin gray pools of her eyes, but then a shadow seemed to fall over her face and she met his eye steadily. "Am I—as beautiful as the girls from the rigs?"

"What?"

He felt as if he'd been sucker punched in the gut

and it hurt, deep and hard. *Damn her intuition—somehow she knows. . . .*

"Sarah, I—"

"Hey, whatcha doin'?" The child's voice was shrill and resonant.

Edward quickly moved to cover Sarah with his body, ignoring her attempts to push him off. He turned and looked over his left shoulder to see Samuel Mast watching them with dancing eyes and his gap-toothed grin.

Edward bent his head into Sarah's gown and muttered a curse, then resumed looking at his small brother-in-law. "Samuel, your sister and I are talking; that's all."

"But Sarah's in her nightgown. . . ."

"I know," Edward said, resisting the urge to grit his teeth for patience; then Sarah's struggles brought her knee into abrupt contact with his groin and he saw stars. He rolled off her, moaning faintly.

"Edward. . . . *Ach*, Edward . . . are you all right? What happened?" She fluttered over him, all virgin white and big gray eyes, and he wanted to throw up with the pain.

"Hey," Samuel said. "*Daed* and Clara and Ernest are *kumming* up the hill."

"Get in the *haus*," Edward managed, not caring who saw him curled up in a fetal position, but Sarah could not be seen outside in her nightclothes by her dolt of a *fater*. . . .

"But . . ." she began.

"*Geh*," he ground out.

He felt the brush of her gown over his hip as she fled, and then he concentrated on straightening his body.

"Are you all right, *Bruder* Edward?" Samuel asked solicitously.

"Fine," Edward coughed, suppressing a gag reflex as he dragged himself into a sitting position exactly in time to see his *fater*-in-law top the breast of the hill. Edward tried to appear nonchalant, but his world was still faintly swimming. He squinted up at Mahlon Mast and saw the derision in the older man's eyes at finding him sitting aimlessly on a bright day with potential for work.

"Be you drunk?" his *fater*-in-law questioned suspiciously.

I wish I was. . . . "*Nee.*" Edward forced a tight smile. "Just sitting a bit—talking to my new—*bruder*—Clara, Ernest, I must get to know you two better as well."

Edward noted that sixteen-year-old Ernest nodded eagerly with a bob of his Adam's apple, while the slightly younger Clara hung back in obvious shyness, her eyes the same pretty gray as Sarah's.

"Well," Mahlon said, a trace of doubt still making his voice ragged, "Anne and I need some things from Coudersport and Mr. Ellis, down at the bottom of the mountain, offered to drive us. We usually have Sarah about to watch the *kinner*, but—" He half-scowled. "Anyway, we wuz wonderin' if the young'uns could spend the afternoon here."

So sorry I took away your built-in babysitter . . . like two teenagers really need watching; they should be minding Samuel themselves. . . . Edward hauled himself to his feet, suppressing his thoughts. "Let's go up to the cabin and check with Sarah," he said.

"You would ask your wife's permission?" Mahlon asked in obvious disbelief, not moving.

Edward wanted to hit him—*one solid blow to knock that royal chip off his shoulder and bring him into the current century. . . .*

"I respect my wife, your *dochder* . . . Of course I ask her permission." Edward started up the rocky path, ignoring Mahlon's grunt of disapproval. *I respect my wife. . . . Is it true? I'd like it to be, but . . .*

"Hey, *Bruder* Edward, can I go look in the stream for crayfish?" Samuel asked, breaking into his thoughts.

"*Jah*, sure," Edward agreed, then concentrated on climbing the steps to the cabin door, his new relatives on his heels. Edward cautiously opened it, hoping that Sarah had had enough time to change, and then allowed everyone to enter the empty kitchen. Seconds later, the curtain leading

111

to the bedroom slid open and Sarah breathlessly emerged with a slight bounce in her step.

Edward noticed that she'd changed into one of her infernal gray dresses and covered it with a clean white apron. Somehow, she'd also found the time to bundle her hair up and pin on her *kapp*. He glanced into her eyes, though, and saw that her question still hung like frost in the air between them. . . . *Am I as beautiful as the other girls . . . the other girls . . .*

He swung away, concentrating on staring out at the pasture beyond the kitchen window, remembering the fleeting joy he'd felt on Sunny's back. Right now he'd give about anything for a drink. *I'll have to visit the still later. . . .*

"Who's horse be that?" Mahlon asked from close beside his right side, and Edward half-jumped, still unused to having no peripheral vision.

"Ben Kauffman's," he answered sourly. "I'm training the horse to a buggy."

"Huh? You got time for that, *buwe*? What about doin' some work 'round this place?"

Edward turned to face his *fater*-in-law, his lips forming a sharp retort, when he felt a slender arm slide about his waist. He forgot what he was going to say at his wife's gentle touch and instead felt his mind sliding to much pleasanter thoughts. It was the first time she'd touched him willingly since the wedding, it seemed, and the muscles in his belly tensed at the nearness of her hand.

"*Fater*, you forget that Edward was able to lay aside plenty of money from his work on the rigs. We will be fine with my work and Edward's gardening."

Suddenly, his world crashed into angry reality and Edward looked down into Sarah's serene face. *Her work . . . my gardening . . . She makes it sound as though she's the provider and I'm the half-blind idiot who . . .*

"Isn't that right, Edward?" She smiled up at him and he looked at her blankly.

"What?"

Her hand convulsed around his side. "You'd be glad to show *Fater* how to use cold frames, wouldn't you?"

No . . . not on your sweet life . . . "Sure . . . anytime."

Mahlon grunted suspiciously. "Seems wrong somehow—taking from the land out of season. Might not be lucky."

"You don't believe in luck," Edward intoned dryly. "Only *Gott*." He felt Sarah's grip again on his side and ignored it. "Your *fater* would like us to . . . watch . . . the *kinner* for the day, sweet. Do you mind?"

"*Nee*," she said with a smile. "I think . . ."

"Great, then I'll see you out, Mahlon." Edward disengaged himself from Sarah's grasp and opened the door in obvious invitation. His *fater*-in-law glared at him but nodded to his children and headed out the door. Edward followed him out onto the porch, closing the door behind him.

"Would you like to see the cold frames before you go?" Edward asked with false cheer.

Mahlon turned and looked at him, then shook his head. "There's a lot you don't know, *buwe*, about life. Maybe a shunning would have taught you. . . ."

"You mean like it taught you?" Edward cursed the words as soon as they were out of his mouth. His *fater* had told him once about Mahlon's shame, but to bring it up on a beautiful autumn morning seemed truly wrong in quick retrospect.

Edward sighed aloud and prepared for the verbal onslaught he knew was both coming and deserved.

Mahlon closed his eyes on Edward's arrogant, hurtful words. Of course the *buwe* would have heard of his shunning in one way or another— *auld* gossip passed down through the years. Yet to be so bold in manner for a *sohn*-in-law . . . *I never would have dreamed of talkin' to Anne's daed so. . . .*

"I'm sorry," Edward muttered, and Mahlon opened his eyes.

"You think it's that easy?"

"*Nee.*" The younger man shook his head.

"Well," Mahlon snorted, "ya got one thing right today." He turned his back on the *buwe*, staring out at the landscape. Then he began to speak, feeling almost compelled for some reason, as he remembered what it was to have been shunned.

"When I was in the *bann*, even my *mamm* stood against me—though she had no choice if she wanted to stay in the church, I s'ppose." He sighed aloud. " 'Twas she who convinced me to go and beg for forgiveness on my knees, to confess that I hadn't meant what I'd done . . . but I did mean it." He turned to look at Edward, who was watching him steadily. "I meant it in the same way that you did, *buwe*—you and Marcellus Shale. Ya wanted to take a shot at the mountain, at what you come from, but it don't work—it won't work."

"I didn't . . ." Edward began, and Mahlon lifted a weary hand to silence him.

"Don't bother none . . . I'd best be going back ta Anne. You keep that eye of yours close on the *kinner*, mind?"

Edward nodded, and Mahlon turned and walked down the wooden steps, concentrating then on the solid, rocky earth beneath his boots.

Sarah closed her mouth when her husband shut the door on her in midsentence. She glanced at her brother and sister, who both were concentrating on anything other than her face, and she forced a quick smile.

"Edward can be abrupt, but he's also really—

affectionate," she said. "I'm sure he only wanted to tell *Fater* good-bye in peace."

Sarah felt the tension lift as Ernest and Clara visibly relaxed, but then the door swung open again and Edward reappeared.

"Your *daed*'s just gone," he said and Sarah nodded.

"I was trying to think of something we might do to entertain the *kinner*," she said brightly, betting that Edward would like nothing more than to sneak off to his still and drink himself into . . .

"How about broom ball?" Edward asked.

"What?"

"Broom ball. You must have played sometime, Sarah. You hit the ball with a broom and . . ."

"I know what it is," she cut him off. "I just thought that you, well . . ." She bit her lip when he edged near her.

"What, sweet? Didn't think I like *kinner*? Actually, you might be surprised," he drawled as he ran a slow finger around the curve of her ear.

Does the man have no modesty to touch me so in front of my siblings? Sarah couldn't control the flush that she knew stained her cheeks and was infinitely glad when Samuel burst open the door.

"Say, *Bruder* Edward, what a horse you've got! Can I have a ride? Sarah, I caught me three crayfish . . . here." He dropped the squirming creatures, and she caught them by instinct, only to recoil a bit from their sliminess.

116

Edward's hand closed over hers quickly, and he'd taken the small creatures from her before she could make a sound.

"Samuel," he said gravely, "never drop something into a lady's hand that she's not prepared to accept. You must learn to be a *gentlemon* and *nee*, you cannot ride Sunny quite yet—he's wild. And take these fellows back to the creek unless you're going to boil them—which I don't suggest."

Samuel pushed his hat back on his head. "Sheesh, *Bruder* Edward, you talk a lot. All right, I'll take 'em back, but I don't want to be no *gentlemon*." The little *buwe* slammed the door on his way out and Sarah was relieved when everyone, including Edward, laughed out loud when he'd gone.

Chapter Fourteen

Edward had no idea what had possessed him to suggest a game of broom ball instead of enjoying a deep drink alone. And further, he soon realized that Ernest was more than eager to talk to him as a *bruder*-in-law and potential friend.

"Joseph says I'm a dab hand at carving wood. He's letting me work on some cabinet legs this week," Ernest announced proudly as he and Edward walked to one of the outdoor sheds in search of a soccer ball.

Edward nodded at Ernest's comment, musing to himself that he knew very little about his *bruder* Joseph's work with some of the young men on the mountain, starting a wood workshop adjacent to the family home. *Not that it's my home anymore . . . I haven't been there in weeks. Not since Joe threw me out.*

"I don't think *Grossmuder* May had much call for a soccer ball." Ernest's strident voice broke into Edward's thoughts and he looked up to see the *buwe* poking about in the shed and looking discouraged.

"Well, then, we'll go and buy one down at Kauffman's. Go run in and tell Sarah we'll be back shortly."

Ernest's thin chest puffed out with obvious pride in being invited to walk alone with his new brother and he took off like a shot back to the *haus*, leaving Edward frowning after him. *I've got no reason to be anything that Ernest could or should admire. . . .* But he had no time to consider further as Ernest huffed back to him.

"Sarah said to get two other brooms as well."

"All right."

Edward turned and they headed down the path that wound around to Ben's store. Edward had the distinctly uncomfortable feeling that he was being not so discreetly scrutinized by his new *bruder*-in-law, and it made him frown and seek desperately for some topic of conversation.

"You sweet on a girl, Ernest?"

To Edward's amazement, the *buwe* solemnly shook his head. "*Nee*, your *bruder* Joseph teaches us at our Wednesday *nacht* group that women should be respected and that being sweet on someone could get you into trouble with having sex before marriage. So, I'll wait until I'm truly in love, not just the feeling of it."

Edward nearly stopped still at Ernest's frank talk. "Leave it to old Joe," he muttered under his breath.

"What?"

"Nothing. Uh, tell me, Ernest, did Joe ever happen to elaborate on how to tell the difference between lust and true love?" *Now, why did I ask that?*

"True love means hope and sacrifice and life and death—the other is a gift from *Gott*, *jah*, but it only lasts for the moment."

"Right," Edward agreed sourly, not knowing whether he was mad at Joe, the *buwe*, or himself, but he was grateful when the big white store came into view.

He mounted the wooden steps with Ernest on his heels and paused outside the big door to listen to the unfamiliar sound of men's voices raised in anger. He looked askance at Ernest, then was almost bowled off his feet when the door was flung open from the inside. Ernest caught his arm as Edward gazed into the reddening face of his own *fater*.

"*Daed*, what is it? What's going on?" Edward asked, regaining his footing.

Abner King threw a harassed glance over his shoulder. "*Kumme* home with me, *buwe*. They're arguing about the Marcellus Shale—that *Englischer*, Jim Hanson, stopped in and the bishop's not around. You'd better not go in right now."

Edward felt himself bristle at the idea of backing down from any fight and moved to ignore his father's words when his *daed* laid a hand on his shoulder. "Edward, *sei se gut* . . . listen for once."

The gentle rebuke stilled him and he looked down at the whitewashed plank floor of the old porch, then shook his head. "I'm sorry, *Daed* . . . I'm not Joe."

He nodded briefly to Ernest, then left them standing on the porch as he squared his shoulders and opened the door to the store.

"Is he a nice man for a husband, Sarah?" Clara asked.

Sarah ran a finger around the edge of the large chipped yellow mixing bowl and smiled faintly at her younger sister. "Nice? Uh . . . sometimes."

Clara visibly shivered. "He looks so—big and scary . . . and that eye patch."

Sarah patted her sensitive sister's hand. "He'd

always be kind to you. And he's not scary to me at all." *At least not often . . .* She sighed to herself as she poured the cake batter into a greased and floured heart-shaped baking tin.

Samuel had begged for a mayonnaise cake before tearing back out to the creek and Sarah hadn't the heart to refuse him the creamy chocolate dessert with its frothy white icing.

"We need to have a wedding quilting for you, Sarah. *Mamm* and I have been talking about it." Clara's eyes shone. "I know the marriage was hasty, and then the—accident, but please say you'll accept a quilting."

Sarah smiled. "Of course, Clara." *Even though I'm not really a wife and am married in name only . . . unless I ask for something different.*

Clara gave a happy clap, then tucked her hands behind her back. "*Ach, gut,* Sarah. *Danki.* Maybe early next month, when the chill really sets in. . . ."

A quick tap on the door interrupted her sister and Sarah turned to open it, wondering if Samuel had brought back something bigger than a crayfish. But, to her surprise, Martha Umble stood there, her left hand swathed in bandages while she held an open bean tin can in her right.

"Hiya, Sarah! Bright morning it was until I cut the tip of my finger off with the ax."

Sarah was aware that Clara had gagged faintly and made for the bedroom.

121

"Well, *kumme* in, Martha, hurry! Where's the bishop?"

"Home. Mad as heck because I won't go down to the hospital. But what's the sense? I'm sure you can give it a fix as quick as any other doctor or nurse."

Sarah pulled out a kitchen chair and gingerly took the tin can. "Kerosene?" she asked, getting a whiff of the pungent stuff. It was an *auld* custom on the mountain that kerosene could cure or preserve just about anything.

"Yep." Martha grinned, revealing a few missing teeth. "Always works."

Sarah nodded, then went to her cupboard and turned up the lamp even though the cabin was flooded with sunshine. She peered down into the murky fluid and saw the fingertip floating casually. It truly was just a sliver of flesh. Sarah chewed her lip.

"All right, Martha. I can stitch it on or disinfect it and duct tape it back into place. I actually suggest the tape."

"Duck 'er up then, luv."

Sarah smiled at her friend's mispronunciation and fetched the big roll of silver tape that Edward had brought home from the rigs. Then she proceeded to gently undo the makeshift bandage Martha had wrapped around her hand.

"Hmmm," Sarah mused aloud. "It's still bleeding, but it is a clean cut. What were you doing with the ax?"

122

"I had that scrawny rooster, Charlie, on the block, and darned if he didn't fly up in my face and get away. I'm lucky the hens didn't get the fingertip—they wuz scrabblin' after it, but I got there first," Martha said triumphantly.

Sarah was cleaning the wound. "Mmm-hmm."

Martha leaned closer. "Where's that man of yours?"

"*Ach*, he went with Ernest to set up for broom ball. We're watching the *kinner* today." Sarah carefully lifted the bit of flesh from the kerosene with tongs.

"Well, if you ask me," Martha whispered, "it won't be long 'til yer watchin' *kinner* of yer own. A big man like that will be *gut* with the children and you."

Sarah frowned as she carefully fit the pieces of flesh together. *I don't want to think about* kinner *with Edward and I don't have to, anyway, not until I say . . . until I ask . . . Never, never, never . . .*

"Nuthin to say, hmmm?" Martha asked knowingly. "Wal, I don't blame you none."

Sarah concentrated on winding the duct tape around the wound, then straightened after a few moments. "There. *Gut* as new." She cleaned up the bits and pieces, then disinfected her hands.

"All right, Clara, you can *kumme* out now."

Martha laughed as Clara slowly emerged from the bedroom, looking even paler than usual. "As different as chalk and cheese, you sisters are—but that's how *Gott*'s made you, so praise be!"

Sarah smiled. "Clara wants to plan a wedding quilting for me, Miss Martha. Perhaps you could help her and *mamm* organize things?"

Martha slapped her thigh with her *gut* hand. "Surely, Sarah. We've got more than enough space at our place and I love the food at a *gut* quiltin'. Clara, we'll talk on it, but now I've got to get back to making lunch."

"Chicken?" Sarah asked.

Martha looked abashed as she held up her silver-tipped finger. "Naw, I suppose that *auld* rooster deserves to live out his time given that he wuz wily enough to escape me. I kinda respect him."

Sarah watched her sister, an animal lover, break into a smile, then turned back to Martha. "All right, my friend." Sarah laughed. "*Kumme* by again when you need that changed, but give it at least eight days to start."

She saw Martha out, then turned back to her younger sister, who was eyeing the bean can with distaste. "*Ach*, Sarah, how can you do this work?"

Sarah shrugged as she emptied the kerosene into a basin. "People need me. How can I not?"

The sound of the men's voices came to a sudden stop when Edward entered Ben Kauffman's store. Edward nodded to those nearest him, perched on counters, their faces both somber and excited. It was a strange atmosphere . . . *and not one that I need two eyes to see,* he thought ruefully.

He proceeded to wade deeper into the gathering of black coats and finally saw Jim Hanson standing by the potbellied woodstove. The *Englischer* had a quick smile for Edward and held out his hand in greeting.

Edward shook hands, almost unwillingly, when he recalled his *fater*'s face from the porch outside, but then shook off the feeling of disquiet and decided to take the proverbial bull by the horns.

"Jim, how are things?"

Another quick smile. "I think things are going fine, Edward. I was just explaining to the men here about the fact that they stand to make a nice tidy sum should R and D decide to drill here."

"Money?" Ben Kauffman snorted. "*Jah*, but at what cost? Our homes? Our way of life? The Ice Mine?"

There was a rumble of accord from some of those gathered, but Edward quickly realized that not everyone was agreeing. He had a sudden sick feeling in his stomach; he hadn't thought truly of losing the mountain, and now guilt flowed over him in waves. Still, he straightened his shoulders, determined to see his actions through.

"There's other land . . ." he announced tightly. "We live in the land of Endless Mountains, don't we? What harm is there in simply listening to Jim here? To give folks a chance to choose?"

"You forget community, Edward," Deacon Keim spoke up from the background. He was usually quiet, so now everyone stilled to hear him speak. "We are not separate; we are one. One in nature, decision, choice. . . . If we separate into individual grains of wheat, we lose the joy of the whole loaf of bread. I don't feel we should be discussing this without Bishop Umble's presence."

"I don't mean to cause trouble," Jim Hanson said affably. "Just talking. That's all."

"You wouldn't be talking at all without this firebrand here," *auld* Solomon Kauffman suddenly spoke up, while pointing an aged finger at Edward.

Edward squared his jaw, ignoring the vague desire he had for the floor to open up and swallow him whole. "That's right," he said. "It's my doing. I accept that."

"And I accept the notion that my family could do with a bit more cash—some security for my grandchildren even." Herr Zook spoke firmly.

Others murmured with him.

"*Gott* provides security," Ben declared loudly from behind the counter.

"*Jah*, easy enough for you to say when you've got the only store on the mountain and a regular income all year round," a slightly raised voice from the back put in.

And then there was chaos as Edward watched the idea of money infiltrate his people and set them against one another. He wished now that he had obeyed his *fater* and gone home with him instead.

Sarah watched her husband gently charm Clara out of her normal reticence as they all sat on the porch, eating forkfuls of the deliciously rich mayonnaise cake. Though Sarah sensed a restlessness in Edward and wondered if he longed for a chance to imbibe instead of drinking in the demure picture of domesticity they all presented, even after a rousing game of broom ball.

Samuel clattered his plate and fork down onto the top of a small barrel and the sound broke into Sarah's wandering thoughts.

"*Nee*," she said, looking intently at her little *bruder*.

"What?" he asked with round, innocent eyes.

"I'm a mind reader," Sarah said dryly. "No more cake. You've had three pieces."

Samuel gave an audible sigh, then marched over to Edward and, much to Sarah's surprise, clambered without comment onto her husband's lap.

Sarah saw the initial tenseness in the lines of Edward's big body and would have said something to Samuel when Edward suddenly smiled—an almost wistful smile that made her heart turn over—as he visibly relaxed and gathered the child close.

Ach, my, he'd make a gut fater. . . . She stiffened in her chair at the naked thought, unprepared for its appearance in her mind. Then she quickly began to rationalize, even as she recalled Frau Umble's words from earlier. *He'll be* gut *with the children . . . the* kinner . . . *But do I want a child of his?* Her belly tightened with primitive pleasure, but her mind spoke with even reason. *He drinks; often and far too much . . . How can I risk having a* boppli *when he might be too drunk at times to even watch over or raise a child?*

She lifted her eyes to the clumps of herbs dancing in the fading sunlight and a thought came to her: dark, easy—satisfying. . . . *If I ever ask him to—consummate the marriage, I could always keep from getting pregnant using* Grossmuder *May's potion, and then, if he changes . . . when he changes . . . I'd stop and he'd never need to know.* She pushed aside her conscience, ignoring the fact that she'd denied Deborah Zook the potion, and forgot for a chosen moment that her people believed *Gott* should be in charge of *kinner* coming. After all, it seemed much more sinful to continue to live as man and wife without true union. . . .

She slanted him a discreet glance beneath lowered lids and absently pressed a hand against

128

her abdomen. *It's a strange thing to realize how much I love him, with the taste of chocolate still in my mouth and the promise of autumn in the air. . . .* Then the moment was lost as Ernest announced that their parents were coming up the hill.

Chapter Fifteen

The following week, fall came early and in earnest to Ice Mountain, and Sarah was often kept busy with the normal seasonal round of allergies and colds. Edward had never realized how often his people must have sought out *Grossmuder* May for one thing or another, but he was glad in a way that Sarah was so occupied. It gave him time to both ride Sunny and to drink.

But if Sarah noticed that he was imbibing more than usual, she didn't mention it and went about her daily chores without speaking of his frequent visits to the still. Then, one bright morning, she cornered him after breakfast.

"Apple butter making today—my own recipe," she announced, gesturing with her fine chin to the large crab apple tree in Sunny's pasture.

"Sarah, those apples aren't even half ready to be picked," he prevaricated, fingering his hat and hoping for a quick exit.

"You're right." She gave him a smug smile.

"They're past ready, and Joseph and Ernest came over and helped me pick them yesterday—while you were—out. We got nearly a bushel."

Edward suppressed a groan. Helping to make apple butter was an all-day job with little opportunity for taking a break, but she looked so excited at the prospect that he didn't have the heart to deny her.

"Is it important to you that it's your own recipe?" he asked finally and had to resist the urge to kiss her when she smiled.

"*Jah*. I've always done it *Mamm*'s way, but I've got an idea for a secret ingredient."

"Not just your usual allspice and cloves, hmm?"

She shook her head. "Nope. Now, you set up the copper pot outside and fetch the oak firewood and I'll start cutting the apples down into snits."

Edward sighed. "All right. Fine."

He found that it was a long day indeed and realized how much he'd come to rely on a drink to make him feel better. *But to feel better from what?* he asked the question, realizing he was deeply uncomfortable with being so intro- spective. *After all,* he slanted Sarah a sidelong glance as loose tendrils of hair escaped her *kapp* while she worked, *I have a beautiful wife, plenty of cash, a fast horse. . . .*

He shook his head, deciding he simply needed a diversion, and dipped a quick finger in a smaller kettle of cooled apple butter.

• • •

Sarah gasped as he took a fingerful of the fresh apple butter and smeared it down her cheek. Then he stepped so close that she had to rely on his strong arm about her waist to keep herself upright.

"Mmm," he murmured. "So sweet." He put his mouth against her cheek and she felt the dual sensations of heat and coolness as he let his tongue lap gently on her skin, drawing away with tight sips of the apple butter. When he was finished, he released her and took a step back, almost as if to gauge her reaction. For some reason, the move angered her . . . *I am not some mare to be tested and tried. . . .*

Impulsively, she reached down and ran her finger through the bucket, then flicked her hand at his clean white shirt, spattering it with apple butter. Suddenly his blue eye shone with a wicked glint, and she realized the implications of what she'd done.

She put her hands up in front of her and started to back away. "Edward, I didn't . . ." But he grinned and mimicked her actions, flinging some of the sweet brown goodness at her before she could speak another word. She felt a splat on her hair and on her dress front, and then he caught her wrists.

"Tit for tat, sweet. *Kumme* . . . taste how you've dampened my shirtfront."

"I—don't know . . ." she began and he laughed,

a low, rich sound that strummed along her spine and then lower.

"I'll show you," he whispered. "Now, pay attention." He spread her arms and bent his head to the spot on her breast. She couldn't help but look down, watching him, his long golden lashes flush against his cheek. The sunlight caught on the wet draw of his tongue as he arched his neck to lap at the apple butter. Then he closed his lips and sucked on the fabric of her apron and dress, directly on the center of her breast, deep pulling patterns of hard then soft that caused a whimpering cry to come from the back of her throat.

Then her mouth watered with want for him to kiss her, hard and deep, but he simply rose to his greater height and stared down at her. "Wait," he murmured after a moment. "It's much better if you wait, sweet Sarah."

She shook her head in mute disagreement and he laughed again. "Baby," he said, then bent to touch her lips with his own. He tasted like sugar and sin and everything she shouldn't want but everything that made her body sing. She arched upward in frustrated appeal, her wrists still held in his iron velvet grasp; then some instinct made her change her tactics. She relaxed her arms and came off her tiptoes to glance upward at him from beneath lowered lashes. Then, not breaking his gaze, she boldly ran her tongue up and down the drip of apple butter on his shirt.

She thrilled to the low growl of approval that reverberated from deep within his chest and she continued her ministrations, moving her mouth in languid strokes, trying her best to mimic him.

Sarah adjusted her apron and clean dress, intent on making an evening visit to her friend Martha Umble with some of the fresh apple butter. Somehow, she and Edward had managed to finish canning the jars of delightful brown goodness without any more play, though the sudden appearance of Ben Kauffman, coming to check on Sunny, surely had something to do with that.

She snuggled into her cloak when she thought of Edward's kisses and knew it would only be a matter of time before she would bring herself to ask him to make love to her. But for now, she was more than content with the rich foreplay he seemed to come up with—licking apple butter from each other indeed!

She climbed the steps to Martha's *haus* with heated cheeks and opened the porch screen door only to stop still in amazement. Martha sat on an old rocker, her head encircled by a thick white cloud, as she puffed happily on a richly aromatic pipe.

"Martha!" Sarah exclaimed.

The older woman choked and hastily dumped the contents of the pipe into a bucket beside the chair. "Well now, ain't this a nice surprise? My new friend!"

"Martha," Sarah said again weakly. "Does—the bishop know that you . . ."

"Smoke like a chimney? He sure does, though he don't say a word so long as I keep it outside. My granny got me smokin' a pipe when I was younger than you. How do you think I stand all those meetings and things I do as the 'perfect' bishop's wife?"

"I don't know," Sarah replied, dropping into a neighboring chair. "I expect I never thought of it."

Martha laughed. "Sure an' we've all got secrets, Sarah. Remember that."

Sarah nodded, thinking of *Grossmuder* May's journal. "I brought you some fresh apple butter. Edward and I made it today."

"And where's that fine figure of a man now?" Martha asked as she accepted the jar Sarah passed her and unscrewed the lid.

Probably drinking . . . "I'm not sure," Sarah said brightly. "He said he had some things to—attend to."

"Sure he did," Martha said dryly, and Sarah frowned.

Did the whole of the mountain know of her husband's drinking? And even so, did it matter?

"Well." Martha sighed. "Lemme taste the apple butter and see what flavor your love's

134

given to it. Apple butter's got to be made with love or it turns to bad, you know?"

"I've heard that."

Sarah watched as Martha dipped a bony finger into the jar and then pulled it out to suck emphatically. The *auld* woman slapped her knee in appreciation.

"Orange zest! Fine and tasty. Did you think that up yourself, child?"

Sarah felt a surge of happiness. "*Jah*. Edward grated the orange peel."

"Well, then, lemme see—your love is zesty like. Full bodied and jest waitin' fer good things. Your apple butter sez yer *kinner* will be full of the flavor of life. What more could ya want?"

Sarah ducked her head at the mention of children but nonetheless felt blessed by her friend's words. It was a fine beginning to the first of what she hoped would be many apple butter makings together between her and Edward.

For the first time in a long while, Edward turned Sunny from the familiar trek to the still and set out for his father and Joe's *haus*. He hadn't visited for any length of time since Joseph had thrown him out for drinking, but now it seemed that so much had changed. And he had an ulterior motive in mind.

He drew rein at the familiar cabin, the huckleberry bushes and sassafras branches near the front beginning to show the first tints of autumn red. He tied Sunny to the hitching post and glanced down the length of the home where he'd been raised. When Joseph had married Priscilla, the community had worked to expand the once small place. And now, Joseph even had a woodshop where the old work *haus* had been. Edward saw the lights from beneath the door of the woodshop and decided he'd try his luck there first. He eased open the wooden door and peered inside, surprised to see Ernest bent in complete con-centration over the lacquering of a chest of drawers. Other *buwes* were working, too, while Joseph stood at the drawing desk, a pencil nub in hand.

"Hiya," Edward called, not entirely sure how he'd be received. But Joe looked up with a smile on his face and moved to welcome Edward with a hearty embrace that made him feel both uncomfortable and grateful at the same time.

"Edward, I'm so glad to see you. And you know Ernest, of course, and Jay and Dan. We're a late crew tonight—I got a special order from down Williamsport way."

Edward nodded, glancing around in appreciation at the orderly place. "I was wondering, Joe, if you had any time to make me something special for Sarah. It's her birthday next month and I was thinking about something small and unusual—a spice box, maybe."

Joseph smiled, clearly pleased, and Edward gave him a wry look. "What?"

"Nothing."

"I know you, big *bruder* . . . what?" Edward asked.

Joseph leaned close and whispered low. "You're in love."

Edward felt himself flush and shook his head. "Are you *narrisch*, Joe? Of course I love my wife." *I love my wife. I love her.* . . . The thought shook him and he longed for a drink to steady himself.

Joe put an arm around his shoulders and turned him back toward the door. "Keep on working, *buwes*. I want to talk with my little *bruder*."

Edward shrugged off Joseph's arm when they'd gotten outside and scowled at him in the light emanating from the shop. "Can you make the spice box or not?"

"Can—but I want to tell you that there's a difference between being in love and loving someone," Joseph said, happiness in his tone.

"So?" Edward demanded.

"So, I was worried for a while about you and how you were forced into the marriage. I know it goes against your grain to be forced and I thought maybe—well—that it might not work out so well. But now, seeing that you're thinking ahead to her birthday, I think you're a little addled after all."

137

"And is it good to be addled and 'in love'?" Edward asked, trying to control the leap in his heart that his *bruder*'s words produced.

Joseph laughed heartily. "You betcha. I'm a particularly addled man myself."

"Yeah, yeah. Whatever. Is *Daed* still up? I'll go in and say hello."

Joseph shook his head. "He goes to bed early, and so do Priscilla and Hollie—my little sweetheart," he added, mentioning his wife's daughter from a previous marriage.

"All right." Edward sighed. "I guess I'll head out. And no talking about the spice box, okay? I want it to be a surprise."

"Sure." Joe grinned. "A surprise."

Edward rolled his eyes and walked over to Sunny, trying to thrust his brother's obvious joy out of his mind.

Chapter Sixteen

On the heels of another glorious fall day, Edward had been drinking—just enough to ward off the chill of the coming *nacht*, he'd told himself, and now his blood felt warm and he hurried his steps toward the cabin, hoping to catch Sarah in the bath. Heated images of her small, well-formed breasts dripping with moisture drove him forward and there was a catch in his breath when he mounted the steps and opened the door. Then he stopped still.

"Edward—I, uh, wasn't expecting you," she stuttered, dropping her hands from the lean body of the handsome half-dressed man before her.

Edward blinked. Stephen Lambert, an *Amischer* a bit older than himself, stood with his shirt off and his suspenders hanging about his waist. His hands were braced on the mantel of the fireplace, splayed far apart, displaying the strong musculature of his forearms and back as the heat from the low fire before him made his dark hair curl and his tall frame glisten with sweat.

"Clearly," Edward bit out as jealousy roared through him. "But don't let me interrupt . . . although I recall a similar situation that ended in a hasty marriage. . . ."

Stephen smiled, displaying even white teeth, obviously oblivious. "Sorry, Edward, to be here after supper, but I took a bad fall today from a barn ladder—stupid mistake."

"*Jah*," Sarah nodded, lifting her slender hands back to the other man's rib cage. "He's badly bruised, but I believe nothing's broken. I was just putting some herbal oil on his side."

Edward swallowed, telling himself that he could bear this torture. *It's her job, right?*

He sat down at the kitchen table, facing the intimate picture of his wife touching another man. Everything seemed to play out in slow motion before him, from Sarah adding more oil to her hands to Stephen arching his back and sighing in obvious pleasure as her fingers worked against his side. It was part arousing, part torment, and all so very much something Edward doubted any husband could sit through. *But I am* . . .

The crackle of the fire and the sensuous smell of the fragrant spiced oil teased at him and he shifted restlessly against the wood of the chair. He half-closed his eye, his mind simmering with images of what it might look like if she ran oiled hands down his own body, touched him until he begged, felt him until he hurt. . . .

"Edward . . . Stephen's leaving now." Her quiet voice was hesitant, and he sat back up at attention, his fantasies doused by the reality of watching Stephen dress and pull on his coat with gingerly movements.

"*Danki*, Sarah," Stephen said, handing her some money, which she accepted with visible reluctance, but the moment irked Edward just the same. *My wife—getting paid for giving a man a* gut *rubdown* . . .

The door had barely closed on Stephen's back when the words were out of his mouth. The whiskey had loosened his tongue and he felt keyed up and angry. "Did you enjoy that?"

She eyed him warily and he gave her a surly smile and rose to round the table to where she stood drying her hands on a linen cloth.

"I don't know what you mean," she said finally.

He ran his hands down the back of her fragile neck and leaned close to her, forcing her to press her skirts against the table. "Oh, I think you know very well, Sarah King," he whispered. "He's built like a damn stud and you spent how long touching his warm skin before I came in?"

She half-turned, her gray eyes lit with rage at his insinuation, and he couldn't help the mockery that he knew glinted in his eye.

"How dare you? I—I'm your wife and you think that I'd . . ." She spluttered to a stop when he placed a finger against her parted lips.

"He paid you for it, too. I wonder if I'd get anywhere going that route? What do you say? Payment for your—services."

"You're drunk," she snapped, jerking her mouth from his hand.

"I'm serious as death."

He watched her swallow, knowing he was goading her, and half-expected a *gut* slap in the mouth for his efforts, but then her demeanor changed, softened, and she turned. He stared at her in bemusement, amazed at her beauty.

"All right, Edward," she whispered, splaying her fingers across his chest. "Pay me."

Sarah knew she was playing with fire, but suddenly she wanted to catch him at his own game, best him at it for once. And by the look of mingled shock and interest on his handsome face, she knew she'd knocked him off guard.

"Very well," he said roughly after a heartbeat of a moment. "I tell you what I want. You tell me how much it costs."

"Done," she murmured, trying hard to come up with a businesslike manner.

She watched him skim his eye down her modest dress; then he looked up with a wicked smile. She braced herself mentally.

"A kiss," he whispered, staring at her mouth, then looking over her head and back again. "One kiss."

She felt herself exhale with relief until he spoke again.

"Here." He tapped himself on the collarbone. "No shirt."

"Five dollars."

He laughed. "You rate your kisses so low, sweet Sarah? I would have easily paid a hundred."

She mentally stood her ground, not moving while he eased out of his suspenders and shirt, then let the fabric fall to the floor behind him.

"Payment first," she said tightly.

He pulled out his pocketbook and found a five-dollar bill. She bit her lip when he held it practically under her mouth.

"Funny, I never thought of you as bearing the sin of avarice, Sarah. We would have rubbed along much better had I known before this."

He is simply trying to make me lose my temper, she warned herself internally. *And I won't . . . I will not.* Yet she couldn't keep herself from practically ripping the bill from his long fingers. Then inspiration seized her and she moved away from him a bit, bending to lift her skirt to reveal her high black wool sock, and she made a show of sliding the money inside.

"This could get interesting," he drawled, and she dropped her skirt to move up close to him, giving him a quick peck on his collarbone.

"There," she announced.

"*Nee*, sweet, that hardly qualifies as a fair kiss."

She pursed her lips and longed to tap her foot against the wooden flooring in irritation, but then she remembered her resolution to win the game he so loved to play and let her lashes fall in demure calculation.

"What is a fair kiss?" she asked softly and almost had to smile at the visible tightening of the muscles surrounding his lean ribs.

"Hot," he exhaled. "Wet . . . hard, then soft, then a thousand things at once and more."

"All that for five dollars?" she mused aloud, deliberately ignoring the lurid images his description conjured up.

"*Jah*," he half-choked when she reached to brush the back of her left hand against the hard male nipple nearest her.

"*Gut*," she whispered, then stretched on tiptoe

to put her mouth against his collarbone, moistening her tongue against the satiny warmth of his skin, then allowing her teeth to edge over him in time to the movement of her fingers against the hard nub of flesh on his chest. She pulled away after long moments, then looked at him to gauge his reaction.

"Sarah, I want . . . would you ask me to . . . ?"

She was unprepared for the raw emotion that flushed the contours of his face and she knew she'd both won the game and lost. *I've pushed him too far and now he wants . . . but it wouldn't be right if I asked him now, not when I know that it would be lust driving him and not love. . . . And no matter what I thought about* Grossmuder May's *potion, I can't . . . not like this . . .*

"Edward, I'm sorry . . . I shouldn't have . . ." She took a definitive step backward, coming up against the table, not touching him but leaving him breathing in ragged gasps.

She automatically reached down, intending to retrieve his money from her sock when he caught her shoulders in a grip of steel.

"Don't," he growled, forcing her upward to meet his gaze. He shook his head, his hair falling over the eye patch that now seemed so much a part of him, and her eyes filled with tears. "You keep that money, Sarah. You earned it well— you deceiving . . ." He half-shook her, and her mouth tightened in anger.

"Deceiving? Me? All you've been to me is deceiving, Edward King. . . . Your women, your drinking, your whole stupid game of push me/pull me, and you get one small taste of your own medicine and you cannot manage it. Why, I should feel sorry for you, right?" She half-choked on a tight sob and he released her abruptly.

"*Gott* save me from a nagging woman," he muttered, loud enough for her to hear as he turned to snatch his shirt off the floor, yanking it back on.

"*Gott* save you from yourself, my husband," she mimicked hotly. "Because you—are your own worst enemy!"

She watched him stomp toward the door; then he turned to look at her with his hand on the latch. "It's getting late," he sneered. "Try not to entertain anyone while I'm gone." Then he slammed the wood behind him and Sarah dropped, furious and crying, into the nearest chair.

Chapter Seventeen

A storm came up fast that *nacht*; the wind howled, rattling windowpanes as early autumn hail and rain took a merciless swipe at Ice Mountain. But the elemental chaos suited Edward's mood fine as he threw a saddle on Sunny and recklessly grabbed the reins. He sensed that the horse's temperament fit the storm and had no fear as they navigated the landscape, illuminated only by momentary flashes of lightning. It was relatively easy to get to the still, and then he sought shelter in a vacant barn with Sunny, three jars of moonshine, and a fast-turning conscience that told him he'd been perhaps less than a *gentlemon* to his wife.

He threw himself down on a moldering pile of hay and took a long pull of the first jar. By the time he'd gotten to the bottom of the Mason glass, he was already feeling the familiar warmth and drift the alcohol typically brought him, but he felt no less uneasy about Sarah. He unscrewed the lid of the second drink, drained it, then tilted his head back to drowse, and somewhere between being drunk and asleep, he began to dream. . . .

He'd broken something, something valuable, and he was scared to death. He needed to run and run, but the brambles and branches of the forest rose up like sirens' arms to tear at him, preventing his escape. Something was behind him—his grandfather's face—gasping and spewing bloody spittle—it tried to speak; he could hear it straining in his ear, but he refused to understand and broke free at last to be swallowed by the darkness of the trees. . . .

Edward woke with a start and stared into the darkness surrounding him. Sunny edged nearer and nudged him, making a low sound that brought some comfort from the dream. He reached up a hand to fondle the horse's nose absently, then reached for another jar. . . .

Sarah had tearfully tucked herself up in bed after banking the fire and listening to the howl of the storm. She was angry with herself that she still felt compelled to pray for Edward's safety, even after his unforgivable behavior earlier that evening.

"Probably out drinking somewhere, as comfortable as a clam," she muttered aloud, then froze when she heard a violent pounding on the front door. She jumped from the bed, knowing that she had not set the latch and assumed that her husband was too drunk to enter, but when she opened the door, she was surprised to see the lanky form of Aaron Zook, Deborah Zook's younger *bruder*. His face was pale, his brown eyes set. "*Mamm* says to fetch you now. . . . Deborah's bleedin' somethin' fierce."

"What? Where is she hurt?"

He dipped his head for a moment, then looked back up. "Woman trouble, Ma says."

"All right." Sarah nodded. "*Kumme* in. I'll get dressed. . . ."

"*Sei se gut.*" The boy caught her arm. "There's no time."

"All right, but I need some supplies." Sarah threw a cloak over her nightdress, slipped her feet into a too-large pair of Edward's tall boots, and then scrambled to grab bottles and linens from the big cupboard, stuffing them all into a large carpetbag.

"I'll take that." Aaron grabbed the bag from her hand. "I only have the one horse. You'll have to ride behind me and hold on. I didn't have time to saddle her." He spoke over his shoulder as Sarah blew out the lantern, then ran out into the onslaught of wind and rain. Her hair was plastered to her face before Aaron even hauled her up behind him and she found herself holding on for dear life, then praying for Deborah.

Aaron let her off near the front porch and she slid to the ground, grabbed her bag, then sloshed through chilling puddles up the rather worn wooden steps. She hugged her sodden cloak close to her as she lifted her hand to knock, but the door was opened before she could make a sound. *Auld* Herr Zook, Deborah and Aaron's *fater*, stood staring down at her, his wrinkled face inscrutable in the half light.

"I . . ." Sarah began, trying to speak over the pounding of the rain.

He jerked his thumb over his shoulder. "They're in the bedroom yonder."

Sarah nodded and tramped into the house, deciding against removing Edward's big boots and revealing her bare feet or wet nightdress to the elder Zook. She made for the indicated door and eased it open. "Deborah?"

A choked sob was the only response as Esther Zook, Deborah's mother, tearfully widened the door. Sarah swallowed at the sight of so much bright red blood staining the older woman' apron front.

"*Kumme* in," Esther whispered in obvious despair. "Dear *Gott*, do something to help her."

Sarah inhaled and caught the unmistakable tang of warm blood in the air. She quickly stepped out of her boots and let her wet cloak drop to the floor. Then she let her gaze sweep the shabby room.

"We need more light. *Sei se gut*, Esther. I will see to Deborah." Sarah kept her voice brisk, leveling her words in the hope of giving the mother something to hold on to as she reluctantly slipped out for more lanterns.

Sarah approached the bed and found Deborah naked, half-covered by a blood-soaked sheet. Her color was a grayish pallor, and as Sarah tried to count her erratic pulse, she knew that the other girl was bleeding badly enough to require surgery. Then Sarah raised the single lantern from the bedside table and carefully lifted the sheet, suppressing a gasp. She'd never seen so much blood. Deborah's legs were splayed and Sarah knew immediately what was wrong. *An early miscarriage . . .* Even as she began to pack the area, the words from *Grossmuder* May's diary entry about her own miscarriage floated eerily through Sarah's mind. . . . *Bled out . . . orange juice . . .* And then Sarah nearly stopped still as she remembered Deborah coming to her, asking for help to prevent pregnancy, but she'd been too angry, too judgmental. . . . Dear *Gott*, her mind screamed. *Let her live. Let her live. . . .*

She was continuing to tear the linen as fast as she could when some small sensation made her look up and she met Deborah's open eyes.

"Deborah, it's going to be all right. We'll get through this. . . ."

"You." Deborah gasped as spittle ran down the side of her now greenish-toned skin.

Sarah wet her lips and leaned closer. "*Jah*, Deborah?"

The other girl lifted a blood-splattered hand and caught Sarah's hair with curled fingers and surprising strength. "Your—fault."

Sarah understood and nodded faintly, longing to draw away and run from the horrific room, the dark *haus*. . . . "I know, Deborah. I'm . . ." She broke off as the other girl's eyes suddenly rolled backward in her head and her body arched, seizing. Then she collapsed, her fingers still knotted in Sarah's hair.

"Deborah?" Sarah whispered, automatically feeling for a pulse she knew wasn't there. She

150

jumped when a hand touched her shoulder moments later.

"She's gone, ain't she?" Esther Zook asked.

Sarah swallowed. "Yes." She worked at untwining her now bloody hair from Deborah's fingers and felt numb with shock.

Esther sank down on the floor by the bed. "This was a babe what killed her—I knows. But I'd dearly 'ppreciate it if ya didn't speak of it to anyone else."

"*Nee*, I won't," Sarah choked out as her gaze happened to light on the black gauze-covered mirror, a common enough thing on the mountain to guard against vanity but now ominous with portent.

And then she was running, barefoot, cloakless, leaving *Grossmuder* May's medical bag behind as she struggled with the front door and ignored Herr Zook's voice. She ran out into the rain and the wind and the *nacht*, careless of anything but getting away.

Edward slouched over the dark horse's saddle, trying to focus his blurred vision on the rough road ahead of him in the dark storm-slashed air. He jerked upright when he saw a flash of white on the road ahead of him, and then Sunny reared. Edward barely kept his seat and then he felt a sickening thud as the horse's hooves made contact with something other than the road.

Edward pulled to a sharp stop, then slid down and staggered back to the puddle of white nightgown lying on the ground. His heart beating in his throat, he knelt and gently turned the body over, knowing already, intuitively, that this vision was somehow his wife, and then he saw the blood streaming down her face, making wet rivulets in her hair and pooling on the ground.

"Sarah," he cried out, his voice sounding low and useless against the power of the storm. "Sarah!"

He was afraid to move her so he screamed helplessly, and then he threw his head back and stared up into the rain. "*Gott*, if you're there, spare her. Dear *Gott*, spare her. Take me instead." He began to sob, his warm tears mingling with the cold rain. He reached up and tore off his eye patch, wanting to be fully revealed to the only Divine Being who could save his wife. And then, clearly, like the stirring, mesmerizing words of a song, he recalled his conversation with Ernest. *What is love? True love means hope and sacrifice and life and death . . . a gift from* Gott *. . . Death, a gift from* Gott *. . .*

"I'll change," he cried out, rocking over her on his knees. "I'll be the sacrifice. Take my life, Dear *Gott*. Take my life. . . ." And then he felt he could see her, even through his vacant eye: flashing vibrant images of her smile, the curve of her cheek, the movement of her small gentle hands. He shuddered and bent his head, sobbing, then looked up again as the unmistakable clip-clop of a horse and buggy came from the road beyond. He saw the light of a buggy lantern and stood up, waving his arms wildly, filled with transcendent gratitude.

Chapter Eighteen

He studied her intently, the subtle rise and fall of her chest in the bluish hospital gown, the heavy braid of her now clean hair, and the deftly placed row of stitches along the top of her forehead. He recalled coming upon a fawn in the woods once, when he was young enough to be charmed by such things, and the memory filled him now and swelled his throat. Where was its mother? Surely some larger prey animal would take it, but to touch it would mean certain rejection from any of its kind—so he merely watched, until the brown hairs became Sarah's delicate brows, arched faintly, as if in pain. . . .

"Edward?"

He heard Joe's voice from far away and chose not to respond. *I just want to watch her. . . . Can't they understand?*

"Edward, you have to get some sleep or something to eat. I'll sit with her."

"*Nee*," he murmured quietly. "*Danki*, Joe. But *nee . . .*"

There was a distinct pause in the air, long enough for Edward to watch her breathe in and out again.

"Do you want your eye patch?" Joe asked after a moment.

Edward felt with curious fingers over his scarred cheek and then the empty eye socket. It was strange that all through the horrific *nacht*, he hadn't thought of covering his eye. . . . He sighed.

"Why was she out there, Joseph?" he asked aloud. "Was she looking for me?"

Joe pulled up a chair and sat down. "I don't know. But you—you can't blame yourself; it was an accident."

Edward snorted. "Let's call it what it was, Joe—I was drunk. I didn't see her. It's the same as if I'd run her over with a car—drunk driving. But I made *Gott* a promise out there on that road . . . a promise. . . ." He let his voice drift off.

"Well, maybe she'd gone to try to help Deborah Zook. I heard the girl passed away during the *nacht*—some kind of woman's thing. . . ."

Edward frowned. "But Sarah was in her nightgown and far from the Zook *haus* . . . and Deborah, she was so young, may *Gott* have mercy on her family. . . ."

Joseph drew an audible breath. "I know, Edward. And we'll piece it together—what happened last *nacht*. The important thing now is that Sarah is going to be well. The concussion is not that bad, and that only her arm was broken after being trampled by so massive a horse is nothing short of miraculous."

"Then why doesn't she wake?" Edward asked, idly sliding on the eye patch his *bruder* had handed him.

"She's in shock," Dr. McCully answered from behind them. The *Englisch* doctor was a *gut* friend to the *Amisch* of Ice Mountain and had been practicing at the Coudersport Hospital for many years. "She'll wake when her body and mind are ready."

"But it's been hours," Edward insisted.

The older man shook his head. "The MRI was clean except for a mild concussion. She'll be fine, Edward, you'll see. . . ."

Mahlon clasped and unclasped his thick fingers as he sat in the quiet of the hospital's chapel. The silence was unnerving and he tried to refocus on praying for Sarah. He'd left Anne with the *kinner* back on the mountain but had felt an urge he couldn't explain to accompany his unconscious *dochder* to the hospital. Now, he wondered why he'd *kumme*. . . .

"Do I intrude, Mahlon?" Bishop Umble's voice echoed from behind him, and Mahlon startled, then leaned back in the cloth-covered chair.

"*Nee*, Bishop. I'd be glad of yer company, truth ta tell."

The older man came forward and sat down beside him, sighing deeply. "Sarah still hasn't woken, but Dr. McCully seems confident things will be all right."

Mahlon nodded, then asked the question that had been plaguing him for the past hours. "Bishop, do you think *Gott* would punish me for how I've treated Sarah? I mean, I think of all the times I might have had a kind word fer her and I let it pass, and the many times I've thought her . . . strange, or a hex even."

Bishop Umble shook his head. "*Nee*, Mahlon, do not trouble yourself. *Gott* doesn't play games depending on how well we've loved one another, but He does give us room to start anew. When Sarah awakens, why not try to start a real and loving relationship with her? It comes to me that your *fater* may have never let you accept yourself, so you've had a hard time accepting the *kinner* for who they are. But it's never too late to do the right thing—never."

"Ye're a wise man," Mahlon said after a moment, drinking in the healing words like balm.

"And a busy one . . . I've sadly got to go back to the mountain for Deborah Zook's funeral, but your *dochder* lives on. See that she has a life full of love, my friend." The bishop patted his shoulder and rose to leave.

Mahlon nodded, his eyes full of unshed tears. "*Jah*, I will."

•••

She was dreaming, but she was awake some how. . . . Deborah's bloody hands reached out to her, clutching her hair. She couldn't break free—maybe she didn't want to be free. She owed Deborah so much—the truth, decency . . . life. And what about the life of the babe lost? She was accountable for both and the devil had sent a gleaming black dragon to hunt her as she ran. She couldn't escape and heard its pounding feet, turned in time to see the roll of its eye before it took her down . . . punishing her, driving her into the earth. . . . She tried to scream but there was only silent terror, a plea for someone to help, but there was no one. There never had been . . .

"Sarah?" Edward kept his voice low, level, as his wife's eyelids fluttered, then opened for the first time since her injury.

It was after midnight and he knew he should probably ring for the nurse, but he couldn't seem to move as he waited for Sarah to say something. Instead, she simply stared ahead, not moving, her gray eyes wide and blank in the dim over-head light.

"Sarah?" He sought for her hand beneath the covers and found her fingers chilled and limp. He tried to squeeze her hand, growing desperate for a response, but she didn't move.

Then he pulled away, got to his feet, and ran to open the room door. "Doctor!" he shouted into the quiet hall, careless of the answering rapid shushing and the hurried fall of footsteps as he swallowed back tears and returned to his bride's side.

"Catatonic state. I've seen it once or twice during my training," Dr. McCully mused aloud as he shone his small flashlight into Sarah's eyes.

"What? What's wrong with her?" Edward asked in desperation, his hands clenching and unclenching the chair back near the bed.

Dr. McCully straightened. "The fancy name's catatonia, and I've seen it in patients with shock. It usually wears off in a few hours." The doctor lifted one of Sarah's hands and then let go.

Her hand remained poised in the air in a strange waxen flexibility that sent a chill down Edward's spine. She was behaving like some weird doll.

"So, we just wait?" Edward asked. "I'm not very *gut* at that."

Dr. McCully replaced her hand on the sheet and glanced at Edward. "Sit by her. Talk to her. I'll go make a phone call to a friend of mine back in Boston who might know more about this sort of thing."

"All right." Edward nodded and sat down next to the bed, drawing the chair close so that he could see the dark pupils in her wide gray eyes. "I'll try."

...

Two days later, there'd been no improvement in Sarah's responsiveness and Edward was frantic.

"What did your friend in Boston have to say?" he asked the *Englisch* doctor for what felt like the fiftieth time.

Dr. McCully exhaled audibly, clearly frustrated himself. "Edward, there's a difference between the brain and the mind. Her brain is not injured, but her mind . . ."

Edward turned from the bed, where he'd been standing vigil, talking himself hoarse for hours. "You mean there's something wrong with her mind? That she's always going to be like this?"

"No, probably not, but her mind needs time and the right stimuli to recover."

"Stimuli?" Edward whispered, then gave a decisive nod. "I'm taking her home to Ice Mountain." To his surprise, Dr. McCully agreed with a faint smile.

"Yes, Edward, if ever there's a place that a person could heal, it would be Ice Mountain, but you've got to promise me that you'll bring her back if you have any new concerns. And I'd like physical therapy to assess her mobility before you go."

"Fine. But tomorrow we leave." Edward turned back to the bed, then looked over his shoulder as Joe entered and Dr. McCully left.

Joseph pulled up a chair. "Any change?"

"None," Edward replied. "But I just got Dr. McCully's blessing to take her back to the mountain tomorrow."

"Do you think that's a *gut* idea? How will you care for her?"

"I will," Edward said simply, shrugging his shoulders. "How was the service today?" He lowered his voice, not wanting Sarah to hear about Deborah Zook's funeral and be unduly upset—*if Sarah could hear.* Her eyes were closed again, as if she slept, but he wasn't sure.

Edward decided not to take a chance and rose to motion his *bruder* out into the hall. "Did you discover anything about why Sarah was out on the road when I hit her with Sunny?"

Joseph nodded. "Maybe . . . Esther Zook brought Sarah's medical bag to the service. I dropped it off at your cabin. It seems that Sarah was at the Zooks' the *nacht* Deborah died, but nobody went into much detail, except to say she ran off without her cloak."

"Why would Sarah run from an ailing patient?" Edward mused aloud.

"I don't know. Maybe *auld* man Zook scared her off. You know he seems a bit rough, and with his *dochder* ill, maybe he—"

"*Nee*, Sarah's more than tenacious when it comes to her patients. It had to be something else."

Edward looked up when a sudden crash from

inside his wife's room echoed in the hall. He ran to open the door and saw Sarah standing next to the bed, the contents of her previously untouched dinner tray lying on the floor.

Chapter Nineteen

Sarah stared out the window of Mr. Ellis's station wagon, the vehicle that would bring her back to the base of Ice Mountain. She watched the trees rush by in a blur and closed her eyes for a moment, ignoring the fact that Edward sat, solid and still, next to her—so close that she could catch his scent. But now there was no alcohol on his breath, only his own manly smell of pine and summer and things promised. *Things lost . . .*

She jumped when he laid a tender hand on her knee and opened her eyes.

"Would you like to stop at the ice mine for a minute before we go up?" he asked softly.

She shrugged, feeling her shoulder touch his. "It doesn't matter."

"*Jah*, it does. You know there's something about the mine that's . . ." She watched him pause, visibly struggling for words, which was so unlike him. But she didn't feel like supplying what he sought and waited.

". . . like *Gott* is there," he finished.

She stared at him. "*Gott*?" she asked. "Since when do you talk about *Gott*?"

His blue eye shone with steadiness. "Since now," he said decisively.

She frowned. "*Jah*, well, as my *fater* would say, you're a day late and a dollar short." *And Deborah's dead . . . and Deborah's dead . . .* The words singsonged in her mind until he reached for her hand and curled his warm fingers through hers. She looked down at their entwined hands and thought how strange it was for him to be so gentle, so considerate.

"Of course I'd be nice, too, if I ran my spouse over with a horse," she muttered. *Not that I didn't deserve it . . .*

"What?" he asked solicitously.

"Never mind." She pulled her hand away, then looked up as Mr. Ellis spoke.

"We're home, folks, or at least I am. You sure you're going to be able to make it back up the mountain?" their *Englisch* friend asked.

"Joseph and some other men are to meet us," Edward explained. "But I'll carry her," he said dismissively.

Like I'm a bushel of dry potatoes, Sarah thought hotly. *But that's just how I feel inside. . . .*

"I'm sure I can walk."

"I'll carry you," Edward repeated.

She glanced ruefully at the lean bulk of his arms beneath his light blue shirt and had no doubt he'd have more than enough strength to carry her the mile trek up the mountain; but right now, she wanted to be left alone.

They got out of the station wagon, thanked Mr. Ellis, and then Edward swung her up into his arms without so much as a word.

"Hey," she squeaked.

"What?"

She could see the skin of his throat and hear the easy pulse of his heart that beat, slow and steady, and she could also feel her right breast pressed tight against his hard chest. It was all too close for her comfort and state of mind.

"Put me down," she said, trying to sound authoritative.

He smiled, a flash of white teeth, as he bent his head to look at her. "Just relax. I've got you."

"That's half the problem." She sighed, reluctantly slipping her arms, cast and all, around his neck.

"You don't have to touch me, Sarah," he said suddenly, as if the thought had just occurred to him.

She gazed up at him, surprised to see him so serious. "I . . ." She paused, unsure of how to continue. She said the first thing that came to mind. "My head hurts."

He lowered his mouth and placed a quick, chaste kiss on her brow. "*Kumme*," he said, beginning to take long strides. "We'll go into the coolness of the ice mine for a moment and you'll feel better. The sun seems hot today, and besides, there's something I have to say to you, Sarah."

She wondered dully if he would ask to leave her, though it was not her people's way. But Edward kept his own ways—she felt a roaring in her ears and couldn't seem to concentrate.

Then they were at the entrance to the mine, and he set her carefully on her feet and turned to remove the blocking boards from the cavelike mouth of the mine. She shivered in spite of herself, crossing her arms and rubbing her hands up and down the sleeves of her gray dress as she felt the chill burst of air from inside the cave, blowing outward. Usually, she found it refreshing and tantalizing to the senses, but today it was only cold.

Edward turned up the kerosene lamp that hung inside the cave, then lifted it high, standing inside the shadows while he watched Sarah for a moment; he noticed her shiver and set the lamp down and moved to lift her into his arms.

"Edward, I'm fine."

"The ground is still slippery in here with the ice melting. I'll hold you."

He carried her into the mine and glanced for a moment at the deep hole that ran a *gut* eighty feet down, where men had mined for silver, not expecting to find ice. He held her a bit closer. "It's strange, isn't it?" he whispered.

"What?"

"The ice . . . how it grows dry in the winter but is so thick in the summer?" He swallowed, unused to being so serious but determined to say what was on his mind. "The ice is miraculous—like you, Sarah."

"Wh—what are you talking about?" she stammered.

"*Gott* made this ice mine—the place pulses with life—and *Gott* made you. I realized that night on the road—you're the color in my blood. I love you." He felt his eye well with tears, but the words were freeing in a way he never could have dreamed. He waited anxiously for her response and was unprepared for the anger in the luminous gray eyes she lifted to him in the lamplight.

"You don't love me, Edward King. You love whiskey and you feel guilty about what you did to me. . . . Well, forget that it happened. I survived." She lifted her casted arm slightly. "A knock in the head and a broken arm are hardly causes for declarations of love. Now put me down—*sei se gut*."

He obeyed, feeling speechless, as if he'd just had the wind knocked out of him. But then he realized how sudden his words must seem to her and lightly reached out to touch her arm. "Sarah, I . . ."

But before he could finish, he watched as she bent to lift the lantern and then stooped to study something on the ground.

"What is it?" he asked, bending over her hunched shoulder.

"Wolfsbane," she whispered, barely loud enough for him to hear, and then she said more clearly, "It's a sign—a sign that I'm right."

He heard the odd note in her voice and bent closer. "Wolfsbane—you mean belladonna. Even I know that's poisonous, Sarah. Don't touch it . . . and right about what?"

She lifted one of the dark berries of the plant, cradling it in her palm in the circle of light. "It's deadly poisonous and proof from *Gott* that I should never practice healing again."

Edward knocked the berry from her hand without thinking and she sobbed aloud, a keening, awful sound. He gathered her close, feeling her helpless resistance, and then she collapsed in a heap against his legs.

"Your *fater*'s here to see you, Sarah. Shall I let him *kumme* in?" Edward asked softly.

She glanced listlessly at him from her bed and shrugged. "It doesn't matter."

She watched his broad shoulders sink a bit at her words and knew he was probably growing weary with her after a long day at home. She'd sobbed in his arms the whole way up from the

mine, but he'd allowed no one else to carry her.
And once home, she'd continued to cry until her
eyes were red and swollen. She'd finally slept in
his arms, not wanting his touch but not seeming
to be able to pull away. She heard his words
from the mine again and longed to purge them
from her mind. . . . *I love you.* . . . *I love you.* . . .

"Sarah? Be thee well, child?"

She stared at her *daed*'s weather-beaten face,
seeing pain and anguish and something light
and raw and new there at the same time.

But she was in no mood to be compassionate
and steeled herself against her thoughts and
discernment.

"What does it matter if I'm well, *Fater*?" she
asked.

He cleared his throat, and she knew he was
taken aback by her question. "It—it matters a
great deal, Sarah. What would the mountain do
without its healer?"

She laughed faintly. "Hasn't Edward told you?
I'm the healer no more. . . ."

He was quiet for so long that she had to turn
her head to peek at him, and she found his gray
eyes, so like her own, bright with unshed tears.
"What I should have said, Sarah, was . . .
What would I, your *fater*, do without you?"

She swallowed. She'd never heard such words
from her *daed* and the power of them resonated
to her heart. "I don't know," she choked at last,

then hiccuped on a sob. "I never thought that I mattered much to you, *Fater*."

"A grave sin on my part, child. Very grave. I feared you—truth to tell. Afeared of your power and your light . . . I didn't know best how to love you before, but I'm gonna learn, if you'll let me, Sarah."

She nodded, the only thing she could do, and he rose to awkwardly bend over the bed and press a kiss to her forehead. His long beard tickled her cheek with alien softness as she watched him pull back.

It was a moment to remember for always. . . .

Mahlon cleared his throat as he entered the kitchen from the bedroom. He stared at Edward, sitting, staring over a cup of coffee at the small table.

He approached the empty second chair but didn't sit. Instead, he let his rough hand fall on the *buwe*'s shoulder. Edward looked up with his keen blue eye.

"How is she?" he asked hoarsely.

"She needs rest, I think . . . and so do you . . . *sohn*."

"*Sohn*?" Edward blinked and Mahlon shifted uncomfortably.

"*Jah, sohn.* I've never called you that before, have I? But it appears ta me that we both need ta be changed men and we might fare better off as friends—if you'd have it?"

Edward lifted a strong hand upward and Mahlon wrung it wordlessly, more of the ice going out of the river of his once-cold heart.

"I'd best be going," he said finally. "Let us know whatever ya might need."

Edward nodded, rising to see him to the door.

Mahlon left, staring out into the autumn dusk, feeling like he'd just discovered his soul.

Chapter Twenty

"Sarah, I think there's someone at the door," Edward muttered, still half-asleep. She frowned mutely down at him where his blond hair lay in tousled strands against the pillow he clutched.

He must be exhausted, she thought, then pushed aside the feeling of pity she had for him. Someone at the door indeed, and he should be tired after all the drinking he'd done for the past weeks, though in truth she had to admit that he'd not touched a drop since they'd been home from the hospital. Instead, he'd gently and tenderly seen to her needs with a solicitousness she found hard to ignore at times.

A knock sounded and she blinked in surprise. There was someone at the door. . . .

She carefully folded back the quilt and was going to swing her legs over the side of the bed when Edward caught her about the waist. "Lie down, sweetheart," he murmured. "I'll go. It's probably somebody sick."

She did as he asked, resolutely telling herself that she didn't care if the bishop himself was ailing, then straining her ears as Edward left the bedroom, shrugging into a shirt over his low-slung pants.

He was back moments later. "Sarah—tell me what to fetch for croup. Lilly Knepp's *sohn* is sick."

She rolled on her side and pulled her pillow over her head only to thrust it away a second later. "*Ach*," she cried. "I can't. I cannot go forward and I cannot go back."

Edward groaned. "Please sweet—the croup?"

"Ipecac," she snapped. "Make him throw up the phlegm and then give him honey and lemon to soothe his throat."

He left again and wasn't back for some time. She drifted off, only to wake to the haunting sensation of his mouth on hers, hot, damp, and longing.

She opened her eyes to find him sound asleep and she turned away, telling herself that she'd been dreaming and did not feel disappointed.

Edward was still half-asleep, aware of the fall of morning sunlight behind his eyelid but still unwilling to give in to its pull. He stretched out a hand and felt her next to him, all warmth and cuddle and more than right. He moved with languid heat, rubbing against her thigh, nuzzling her neck, and then lifting his weight until she was beneath him.

"*Ach*, Sarah, you feel so *gut*." He kissed her with raw passion, then moved between her legs, but for some reason, she was not ready for him. He tried again, growing frantic. "Please," he whispered.

It was a small squeak of pain that brought him fully awake and he stared down at Sarah in growing horror. He pulled back on his knees between her sprawled thighs and ran a hand through his sweat-dampened hair. "Sarah, I'm sorry—I was half-asleep. Did I hurt you?"

"Only a bit," she said, trying to work her night-dress from beneath his knee.

He scrambled backward and covered his nakedness with the tangled sheet. "I—I'd better make my bed in front of the fire for now," he offered, then swallowed when she gave a small nod of acceptance. Clearly, she was embarrassed and he felt like a fool.

"You were probably exhausted," she said in quiet tones when he left the bed to hastily clamber into his pants. "I mean, after helping Lilly's *sohn* last *nacht* when I—when I wouldn't."

He heard the anguish in her voice and sighed, then sat back down on the edge of the bed. "Wouldn't? Or couldn't, Sarah? There's a difference, you know." He reached to touch her hand and thought hard. "That day in the ice mine, Sarah, when you found the belladonna, I found something, too."

"What?" she sniffed.

He got up, crossed to his dresser, and pulled a folded piece of tinfoil from the top drawer, then came back to the bed.

"What is it?" she asked when he handed it to her.

"I found it in the mine. At first I thought it was a piece of trash, but then I unfolded it. It's a note from Hollie, Joseph and Priscilla's *dochder*."

"Hollie? Why would she leave a note in the mine?" She gave him a puzzled look.

"I asked Joseph when you slept yesterday. He said it was for the angel Hollie said she thought she saw there once." He shrugged. "You're the closest thing to an angel that I can see, Sarah. So read it."

He watched her open the foil with hands that shook a bit and then she began to read:

To My Angel,
   You help me and watch over me. You watch over all of us and I love you for it. You are good. . . .

"But I'm not," she whispered, clutching the paper. "I didn't go to Lilly's *sohn* and I let Deborah . . ." She broke off, and he stared at her hard.

"Deborah? Deborah Zook?"

She nodded, tears welling up in her gray eyes.

"What happened that *nacht* with Deborah, Sarah? Tell me."

"You'd hate me."

"Do you really think you have the power of life and death in your hands as healer? Because she died?"

"*Nee*." She looked him square in the eye. "Because I killed her."

Sarah saw the incredulity on her husband's face and forced herself to continue holding his gaze.

"What?" he asked in confusion.

She reached to her bedside table and brought *Grossmuder* May's journal onto her lap. Quickly, she found the right page. "Here." She handed the open book to Edward.

"Frau Zug's potion? What's this?"

"Something to prevent pregnancy. Something I withheld from Deborah Zook. Her death was my doing."

She watched him through her tears, staring at the old page, until he lifted his head. "So you think you're guilty of murder because Deborah was too—passionate—and because she and her beau didn't use a simple condom?" He sighed. "And sweetheart, did you ever stop to think that for her to die from a miscarriage, the pregnancy must have been somewhat advanced? I mean—

I'm no healer, but suppose she was already pregnant when she came seeking that potion from you?"

A slow dawning lifted at her consciousness with her husband's words. . . . *I didn't have time to think that* nacht, *but she must have been more advanced in the pregnancy.* . . . She stared at him. "The pregnancy was further along . . . you're right. With that much blood . . . *ach*, Edward," she half-sobbed, feeling some relief ebb into her soul.

He squeezed her hand. "Everyone has a *Gott-*appointed time to die."

She nodded, then thought of something else she knew she must tell him. "What would you say if you knew I thought about using Frau Zug's potion myself?"

"To prevent pregnancy?"

"*Jah*." She felt her cheeks flush.

He shrugged. "I'd like *kinner*, but I would have been glad of some time with you alone."

"You mean you wouldn't have been angry?" she cried.

He laid the book aside, then leaned in close to her until she was forced to lift her fingertips to his bare shoulders. "*Nee*," he whispered, bending to brush his lips across hers. "Not angry."

She choked on a sob and he kissed away tears, finding their tracks up and down her face, slowly enticing her to hesitantly lift her mouth to his.

He was reciting math facts in his head, trying to do anything to slow his heated body down, but he couldn't suppress a groan as she threaded her fingers through the hair at the back of his neck.

He didn't want to make love to her with her injuries so fresh and wondered why he'd started the whole process, but he hadn't expected her uninhibited responsiveness. It was as if her confession to him about the potion and Deborah had released some storm inside her, and he didn't want her to regret her actions later.

The decision was taken from him when someone knocked loudly at the door. He made a low sound in his throat, then pulled from her with reluctance. "Duty calls, sweet. You just tell me what to do if it's—whatever people get at this time of night."

She smiled up at him sweetly, her lips red and swollen. "You go back to sleep, my husband. I will handle it."

"As healer?"

"*Jah*." She nodded.

He grinned. "Let's handle it together."

Her answering kiss told him that she agreed.

I have been reading the Book of Job, trying to find my way, trying to love Elias despite the way he hurts me. *Ach*, a thousand hurts a day and more—his words, his hands, and at *nacht.* . . . I cannot even write of the horrors he perpetrates on me. I want to be safe. I want to be young and carefree and happy and home. But I am alone save for *Gott*, and at times, I wonder if He has left me. But *nee*, he promises not to leave. . . .

May

Chapter Twenty-One

The next week, Sarah felt well enough to walk to Ben Kauffman's store alone. Edward had been reluctant, but then one of the Graber men had *kumme* asking for help building cold frames to satisfy a late taste for fresh salad and her husband had uneasily let her go.

She'd been glad. She had it in mind to do a certain thing that *Gott* had been pressing on her heart lately and hoped her plan would work out all right. She realized that Edward hadn't said he loved her again since the ice mine, but he'd been kindness itself to her in both word and deed. Now she felt the need to let him know her true feelings about him and not act with the anger she had when he'd spoken before. She was also hoping that her plan would move him from where he stretched his lean body before the fire each night back to their cozy bed. . . .

As she walked, she had the sudden uneasy

sense that she was being followed and spun around to find the engineer from Marcellus Shale, Jim Hanson, only a few steps behind.

"You startled me." She laughed, putting a hand to her throat.

He gave her a nice smile. "I'm sorry—you're Edward King's wife, right? I'm Jim. I don't think we've ever formally met." He held out a hand and she took it slowly, unfamiliar with such doings.

"I'm Sarah."

His handshake was light and reassuring and she let him fall into step beside her as she walked.

"You're the local healer, aren't you?"

She must have looked surprised because he laughed. "I hear a lot of men talk and general gossip down at the store and in different homes."

"*Ach*, well . . . yes, I am."

Jim Hanson nodded, and she couldn't help but ask the question that drifted at the back of her mind.

"You've been invited to individual homes, Mr. Hanson? I mean—not that my people are closed here—my own *bruder*-in-law, Jude, was *Englisch*. But I'm surprised . . . that's all."

"Call me Jim. . . . Of course you wonder because the Marcellus Shale business is rather a sticky topic. . . . Well, in fact, several families have already invested the initial fee with R and D to become shareholders in a well site. The well we'd like to drill would allow them to keep their homes and would not destroy the beauty of your mountain here."

"Invested?" Sarah kept her voice casual, though she felt a sudden alarm in her heart. Her people were honest and trusting when it came to money and largely dealt with cash when making their payments in the world.

"Sure," Jim went on. "Only a few thousand . . . I should have approached Edward and you about it first, I guess. But things are looking good."

They'd nearly reached the store when Sarah knew she had to go home to talk to Edward immediately about the money folks had given to Jim Hanson.

"Uh, if you'll excuse me—Jim. I just thought of something . . ."

She told herself that she was imagining the speculation in his glance, but he gave her a polite nod and a kind farewell, leaving her to hurry back along the path home.

Edward closed the lid on the burgeoning cold frame garden with satisfaction. Emmet Graber had *kumme* over, wanting to see this technique that would extend the growing season for many plants far into the next year.

"You've got an ongoing salad garden and then some growing there," Emmet said with a grin. "You plan on cultivating those back fields next year?"

Edward nodded. "I can't wait to get my hands on that *auld* plow in the barn."

"Well, truth to tell, I'd be glad to pay you to *kumme* over to my place to help me set up a few of these cold frames. . . . The missus would be right grateful to have fresh vegetables for the *kinner* throughout the winter."

"I'd be glad to, Emmet. How about on . . ." Edward broke off when he saw Sarah hurrying up the path. "Uh, excuse me . . . my wife."

Emmet smiled faintly. "You go on now. I remember what it was to be first married."

Edward smiled, wishing Sarah hurried to him for a *gut* reason, and went to meet her.

"Several thousand dollars?" Edward repeated the phrase as he sat at the kitchen table, his head bowed.

Sarah watched him sorrowfully, knowing he was in pain but unsure how to make it right. "Edward, we all sin. But maybe, as my *daed* said the bishop mentioned, *Gott* will turn that letter you wrote into *gut* somehow."

He shook his head. "Not if it's going to cost my people their savings . . . I . . . I made so many mistakes because of drinking. I don't know how to fix . . ." He broke off when she moved to stand next to him, pressing her belly into his arm, and he leaned his head back to look up at her. She bent and boldly pressed her mouth to his, kissing

179

him hard and deep, until she felt the tension ease and change in him. He broke away with a gasp. "Sarah—what?"

She smiled. "Do you know why I hurried back here, Edward King?"

"To tell me about Jim Hanson?" he whispered.

She shook her head, moving even closer to him, until she could feel his arm press hard against her.

"*Nee,* because there was no one else I wanted to *kumme* to with my trouble but you. . . . I trust you. I love you, Edward."

She watched the expression of mingled joy and disbelief on his handsome face and felt a tingle down her spine. Impulsively, she tugged on the fabric of his cream-colored shirt until he turned, the *auld* chair making a faintly screeching noise against the floor. He moved to stand, but she pushed his shoulders back lightly, then let her capable fingers find the pins in his shirt, moving to undo each one with relative haste. She eased his suspenders down and pushed the fabric off his broad shoulders, revealing the taut skin beneath. She touched him as she'd always wanted to, running her hands down his arms, finding each superbly lined muscle, then back up to let her hands rest on the pulse of his throat for a moment, reveling in the galloping beat she felt there. Then she leaned close to his mouth again and said the words she'd sworn never to say—"Edward King, my husband, my life, will you make love to me?"

• • •

He stood, his arms still hampered by his shirt, then arched his neck in pleasure when her small, clever fingers found his nipples on his chest, gently pulling and squeezing. He groaned, then shrugged out of the shirt and bent to kiss her, his tongue delving into the dark softness of her mouth as he lifted her easily into his arms.

He walked into the bedroom, not breaking the kiss, and lay her gently on the bed. Almost everything in him wanted things to go fast and hard, but he also realized what a gift it was to truly be with the woman he loved, and his frantic breathing slowed as he began to undress her. He banished her apron and infernal gray dress to the floor, promising himself that one day soon he'd buy her colored fabric for new dresses, a new life . . . and then he paused, hanging over her on outstretched arms.

"Sarah . . . do you want . . . how long does Frau Zug's potion take to work?"

And then he was lost when she smiled tenderly and reached her uncasted arm up to encircle his neck. "Nothing would please me more than to be filled with your *boppli*, my love."

He kissed her then, lifting her so that his big hands spanned her small waist, and she parted her legs for him; a sweet, open homecoming, begging him for entry.

He bit his lip until he tasted blood, moving

gently against her hidden barrier, then backing away, wanting her pain to be minimal.

"Edward . . ." She wiped the blood from his mouth, then stroked his cheek. "I want you so much. . . ." She lifted her hips and he heard a choked sound come from the back of his throat, half sob, half groan, and then he plunged forward into a tight storm, trying to keep his eye open so he might see her pleasure, but he was helpless when she began to move with him, all fire and tenderness until the moment burst into fluid movement and he collapsed, replete with the knowledge of mutual sustenance, on the bare fullness of her breast.

Chapter Twenty-Two

He wanted a drink. . . . *Dear* Gott, *I spent the first* nacht *with my wife; it's a fine autumn day; I'm dressing for church and I want a drink.* The need burned through him with such intensity that his hands shook as he pinned his shirt. He turned away from Sarah, who was making up the bed, not wanting her to see. Then he had to escape the room, get out somewhere—anywhere. . . .

"Sarah, if you don't mind, I think I'll take a quick walk before church."

She came into his arms, all warmth and softness, and stretched up to meet his mouth.

"What's wrong?" she asked, pulling away after a moment.

He shook his head. "Nothing." *She reads me so easily . . . maybe I should tell her. But what would she think of me?*

He kissed her again. "I'll be back to walk you to church."

He escaped the room, knowing her keen gray eyes followed him but unable to stop or slow his steps as he went outside into the briskness of the sunshiny air. He'd turned in the direction of his still when he reached out and caught hold of a slender oak tree, his breathing ragged. Derr Herr*, help me; help me because I cannot help myself. . . .*

"Hello, Edward."

He spun round and saw Bishop Umble standing not more than ten feet away. Then he swallowed and straightened from his hold on the tree. "What . . . shouldn't you be preparing for service?"

"*Ach*, I am." The bishop's wizened face broke out in an enigmatic smile.

Edward frowned. "I don't . . ."

"What, *sohn*? What don't you want to lose? What do you want to do?"

He didn't ask how the *auld* man knew but simply bowed his head and choked out the words that had been haunting him all morning. "I want a drink."

"Yet you've gone for quite a while without one,

but I know the power of addiction." The bishop stepped closer, and Edward had to resist the urge to back away.

"I'm a monster," he rasped.

The bishop shook his head. "No, Edward, you're a man, and you've been commanded by *Derr Herr* to love your neighbor as yourself . . . but you seem to have a great deal of trouble loving yourself."

Something clicked in Edward's brain and he stared at his spiritual leader, asking the painful questions with all the plaintiveness of a child. "Why? Why am I like this? And why would you ever tell me to lengthen the distillate—to make the still better? Why hurt me?"

The bishop spread his hands before him. "I told you a fact, but was it the truth?"

Edward rubbed his head in confusion. "I cannot talk in riddles now."

"*Nee*." Bishop Umble sighed. "Nor should I make you try. The point is, Edward King, that *Gott* is the only thing stronger than your addiction. To love Him more, to surrender each time to Him, requires a bravery of the spirit. It also needs bravery to love yourself, your wife, your one-day children . . . bravery to be kind to yourself. . . . Can you understand that?"

A gentle breeze blew through the trees, clearing Edward's thoughts, easing his desire to drink. He straightened and looked the bishop in the

184

face and slowly nodded. "I can try—every day."

"*Jah*, my *sohn*, and you can start today."

Edward thought for a moment, watching the drift of a yellow leaf as it swirled peacefully to the ground. "May I speak before the church family today, Bishop?"

Bishop Umble moved to catch him in a hearty embrace. "You certainly may, Edward. You certainly may. . . ."

Sarah sat down on the edge of the now-made bed and began to pray out of her heart for Edward. There was something he wasn't telling her, and even after the amazing intimacy of last *nacht*, she knew there were shadows in his soul. And, as her spirit prompted her, she went to *Grossmuder* May's journal, which in its latter entries had become rather a log of care for the different folks she saw on the mountain.

Sarah scanned the spiderwebbed handwriting, not knowing what she was looking for but feeling it was important all the same. And then she came across the name Elijah King . . . Of course there was no telling if this was any direct relation to Edward and his family. The King surname was prevalent in *Amisch* communities everywhere, but she read the entry all the same.

Saw Elijah King today for chest pains again. He refuses to get any help from a hospital and

185

swears he will not give up drinking. There is little I can do for him.

Something about the mention of drinking spurred Sarah on, and she turned the page, finding another entry not long after.

Dressed Elijah King for burial today. He was found in his cabin yesterday—his spirit gone. Also treated young Edward King for shock and near freezing. The *buwe* was found in the Bear's Cave, apparently lost for almost twenty-four hours. We believe he found his *grossdaudi* dead.

Sarah reread the entry and tried to puzzle out how old Edward might have been. *Grossmuder* May was sketchy on dates in the latter part of the journal. Then she flipped the pages idly backward to when *Grossmuder* May was still bearing the brunt of Elias's anger.

He broke two ribs today—mine of course. I could almost laugh if it didn't hurt so much at the idea of me cracking his ribs for once. Not that I haven't thought of it. Dear *Gott*, forgive me, I've thought of it when he sleeps beside me . . . to break his ribs, his head, his heart. But I will not; I cannot become the monster that he is. . . . I've started to pray about leaving him. Again, *Gott*'s mercy upon me . . .

"Sarah?"

She looked up at Edward's call from the next room and hastily closed the book, determined to figure out things about the past if it might mean helping her husband.

Edward was nervous. He listened to the regular order of hymns, trying to let the sound of his people's voices soothe him as he'd been soothed in the woods that morning. He hadn't been able to work up the courage to tell Sarah that he was going to speak at the end of the service but decided it might be better this way.

The bishop preached, but Edward could absorb none of it. Instead, he simply waited until the time was his.

Bishop Umble rose again after a prayer for unity, then turned to face the group. "A few weeks ago, I talked about forgiving ourselves. Well, today one *kummes* with the fulfillment of that sermon—young Edward King."

Edward rose, sensing Joe's surprise beside him but concentrating on simply getting to where the bishop stood, and then his eye swept the crowd and he found Sarah's beautiful face, looking expectant and encouraging as she sat next to Martha Umble.

Edward drew a deep breath. *Help me,* Gott. *Help me to remember what it is I wanted to say here, that it might even help someone else. . . .*

"I'm an addict," he said baldly. "I'm addicted to alcohol. And after time with my lovely bride these past weeks, I thought that I could control it. Control the wanting and the fever that seems to get in my blood when I feel like I need a drink." He swallowed hard.

"But I learned this morning that I cannot control it—I can only turn to *Gott*, each time, every day, and ask Him to stay my hand. I've also made a lot of mistakes that have hurt many of you—my wife . . ." He struggled for words. "My language has been coarse. My *daed*, I've dishonored. My *bruder*, I've struck and berated. And you, all of you, I've broken community with you all through my letter to Marcellus Shale." He held out his hands in supplication. "I want to beg forgiveness for these and a million other sins, but I know that forgiveness only *kummes* in truth through *Derr Herr*." He glanced at Bishop Umble to find that man smiling and nodding. Edward bowed his head. "That's all, I guess."

He was unprepared for the surge of people around him, hugging him and clapping him on the back. And then Joseph and his *fater* were there, Mahlon Mast and Ernest, and then, finally, Sarah reached for his hand. He took her cool fingers in his, feeling as if he'd just grasped a lifeline. She stood with him until the service began to break up, small groups of men and

188

families, pausing for a bit more chatter before heading over to the Umbles' farm for volleyball and the usual huge bimonthly Sunday gathering.

"*Danki*, Sarah," he whispered, bending his head to brush his mouth across hers.

"I love you," she said simply. And he knew a temporary cleansing in his heart.

Jim Hanson showed up at Bishop Umble's, much to Sarah's surprise. She offered him his plate of potato salad, deviled eggs, baked beans, and pulled pork with a smile, though, wondering if he knew that the community was divided over the idea of buying shares in the well.

She was washing dishes in a large tub when she saw the man approach Edward and hastily got to her feet, unsure of what alarmed her but feeling the need to be close to her husband.

She reached the two men in time to hear Jim present his idea for a share in the well to Edward.

"Do you have any paperwork to back this up? Drilling specs? Fracking? Anything?" Edward asked, slipping an arm around her.

"Sure." Jim smiled. "I'll get all that to you soon." He looked down at her. "Hello, Sarah."

Sarah felt Edward's arm tighten possessively around her waist and nodded a brief greeting. "You'll have to excuse us, Mr.—uh—Jim. My *bruders* want Edward on their side for volleyball."

"Surely," the *Englischer* said agreeably. "I'll talk with you soon."

"You don't trust him?" Sarah asked in a whisper as they walked away.

"Not as far as I can throw him, sweet. But let's forget him for a moment and see how well a one-eyed man can play volleyball."

She swatted at his arm and he laughed, then pulled her close with a nuzzling promise for that *nacht*.

The next morning, Edward listened to Sarah's happy chatter at breakfast, but his gaze strayed throughout the meal to the innocent, half-undone slip of ribbon at the throat of her *nacht* shift. For some reason, it spoke to him of things secret and sweet, and he played idly with the honey spoon while his thoughts strayed and he felt as if he was coming apart, held in painful abeyance, until he could make his fantasy come true. . . .

"Would you like anything else?" she asked, eyeing him quizzically.

"Latch the door and *kumme* sit on my lap," he commanded in a rasp.

A slow smile spread across her face as she hurriedly rose to obey. His keen eye traced the curve of her hips and bottom when she turned in the thin fabric, then he watched in equal fascination as her breasts bounced with each step she took back toward him.

He slid his chair back a bit but he didn't rise, instead patting his thighs. "Sit down."

She complied, nestling close to his chest, with her legs pressed tight together. He savored her nearness and the fresh, heady scent of her hair, but then he inched her upright, turning her shoulders slightly until she faced him. He reached out a hand and slid the honey pot closer. . . .

Sarah shivered in excitement when he let go of the little jar of honey and lifted his big hands to her shoulders, massaging gently.

"Remind me," he whispered casually, "that I owe you a new *nacht* shift. . . ."

"What?" she murmured, then gasped as he tore the thin gown from her shoulders in one easy move, leaving her bare from the waist up. "Edward . . ." she stammered in surprise.

"I've needed to do that since you sat down to breakfast, sweet. And now it occurs to me that I'm wanting more honey. . . . Will you oblige?"

She felt breathless with excitement and reached an unsteady hand toward the table.

He caught her arm. "Ahh . . . not quite what I'm thinking. Let me show you."

A sunbeam shot through the window, bathing them both in a halo of light. And Sarah watched in fascination as he drew the long honey spoon from its jar. The sunlight played through the golden goodness as he pulled a long strand onto the spoon. She thought he meant to suck the spoon and then perhaps have her kiss his lips, but instead he drizzled the dripping honey down the full curve of her left breast.

She gasped at the sudden warmth and sensation, her senses overflowing at the decadence of his action.

"*Ach . . .*" she whispered.

He grinned at her, a tender, wolfish look, then continued to bathe her breast with honey, finally laying the spoon full against her taut nipple. She felt giddy and awkward and a thousand other things at once when he put the spoon aside and slid his hands around her waist.

"Arch your back, sweet."

She put her fingertips on his shoulders and did as he asked. She'd never been more proud nor more conscious of her breasts as he lavished her skin with his tongue—first wet, then hot, then he blew softly on her nipple before closing his teeth over her, edging and then sucking hard at the same time until she felt a cramping response deep inside.

She pressed her legs tighter together, and he dropped his hand to caress her belly and then lower. She sobbed with passion and instinctively knew what she wanted. She scrambled from him, despite his groan of protest, and let the remains of her gown fall to the floor. Then she bent and helped him work the hooks and eyes on his dark pants, just enough to reach him, heavy and hard. She changed her position, straddling him delicately, moving against him in frantic desperation. He helped her, and then she was in control, experimenting with the feel and depth of him as she pressed her tiptoes against the floor.

"*Ach*, Edward—I love you so."

She smiled in tender triumph when he could barely form the words to give back to her and then she moved harder and they came together in the meeting of a thousand suns, each burning more brightly than the last, until she cuddled quietly against him, honey-sticky, content in the aftermath of their love.

Chapter Twenty-Three

Edward suppressed a frustrated sigh and wondered why he'd *kumme* to Martha Umble's *haus* for this very early morning visit. When Sarah's older friend wanted to, she could be as obstinate as a mule, and he had no doubt she was enjoying herself a little at his expense as well. But Sarah was more than worth it. . . .

"So ya want a quilting fer yer bride?" Martha asked for the third time as she munched on some chestnuts she'd freed from their green spiny shells.

"*Nee* . . . not a quilting. A—a dressing."

"Ya want us ta dress her? You've got no problem with the undressin' part, I'd wager." She laughed aloud at her own bawdy humor, and he wondered helplessly where the bishop was.

"Okay, almost all that Sarah wears is gray . . ." he started again.

"Looks *gut* on her; matches her eyes." Martha chewed louder than a woodchuck.

"Right, but she never had the royal blue dress of a real bride. . . ."

"That's because ya was undressed in her presencelike, young man."

"Right, but what I'm wanting to do is get rid of all of her gray dresses, buy some colorful new fabrics, and have all of you women get together. Instead of quilting, I thought you could all sew dresses for Sarah. . . . So . . . a dressing, and I wanted it to be a surprise. I don't know; maybe it's a dumb idea." He leaned his chin into his palm with some dejection that must have struck a chord with the *auld* woman.

"Now, now . . . I think it's a fine idea. Strange . . . but fine! What woman wouldn't want to be made a whole new wardrobe?"

"Probably my wife." He smiled. "But I want it for her."

Martha reached out to pat his knee. "Ye're a fine strappin' man, Edward King. Jest fine."

Edward felt in strange accord with her complimentary words and rose to take his leave, only to turn back at the last moment to bend and press a kiss on her wrinkled cheek. She gasped and smacked at him, but he only laughed, whispering softly, "Our secret, Miss Martha."

"*Jah*," she agreed with a smile. "Our secret."

Edward swatted Sarah's bottom and she squeaked, then laughed out loud. "I mean it, sir, I'm not going until you tell me what this is all about."

He was practically chasing her around the kitchen table once back at home from his visit to Martha Umble's, but he didn't want to reveal that he'd gotten Ben Kauffman to open up an hour early. Nor did he tell her that he wanted to be there that morning for her to pick from the myriad colors of fabric for the surprise dressing.

"Let's say that left to your own devices, you'd turn this fine autumn morning into a gray day," he joked until she ran full tilt into his arms.

She smiled up at him, obviously feigning coyness, and he bent to kiss her once and hard. "I think you're mocking my dress with your gray-day comment," she pouted.

"Now, sweet, would I do that?" he asked her merrily, catching her arm and steering her toward the door.

"*Jah*." She giggled. "You would."

Sarah reveled in Edward's hold on her arm as they slowly walked the rocky path down from the cabin. She thought of the plan Jim Hanson had interrupted several days before and cast a warm smile up at her husband.

"What?"

"Nothing." She shrugged. "But I might have my own secret this day as well."

"I'll take anything from your hand, Sarah."

She hugged his arm and thanked *Gott* for the fact that they'd been able to find a way to love.

He led her to the steps of Ben Kauffman's store and she paused, doubtfully looking up at the big windows. "Does Ben open so early now?" she asked.

"He might, if a fella makes it worth his while. *Kumme*."

Sarah tripped gaily up the steps and was surprised when Ben met them at the door. "*Kumme* right in, folks," he said in his booming, good-natured voice.

The strategically placed kerosene lamps lit up the familiar and comforting store as Sarah drew in an appreciative breath of mingled scents: wood, leather, spices, and dried fruit tantalized the nose and made her stomach rumble a bit for want of breakfast. But she was most surprised when Edward made a straight line for the large counter that stood before the myriad bolts of fabric available. She followed him, wondering what he was up to, when Ben, too, edged his bulk near the fabrics and looked expectant.

196

"Royal blue first," Edward said.

Ben drew the beautiful bolt of fabric down from a selection of blues and then gave a professional, appraising look at Sarah.

"What is it?" she asked in confusion.

"About seven yards give or take," Ben muttered, measuring out the blue material against the notches carved along the edge of the table. His shears flashed with authority, and then he neatly folded and pinned the fabric and looked back to Edward. "Next?"

Sarah was about to catch Edward's arm when a tiny whimpering sound caught her attention. She turned and followed the faint noise to a box on the floor near a stand of cedar sachets. "*Ach*, Ben, what's this?" she cried.

She knelt, careless of her dress, and gently lifted the dirty and matted little black dog into her arms.

"Found him last *nacht* on a walk after that brief shower we had. I imagine he's run off from somewhere, though he don't have a collar. You're welcome to him, missus."

"*Ach*, he's darling. Edward, *kumme* and see."

She sensed her husband's reluctance as he knelt down next to her. "Dogs don't usually take to me except Joe's Bear, and our cabin is pretty small, Sarah."

"Oooh, his eyes are black as coal on a winter's day. I'll call him Blackie. Can we take him, Edward, *sei se gut*?"

She gave her husband her most winsome smile and saw a reluctant grin tug at his lips. "Anything for you, sweet." He sighed and then lifted a gentle hand to stroke the dog's strangely wispy-haired ears.

"What sort do you say he is, Ben?" Edward asked.

"An oddball, that's what." Ben laughed, coming to stand over them as he patted his stomach. "But he'll do with some bathing and love."

"I think he's beautiful," Sarah murmured, clutching the little animal closer.

"Ah . . . will you be wanting to continue now with yer shopping or would you both—with, uh, Blackie of course, care to join the family for a bit of breakfast?"

Sarah looked up at Edward. "I'm sorry," she cried. "I interrupted your fabric shopping."

He rolled his eye at her, then laughed. "I think we'll take that breakfast first, Ben. I can hear your belly rumbling from here."

Sarah nodded and cuddled the little *hund* closer.

The Kauffman family was huge, but as Frau Kauffman put it, there was "always room at the table for more."

Edward thanked his hostess while he watched his wife show off her new pet to the children and took joy in her simple happiness. And he realized she didn't fuss about keeping her apron perfectly white. As much as he wanted her to wear colors like the ones she added to his life, a few muddy little paw prints on her breast did a lot to add to her own sweet attractiveness. He found himself beginning to slip into the pleasant lassitude that usually accompanied his fantasies about Sarah when Ben clapped him on the shoulder.

"*Kumme* sit by *Fater*, Edward. I think yer wife is happiest amongst the *kinner*." Edward nodded and slipped over to the bench next to Solomon Kauffman, who was as near to ninety as a man could be. Everyone on the mountain knew that the old man suffered from bouts of senility, but he was always treated with the greatest respect, as any elder should be.

"You like toast?" the *auld* man asked in a patronizing tone during the silence of grace. Edward tried not to smile and opened his eye to give a quick nod. A few of the younger *kinner* giggled and Ben cleared his throat. "What about weasels? You like weasels?" Edward shook his head, then breathed a faint sigh of relief when the exact twenty-one seconds of grace were over.

"Elijah King here, he don't like weasels!" Solomon crowed to the now busy table. No one seemed to mind much, but Edward froze. *Elijah King . . . my grandfather . . .* He passed the steaming platter of scrambled eggs and glanced down the table to Sarah. She was staring at him, her beautiful face serious. *But she doesn't know* . . . He pushed aside the insidiously dark thought, trying not to analyze exactly what it was she didn't know and accepted a fresh biscuit from Solomon.

"You still runnin' shine, Elijah?" Solomon asked conversationally. "I'll take a jar or two if you've got it handy."

Edward stared down at his plate and shook his head.

"*Daed*! That's not Elijah King—it's Edward, his grandson," Ben called down the table as he chewed a piece of ham steak.

"What?" Solomon yelled back. Then he muttered to Edward, "These young folks all mumble, Elijah. Now, what about that 'shine?"

Sarah didn't question Edward when he told Ben that they would finish shopping another time. Instead, she followed him outside as he absently took her free hand and helped her down the steps while she carried the dog.

Edward's head was bowed and he appeared deep in thought, and she hated to intrude. So, instead, she silently prayed for him until they'd turned the bend in the road. Then she stopped and Edward did likewise, but she could tell he was paying no attention to where they were.

She let go of his hand, then reached up to encircle his neck with her free arm. "Hey," she whispered.

He looked at her then, his tiger's eye veiled and hurting. "What?"

"I love you," she said clearly as a light breeze stirred up the brown and red leaves at her feet.

"I love you, too."

She heard the expected answer but knew it lacked focus, so she tried again, stretching to place a warm kiss on his lips, then using the tip of her tongue to tease at his mouth. She could tell when he came back to her, suddenly deepening the kiss, slanting his head to taste more of her until Blackie yelped at the closeness.

Edward drew back with visible reluctance and Sarah gestured to the brown paper–wrapped fabric he carried.

"That bridal fabric, Edward . . . would you like to see me in it?"

"*Jah*," he said simply, but she let her lashes fall, then glanced up at him with desire sparking through her at her intimate thoughts.

I know I can reach him with my body and heart even if I can't with my mind. . . . "I thought how nice the blue would look spread out on our bed," she confided in seductive tones. "What do you think?"

He blinked. "I never thought of that. . . ."

He sounded so surprised that she laughed, then kissed him once more.

"Well, I'm glad I've got a creative mind," she said, and the morning seemed much brighter.

Chapter Twenty-Four

Sometime later, Edward smiled in sleepy contentment when Sarah bent to murmur in his ear.

"I forgot something at Ben's."

"Mmm . . . 'k," he slurred, then began rewinding the past half hour in his thoughts like a long gossamer strand.

Sarah had deposited the little dog into a convenient basket, where it had settled comfortably; then she went to wash her hands at the pump sink.

He'd watched her, clutching the paper-wrapped fabric, seeing the play of liquid and sunshine between her delicate fingers, and he'd felt more charged and excited than he could ever remember. It was the first time she'd suggested their lovemaking and in such a creative fashion that he could hardly wait to undress her. But then she'd dried her hands and walked toward him, loosening her *kapp* and hair until the entire shiny mass had fallen to brush at her hips as she neared him.

His nostrils were filled with the fresh scent of her, and he reached out a hand to caress her hip through the usual gray dress. But she forestalled him by reaching to take the fabric from his hand. She turned and he helplessly followed the swing of her hips into the bedroom. She'd opened the fabric with tantalizing slowness, the sounds magnified in his ears, his senses heightened. And then she'd dropped the wrapper and approached the bed to shake out the fall of royal blue and then carefully begun to spread it out on the bed.

He'd moved again, coming up behind her to catch her hips, but she somehow stepped away. "Help me," she'd whispered, and he ground his teeth but obeyed. When the fabric was in vibrant place, she'd undone her apron and he'd gotten the point in his brain that he was to be treated to the sight of Sarah undressing herself in the bright slant of morning sunlight. . . .

The sudden sound of Blackie the dog whining interrupted his pleasant thoughts and he glanced ruefully toward the basket, where the little whiskery face looked up expectantly.

"You need a bath," Edward said. "And I could use a cold dip in the creek."

"I tell you, Sarah," Ben Kauffman shook his head, "I was going to take that horse back to market this coming Saturday."

"*Ach*, please don't, Ben. I mean it. I really do want to barter with you for Sunny so that Edward can find happiness when he rides." Sarah struggled to keep the note of desperation out of her voice as she glanced through the store window to the pasture beyond, where Sunny grazed.

Ben had taken the huge black gelding back after the accident on the road, but Sarah knew in her heart that Edward missed the animal, though he would never speak of it.

"And frankly, Sarah, yer arm's still in a cast. . . . Would you really want the big brute that ran you down around the farm?"

"*Jah*, I would." She nodded. "Now let's barter. I give you, for all nine children and you and your wife and Solomon, of course, a lifetime of care as you need healing and you give me Sunny."

Ben smiled. "I'm a business owner, Sarah. I can't put stock in a future like that—suppose the *kinner* remain healthy as dirt?"

She gave him an arch look and began to tick off ailments on one hand. "Toothache, insomnia, cold in the lungs, headache . . ."

Ben held his hands up in a placating manner. "*Jah, jah* . . . all right."

"Annnd . . ." She kept her tone low. "I think I have an herbal mixture that might help Solomon sleep better at *nacht*."

Ben's face took on a look of intense interest. Sarah had heard through Martha Umble that many was the time Ben had stubbed a bare toe at night following after his *fater*, who sleepwalked, and Ben loved his sleep. Sarah was not above wielding a little herbal power if it meant fetching Sunny back where he belonged.

"*Ach*, all right." Ben groaned. "The horse is

yours. I haven't been able to break him in a whit anyway, and I want something gentler for the missus." He stuck out a hamlike hand and Sarah took it firmly.

"Deal." She smiled.

"I'll get one of the *buwes* to walk Sunny over for you. No sense you takin' a chance with that arm."

"No need, Ben," Sarah's *fater* spoke up from behind her. "I'll take the horse and see Sarah home."

Sarah turned to smile in grateful surprise at her *daed* but realized that she was still a bit uncertain around him after his newly expressed tenderness toward her. Yet she knew that they needed time together, and she was more than happy to give it.

Mahlon held the reins of the black horse carefully and glanced over at Sarah as she walked a bit apart along the dirt road.

"I don't know if ya remember the time I cut down that big horse chestnut tree we had towerin' over the cabin?" he asked.

"I do," she replied simply, and he knew why her answer was brief.

He cleared his throat. "I've been doin' some rememberin', Sarah. It *kummes* to me that I was harsh with ya that day. . . ."

She smiled slightly. "I wanted to make a necklace out of the horse chestnuts, but we don't wear jewelry—of course."

Mahlon shuffled a bit, then reached into his pocket. He pulled out a wonderful chunky necklace of rich brown horse chestnuts, each carefully strung next to the other to form a beautiful link with nature's abundance. "Here ya go, child."

He was pleased when she stopped and reached out a shaking hand to take the offering. "*Ach, Daed* . . . why . . ."

He smiled, feeling his throat tighten. "We only got so much time to make things right, Sarah, and I'd like to start. There's no harm in a necklace made of *Gott*'s bounty. It would please me if you'd wear it."

Sunny whinnied a bit when she came into Mahlon's arms, tears falling gently down her pretty cheeks. "*Danki, Daddi. Ach, danki* . . ."

He patted her soft head and knew peace in his heart. "You be welcome, child."

"What *en der weldt* are you doing?" Joseph asked, walking through the leaves.

Edward looked up from the old tub he'd decided to use to bathe Blackie. The little *hund* seemed to have a particular aversion to the water and had all four feet stretched out, looking like some dripping rat instead of a respectable dog.

"Sarah found a pet," Edward said with a half smile as Blackie shook, spraying water all about.

Joseph laughed. "Well, you'll have to introduce it, er, him, to Bear. Priscilla wanted me to *kumme* over and invite you both for supper tonight."

"I'd like that," Edward said honestly. "I feel like I haven't talked to *Daed* in a while."

"He misses you, but he doesn't want to intrude on you and Sarah. I remember what it was to be a newlywed—you're kind of in your own little world."

Edward arched a brow at his big *bruder*. "What are you talking about? You're still a newlywed." He lifted a towel from the ground and swathed the little dog in it, hugging the animal close to his bare chest when he felt it shivering through the cotton.

"I guess I am," Joseph agreed good-naturedly, then appeared serious. "Say, that Jim Hanson came around and talked to *Daed* when I wasn't home. . . . Almost has him convinced to invest in this Marcellus Shale thing."

Edward got to his feet and shook his head. "I'm sorry, Joe. I need to get rid of that guy or the community is going to be hurt."

"But what if he's on the up-and-up?" Joseph asked idly, bending to tip the tub into the grass.

"He's not," Edward said flatly. "I can feel it."

"Well, he sure seems . . ." Joseph broke off, and a grin stretched across his face.

"What?" Edward asked, trying to dry the squirming dog.

"Here *kummes* your bride, and I think she may have a present for you."

207

• • •

Later that afternoon, they walked out to the barn together. Sarah still wore her chestnut necklace and Edward had rejoiced with her when she'd explained its origin. But now she knew great pleasure in watching him feed first *auld* Mollie and then Sunny a bit of carrot, making low, soothing sounds from the back of his throat that caused Sarah herself to shiver with delight.

"Do you like your gift?" she asked lightly.

Edward turned and caught her in his arms. "I do indeed, sweet. I wonder if you'd trust me enough to go riding with me on Sunny?" He touched her casted arm, then bent to kiss it with a penitent gesture that moved her heart.

She still felt leery of the tall horse, but she trusted Edward more than she'd ever thought possible. "Of course . . . or at least I'll try."

He drew a deep breath and nodded, staring down at her with his heated tiger's eye. "I can't promise never to hurt you again, Sarah."

"And I wouldn't want you to," she protested earnestly.

"I know. But I can promise to always trust *Gott* with my actions, and I pray that I will bring you the honor you deserve both as my wife and as my best friend."

She smiled up at him, joy trembling on her lips. "I couldn't ask for anything more."

I've begun to pester Frau Zug about the ways of being a healer, sneaking off to see her even though it means a beating when I get home. But this healing of others may be a way to heal myself, and I must keep learning, keep trying to separate myself from this man who hurts me without care or caution. And then, one day, as *Derr Herr* wills—freedom. I must seek freedom. What more could I ask for?

May

Chapter Twenty-Five

Edward glanced down at Sarah standing straight beside him before he lifted a hand to knock at the door of his *auld* home. It was a funny thing, he reflected, that Joseph had thrown him out for drinking not all that long ago, and here he was, coming back, with an enchanting frau, an almost turned-around life, and a domestic dog that still resembled a whiskery rat, even though he was now perfectly dry.

Joseph opened the door and gave him a bone-crunching hug, then pulled them inside. After the quiet of only the two of them, his *fater*'s *haus* seemed to pulse with activity.

Six-year-*auld* Hollie ran past with Bear, the big black wolf dog, chasing her merrily. Bear only paused a moment to stretch up to Sarah's arms, his discerning snout seeking and then giving Blackie a yip of approval, which the little dog seemed to understand. When Sarah put him carefully down, he joined in the rough-and-tumble play, barking in shrill tones and running with all his might.

Edward gave his *daed* a long embrace, somehow feeling that Abner had grown older even in the short time since the last church service. *I'm growing up,* Edward thought in confusion, unsure whether he were comfortable with the feeling or not. *What is it to be accountable for your own life, to take care of yourself and others?* . . . His gaze strayed to Sarah. *And to let* Gott *take care of all* . . . He shook the serious thoughts out of his head as Priscilla, Joseph's frau, came to greet him, her stomach nicely rounded in pregnancy.

She patted her belly and smiled. "Soon this will be your Sarah, Edward, with God's blessing."

He felt himself flush as he recalled his love-making with Sarah that morning on the bridal fabric. "We'll see, but I hope you're well."

Priscilla's eyes moved to Joseph. "Very well," she murmured.

Edward knew that she and Hollie had lived a terrible existence in the *Englisch* world before Joseph came into their lives. Priscilla had been in an abusive relationship with her ex-husband, but Edward also knew that his *bruder* was more than making up for the unhappy times she'd had.

He joined everyone at the well-laden table, his eyes roving with pleasure over the multitude of dishes—stuffed meatloaf, mashed potatoes mounded and dripping with butter, sweet macaroni salad, candied carrots, and fresh salad.

The silent grace over, he lifted his fork to eat, then looked up with everyone else at the sudden pounding on the front door.

Edward put down his fork. "I'll get it," he offered, getting up quickly. He had to hold Bear back with his leg as he opened the door, only to find Ernest, Sarah's young *bruder*, standing there, breathing heavily.

"Ernest, *kumme* in. What is it?"

The *buwe* shook his head. "I can't . . . Samuel's missing and there's a storm due to *kumme* up tonight. *Fater*'s out already, trying to search. He didn't want to ring the school bell and cause a big alarm."

Edward put his arm around Sarah as she came to the door. "Where would Samuel go and why wouldn't he be home for supper?" she asked, her body tense with concern.

Ernest drew a deep breath. "He may be lying hurt somewhere, Sarah. Maybe you'd better come."

"*Nee*," Edward said. "Let the men search." But Sarah pulled on his shirtsleeve and he turned to look down into her big gray eyes, reluctant to see the protest he knew he'd find there.

"Please, Edward," she whispered. "It's my little *bruder*."

He nodded, much against his will; then Joseph was there with heavy coats and several lanterns.

"Best take a blanket or two," Abner said, offering them the warm folded wool. "The *buwe* might be cold. And take Bear with you; I'll watch yer little dog."

"We'd better ring the school bell, too," Edward said.

"But *Fater* said . . ." Ernest began.

"I'll take the consequences," Edward promised, clapping the scared *buwe* on the shoulder. "Don't worry. We'll find him."

"The Bear's Cave," Sarah said suddenly.

Edward turned to stare down at her, a sudden sick feeling in the pit of his stomach that he couldn't explain. "What did you say?"

Sarah laid an urgent hand on his arm. "*Sei se gut*, Edward. I know it somehow. I know he's there."

Edward paused for only a second. "Let's go there. If Sarah feels it, it's probably true." He pushed aside the eerie chord that resonated through his mind at the thought of going to the place, then set out with his family, grimly determined to hike the mile to the Bear's Cave and find his young *bruder*-in-law well.

Sarah was dimly aware of the ringing echo of the school bell over the mountain and knew that soon the woods would be filled with searchers. Her mother and Clara would no doubt be at the school, helping to provide coffee and sandwiches to all who came to look for Samuel. But Sarah knew in her heart and spirit that her *bruder* was at the Bear's Cave, as sure as she had read the name of the place in *Grossmuder* May's journal. She, Edward, Joseph, and Ernest had set out for the cave immediately.

She wondered as she walked whether or not Edward remembered being found at the cave. The place had been, according to local legend, truly a bear's den at one time, and there were even more recent stories that the cave was home to a mountain lion or two. Mostly, the legends were only that, but Sarah knew the rocks leading up to the cave were still treacherous, and it would be very easy for a small *buwe*'s foot to slip or become lodged in a crevice.

They were beginning the climb over the first of the large exposed roots and rocks when lightning struck a tall pine tree nearby, momentarily lighting up their footsteps and searing off a tall upper branch. Sarah watched as the charred embers floated to the ground, causing no damage because it had begun to pour—large fat droplets that caught in the wind and made visibility poor. She was glad of Joseph's big coat, happy that her cast wasn't being soaked, when she heard the first fretful cry over the roar of the storm.

"Listen," she called, catching Edward's arm.

She watched him cock his ear, and then he shook his head, pulling her over some slippery mud, and she tried in vain to hear her *bruder*'s voice again. But when they neared the entrance of the cave, slipping inside the dark cavern, their lanterns giving off a welcome glow, Sarah was thrilled to hear Samuel's call.

She rushed headlong into the darkness, careless of her steps, and only heard the rattle when she felt something move beneath her feet. She stopped dead, feeling queasy, and the lantern fell from her hand, illuminating a huge half-curled timber rattler.

She tried not to scream, then felt a sudden push from behind. She staggered forward, looking back in the haloed light of the lantern to see Edward lose his footing, but not before he'd broken the menacing snake's neck in one quick move.

"*Ach*, Edward," she gasped. "Did it strike you?"

"*Nee*, but I've twisted my ankle on this uneven cave floor. . . . Go to Samuel."

Then Sarah was back in the moment and heard her *bruder*'s cries. She clambered behind a large boulder, glad for the light of Ernest's lantern, and found Samuel huddled and cold against the dripping cave wall.

"*Ach*, Samuel," she cried. "Are you hurt?" She felt anxiously down his chilled arms.

"*Nee*, but I was afraid to move because of that snake, and then it started to get dark and I knew the snake was over there somewhere. Did Edward get it?"

"*Jah*," Sarah said, pulling him close for a hug. He allowed it for a moment, then squirmed out of her grasp.

"*Ach*, Sarah, I'm too big for loves."

"A real man is never too big for loves," Edward said from where he leaned on the boulder.

Sarah smiled and went to him while Joseph moved outside the cave and fired off two gunshots: notice to the searchers that the lost had been found.

Edward knew it was a bad sprain, but his ankle bothered him far less than the chills he had inside and the strange feeling that he was having difficulty swallowing. His heart raced and he felt himself break out in a cold sweat though his black wool coat was plenty warm. *Maybe it's just a delayed reaction to Sarah stepping on that snake. . . .*

Sarah came up beside him, and he felt her study him intently in the light of the lantern he held. "Edward, are you all right? You look flushed and you're sweating."

"I—I don't know," he managed to say, having the strange sensation in his chest that he was dying. *Maybe I'm having a heart attack . . .*

215

gonna die, right here. . . . Help me, Gott. . . .

"You must be coming down with something," Sarah said, sliding her arm around his waist. "Are you sure you can walk?"

"*Jah.*" He gritted his teeth to keep them from chattering and tried to focus on slowing his breathing. He was glad for the pain in his ankle because it distracted him from all the other worrisome feelings he was having.

He didn't want to tell Sarah, but he was immensely relieved to leave the Bear's Cave behind, though it meant leaning hard on Joseph to make it back over the rocks at the entrance. The rain had slowed to a cold mist, and soon there were other hands of help from the community to take Samuel safely home. Sarah gave him a stern admonishment to stay in bed the next day, and Edward felt some lessening of his unease when Mahlon, back at the school *haus*, hugged both him and Sarah in gratitude.

After everyone in the community dispersed to seek their beds, Sarah and Edward walked slowly home. Joseph had given him a stick to limp along with and now he was truly aware of the throbbing in his ankle, though the odd feelings from before had seemingly abated.

But once back at the cabin, his ankle expertly strapped, he found it hard to close his eye to sleep. He told himself that he was probably too keyed up from the *nacht*'s happenings, but then he felt his heart begin to race again and raw panic kept him frozen and stiff in the bed next to his wife.

Sarah could sense that Edward wasn't asleep, though she was tired herself. She leaned over in the dark to quietly turn up the kerosene lamp, then turned back to him to lay a gentle hand on his chest.

"Are you sick, Edward?"

"*Nee*; at least . . . I don't think so."

She reached and felt his forehead, only to find it damp with sweat. "Edward, I'm worried about you. I'm going to brew you some tea."

She paused when he reached out and caught her arm. "*Nee*, Sarah. Please . . . please don't go. There's something wrong with me."

She listened as he began to tell her of his strange feelings. "And all of this started at the Bear's Cave?" she asked.

He nodded, clearly miserable.

"Things happen for a reason," she said finally. "Maybe Samuel getting lost had nothing to do with him, in one sense, and had everything to do with *Gott* wanting to reveal things to your own heart."

"What do you mean?" he asked, his brow wrinkling in confusion.

She drew a deep breath. "Edward, when you were young, do you remember being lost at the Bear's Cave?"

"I remember *Daed* telling me a story about it, but I don't really remember being there. Why?"

"Because I think your body remembers, or some part of your mind. I believe when you were there tonight you had a panic attack, and I think you're having another one now."

"Panic attack? I remember there was a guy on the rigs who had what he called panic attacks. He eventually had to go home. . . . Suppose you're right, Sarah. . . . I—I'm afraid of this, that there's something wrong with me."

" 'For *Gott* has not given us a spirit of fear, but of power and love and a sound mind,' " she quoted quietly from the Bible. "You'll be all right, Edward. I'll take care of you, but I think the best thing you can do is actually try to remember what you can from when you were young . . . like what happened at the Bear's Cave. Now I'll brew you that tea and it will help relax you."

She bent forward and kissed him with tenderness, then slid out of the bed to go to the kitchen.

He realized that he'd forgotten to ask her how she'd suspected about him and the Bear's Cave, then drifted into a fitful sleep instead.

I've heard tell of a place called Ice Mountain, far away, up in the mountains. I could hide there and never be found. But leaving . . . it's harder than I thought, though I continue to study with Frau Zug. . . . What if Elias came after me? He'd kill me, but surely I am already dead a bit inside. *Nee*, I must plan and seek the freedom of *Derr Herr*. . . .

May

Chapter Twenty-Six

The next morning dawned clear and bright, and Edward woke feeling better. He found Sarah had been up for some time, making pancakes and bacon, and he dressed with ease, despite his ankle, after she'd brought him a large mug of tea.

"I can't leave the stove," she teased. "Or I might hide your clothes and keep you in bed all day."

"To rest or to work?" he quipped, and she giggled as she went back into the kitchen.

They'd nearly finished the delicious food when there was a knock on the door. One of their more distant neighbors, John Beider, had *kumme*, and Sarah kindly invited him in for breakfast.

"Well, I'd like to," the older man said, "but the missus is down with bad sinuses. Felt too sick to *kumme* to see you here, Sarah. I'm sorry."

Edward watched Sarah begin to assemble things in her bag. "I'll go to her of course, John."

"Well, then, maybe I'll keep your husband

company. Heard about your ankle last *nacht*, Edward, and I know just the cure."

Edward had to smile. John Beider was known as the best storyteller on the mountain, and his kind face held suppressed excitement at his obvious suggestion of a cure.

"You got a new story, John?" Edward asked, handing the other man a cup of tea.

"I might . . ."

Sarah bent and kissed him good-bye, then set out for the Beiders' while Edward turned to his friend. It was nice to listen to the melodic voice of the storyteller, clearly gifted with the craft of weaving a tale to stop time for a bit, and Edward was grateful.

"Well, you know the craft of being a potter, I suppose?" John asked, squinting a bit at Edward.

"*Jah*, though I don't know of anyone who does it around here still."

"*Nee.*" John shook his head. "It's a fast-disappearing art, but I hear tell of two *bruders* over in Elk County living way back in a hollow who still practice spinning their wheels and making all sorts of pottery. I got this story about them when we was down Renovo way, and the missus found an apple pie plate, glazed and wonderful in design."

Edward offered him a short stack of pancakes, fresh butter, and syrup, and John continued to talk while chewing with decorum.

220

"*Jah*, so I hear they fire their kiln with a mixture of poplar, oak, cherry, and chestnut wood to produce a steady white flame, and then they go to work, shaping and spinning the clay they haul out of the creek bed. But the funny thing about these two *auld* men is the sayings they like to carve on their works."

Edward smiled. "Hmm . . . I would have thought their bishop might see that as some kind of vanity, unless he's a *gut* man like Bishop Umble."

"Well, apparently he is. The missus's pie plate, when you turn it over, says WER NICHT LIEBT SEIN GOTT AND WEIB, DER HAT KEIN RUH IN EWIGKEIT."

Edward laughed. " 'Who doesn't love his God and wife won't have any rest for eternity'?"

"*Jah*," John returned dryly. "I can't seem to get away from that thought now at my *haus*."

"Well, maybe there's some truth in it," Edward teased.

"Bah!" John flung out a hand. "You're still newly married. What do you know? But I will say that by engraving their pots and things, those two are leaving a speaking legacy that could last as long as the glazed clay does."

"Maybe you should do the same, John," Edward encouraged him after a moment. "Why not write down some of your stories?"

"*Ach*, I tell 'em . . . that's my legacy, and

someday somebody else can tell 'em when I'm gone."

"True enough," Edward admitted. Then he enjoyed the rest of John's tales of the two potters until the pancakes were gone and the tea had long grown cold.

"Well," John said reluctantly, "I'd best head back. I imagine Sarah will return soon. *Danki* for breakfast."

"Thank you for the story," Edward said, struggling a bit to get to his feet.

John kindly pressed him back in his chair. "Take it easy, Edward. I'll see myself out."

Edward bid him good-bye, then sat, grateful for Blackie's company when the little dog jumped up on his lap. He was grateful to *Gott* that the panic attack, if that was what it was, had left him for the moment, and in a few minutes he'd stretched out, falling asleep in the uncomfortable kitchen chair.

Sarah kissed his handsome mouth upside down, gently stroking her tongue across his lips until he returned her kisses, still obviously half-asleep.

"Mmm," he muttered. "Am I dreaming?"

"Yes, you are," Sarah answered, continuing to kiss him until he was fully awake and Blackie hopped down, obviously disgusted with this display of human affection.

"You need to be in bed today," she told him in a honeyed whisper.

"Fine with me . . . but only if I have some company."

"And what if someone should *kumme* needing healing?" she asked, shivering a bit as his big hands spanned her hips and then found the curves of her breasts.

"Latch the door. You're used to dressing in a hurry," he said, leaning upward to trail damp kisses over the line of her throat.

"Mmm," she agreed after a moment. "I'm used to undressing in a hurry, too."

"Then do it." He opened his blue eye and smiled at her encouragingly.

She exhaled softly and hurried to draw the latch on the door. Then she turned back to him and slowly began to remove the complicated pins that held her dress together. She sensed his eagerness as he sat, poised, like a big cat on a short chain.

When she'd removed everything but her stockings, his hoarse voice stopped her. "Leave the stockings, sweet. I like the dark wool against your white skin, and I think I can find a more creative way to get them off."

And he did, leaving her in sweet abandon while he trailed kisses down the line of her thigh, deliberately avoiding that part of her that begged for his mouth. Then he caught the top of her stocking between his teeth and slowly pulled it down. By the time he'd done the second in a similar leisurely fashion, she was panting with want, and he knew it by the slow smile he gave her.

"Are you ready, sweet?"

"Please," she gasped, unable to help herself.

"Anything you say," he muttered, then obliged her desire with hard, deft strokes that made her cry out with passion and then collapse lazily into the shelter of his arms.

Sarah couldn't believe it when she heard the knock on the door. She glanced at Edward and saw that he was fast asleep. She hurriedly dressed, bundling up her hair and pinning her *kapp*, then scooping up Blackie before he could yip more than he was already doing. She undid the latch and opened the door but drew back in both surprise and alarm.

Edward came awake in slow degrees to realize that Blackie was licking his nose. He gently pushed the little dog away, then rose up on one elbow to call for Sarah. When he got no response, he dressed slowly, his ankle still quite painful, and went out into the kitchen. There was a curious stillness to the place that jangled his nerves, and then he saw the letter on the table.

It was obviously written in Sarah's neat hand, but he had to read it twice before he could fathom what it said.

Dear Edward,

I've been arrested for making moonshine. The sheriff and his deputy are taking me to the Coudersport jail. They found my still in the woods and the jars of moonshine. I admitted that I've sold it to *Englischers* in the past and to my own people. Please forgive me.

Love,
Sarah

Edward squeezed his eye shut and shook his head, only to look again and read the note for a third time. *Her still . . . her moonshine . . .*

And then his eye burned with angry tears and he drew a deep breath. *Sarah went to jail to protect me. . . . What was she thinking to sacrifice herself to keep me safe?*

He wanted to curse, but nothing except a choked sob would *kumme* as he hastily found his walking stick and set out for Bishop Umble's, amazed at the kind of wife he'd married . . . *the wife of my heart . . . and I could wring her neck. . . .*

After the long trek down the mountain and then a car ride with the kind and reluctant sheriff, Sarah breathed a sigh of actual relief to be placed in a holding cell with two other women. Obviously, from some tip, the sheriff had believed it was Edward's still . . . *but I kept my husband safe. . . .*

It had been all she could think about, especially in light of his recent panic attacks.

Now she glanced with some hesitancy at her cellmates, unsure of what to expect. To her surprise, they both seemed disposed to talk.

"Say, ye're Aim-ish, right?"

Sarah looked at the woman, who must have been in her late forties. She had a black eye and strangely dyed brownish orange hair and she wore a pair of blue jeans and a flowered top with buttons shaped into tiny garden spades.

"*Jah* or yes . . . What happened to your eye?" Sarah asked kindly, wishing she had a poultice with her to give the woman some relief from the swelling.

The woman snorted. "My old man did it. Can't do anything to please him when he drinks."

Sarah felt a jolt in her chest. *Here, too, is someone else whose husband struggles with drinking . . . but to hit her . . . I cannot believe it, though I know it happens all the time.*

"My name's Carla," the woman went on. "And I'm in here 'cause this time I hit him back, and then I got all riled when he called the cops. Domestic dispute, they say, but he's free and I'm not . . . What'd you do?"

"Well," Sarah swallowed, "I'm Sarah and I was making moonshine and . . ."

Carla started to laugh, revealing surprisingly white teeth. "You? Makin' 'shine? You look like

226

some ad for *Little House on the Prairie*. . . . How'd you even know how to do it?"

The other woman spoke up, then. Sarah looked at her and saw someone who might be called pretty in the *Englisch* world, except for her hair, which seemed too. . . . big—and the short cut of her skirt. "Ain't nuthin' to makin' 'shine. My granpappy taught me."

To Sarah's surprise, Carla extended a hand in introduction. "This is Shelley."

"Hello, Shelley," Sarah responded with gentleness. *Both women seem so hurt and tired in a way.* . . .

Shelley chewed a piece of gum loudly, then moved to touch the edge of Sarah's clean apron. "My ma had an apron like this. . . . She died when I wuz fifteen. Don't know what happened to her apron."

"*Ach*, I'm so sorry about your mother," Sarah said, genuineness in her voice as she reached out a hand to touch Shelley's.

The other woman allowed Sarah's touch for a moment but then jerked away. "It don't matter now, though I've had a harder life than some—I get by."

"I'm sure you do," Sarah replied warmly. "Can I ask what you—um—did to be here?"

"Sure, honey." Shelley laughed and Carla joined in. "I'm a prostitute."

Chapter Twenty-Seven

Mr. Ellis was only too happy to oblige Edward and the bishop with a ride to Coudersport. To Edward's chagrin, Bishop Umble seemed unconcerned about Sarah's predicament and even faintly amused. But Edward never felt a car went so slow on a drive.

Once outside the town, the bishop directed Mr. Ellis to go to a yellow building on a side street instead of the jail. Edward read the ornate sign in frustration: DISTRICT ATTORNEY: DANIEL MILLER.

"Do you really think we should be here, Bishop?" Edward asked, his nerves fraught.

"*Ach*, just wait here and give me a few minutes inside, and then we'll go to the jail and visit your, ah—errant frau."

So Edward had to wait helplessly while Mr. Ellis made small talk until the bishop emerged with a tall *Englischer* in a brown suit who piled in the station wagon with apparent ease.

The bishop made introductions with a smile on his face and a twinkle in his blue eyes. "Folks, meet Dan Miller, my fishing buddy and a *gut* friend."

Edward shook hands, still not sure what it all meant until Dan Miller explained. "Your wife will be cleared of all charges, Mr. King, because her alcohol is used for medicinal purposes and because we have no actual proof that she did anything with the moonshine but by her own insistence, which I think may have been for your—er—another's benefit. In any case, we'll go over and see that she's released right now."

Edward felt a surge of intense relief. "Thank you, sir. I—I don't know what to say."

Dan Miller grinned. "Say you'll show me a new fishing spot sometime."

"Done."

The kind sheriff seemed only too happy to lead the way to the holding cell where Edward saw his wife seated on a narrow bench along the wall between two other women. She looked rumpled but was talking earnestly and didn't even appear to hear him when he came in.

The sheriff rattled the keys in the lock. "Mrs. King. Your husband's here. You're free to go."

Then she did look up and met Edward's eye. He saw her swallow, and all anger at her washed away at the weariness in her beautiful face.

Her cellmates seemed reluctant to have her leave, and it shouldn't have surprised him that she'd made friends with women so visibly different from her. *She found a way to connect, to meet them where they're at. . . .*

"Take care, luv," the one with the black eye

called. "And thanks for the tip about the husband."

"Yeah, and thanks for talkin' about my ma . . . I won't forget it," the one in the short skirt said.

"Good-bye," Sarah called, and Edward couldn't help but put an arm around her even while he still held a walking stick with the other.

"I'm sorry, Edward," she whispered as they walked to the outer office and he bent and kissed her forehead in response.

There were some papers to sign and then the sheriff waved them off. Dan Miller shook hands all around and the bishop announced that he had some errands he had to take care of in town if Mr. Ellis didn't mind the wait.

"Not at all," the *gut Englischer* replied. "I've got a bit of business, too. So I guess that leaves you two with an afternoon in town." He gestured to Sarah and Edward.

Edward couldn't help but sense her renewed vitality; probably she hadn't gotten to go to town that often, and suddenly the day was looking better.

"We'll have a *gut* time," he promised as they parted ways from their friends. Then he looked down at Sarah with a smile. "How about a nice lunch?"

Following an elegant little luncheon in a tearoom that delighted her, Sarah asked him if they might go to the library.

"I've never been there, and the little library at the mountain school is so small."

"Surely, sweet," he said, lifting her hand to kiss it. "Joe was always the big reader at our house. He sent away for books, then forced me to read them. I suppose I should thank him for it now."

The library was a long, low squat white building with a mild-looking single lion outside standing guard, but the oaken door was heavy and sported a gold handle. Edward gave the door a push. "After you," he said formally.

Sarah entered, her heart beating with excitement. The place smelled of books, both old and new, and filled her heart and mind with possibilities. She met the beady brown eyes of a woman at the main desk with the nameplate MISS BETTY and went forward hesitantly.

"Hello," Sarah said softly. "I wondered if we could look around a bit. I've never been here before. It seems lovely."

Miss Betty's stern face softened. "Of course, child. Would you want a library card?"

"Oh, no. We don't get down from the mountain enough, but just looking would be wonderful."

Miss Betty nodded. "Well, our children's section is to the left and the adult's is to the right. You can find about anything you want from crafts to King Arthur, and if you have any questions, let me know."

Sarah walked to the right down a slightly

sloping ramp covered with a rich red carpet. There was a sitting area to the left with large black leather chairs and a carousel of magazines, and then there were inexpensive brown wooden tables where three teenage boys were working and talking quietly. The bulk of the library consisted of seven eight-foot-high blue shelves, packed front and back with books of all shapes and sizes. Hand-printed labels across the ends of the shelves told what was what in terms of subjects.

Sarah was immediately drawn to the first shelf in the crafting and sewing section. Her fingers traced the fine spines of the books with excitement, finally settling on a huge yellow book entitled *Costumes through the Centuries* to look at. She took the book down the aisle into a small alcove, which had a bright window with a standing podium and a green potted plant. Edward followed, his stick making light tapping sounds behind her. She'd opened the book and was eagerly scanning its contents when she felt Edward's hand on her shoulder and his warm breath in her ear.

"I think there's something stimulating about libraries, don't you, sweet? All this quiet and stillness?" He kissed her ear gently and she shivered, trying to concentrate on the book.

"Edward," she warned.

"Just stand still, my little jailbird, and let me have the nape of your neck."

She was about to obey, her senses heightened by her surroundings, when she suddenly felt him pull away.

"What is it?" she asked.

"Shh . . . listen."

And then she heard a man's voice, obviously speaking on a cell phone in one of the next rows. She thought she recognized the tone, but she wasn't sure, so she listened intently.

"Yeah, these Amish are truly a bunch of rubes. I've got fifty thousand dollars in cash now and plan to get more. The only one smart enough to figure out what's going on was just arrested for running moonshine courtesy of my tip . . . yeah, I know. Don't worry. It'll all work out. All right. I've got to go . . . 'bye."

Sarah realized it had been Jim Hanson speaking even as Edward turned and walked off. She followed, trying to stop him while being as quiet as possible, but he was fast, even with his stick. She caught up with him in the third aisle, where he had hold of Jim's coat.

"You worthless scum," Edward gritted out.

"Hey," Jim said nervously. "I don't know . . ."

"Edward, *sei se gut*," Sarah whispered. "*Nee* violence."

She realized she must have made sense to him because he finally let Jim go, but the other man took a step backward and lost his footing. His back hit the fourth shelf, which began to teeter ominously. Both she and Edward made a grab for some of the larger books, but it was too late. The fourth shelf fell into the fifth and into the sixth and so on, like a giant, resounding row of dominoes.

Sarah watched in mute horror as the four shelves slid into one another and then slammed against the cement wall on the far side of the library. Jim Hanson attempted to scramble away over the piles of books, but Edward tripped him with his walking stick, then caught him by the nape of the neck.

One of the high school kids stood up and was taking photos with his cell phone. "Dude! No way. My mom works at the newspaper. She can write LIBRARY TRASHED BY AMISH."

Sarah met Miss Betty's outraged eyes and tried to think of something to say, but no words would come. Instead she bent and picked up the first book she came to: *Organizing Your Home*. . . .

Chapter Twenty-Eight

They were late getting home to their cabin on the mountain that evening. Jim Hanson had finally confessed, explaining that he had been fired from R & D shortly into the Ice Mountain job. He knew the company had decided to look else-where for gas, but he hadn't wanted to let go of the opportunity to take cash from the community. Dan Miller found that the money was pretty much all intact in a local bank and made plans with the bishop to return it to the people who'd invested as soon as possible.

Edward had brushed aside the bishop's encouraging words that he had helped to make things right and had concentrated instead on his wife's continued dismay about the library. They'd finally agreed to *kumme* down one day soon and help Miss Betty reshelve the books, possibly getting the community involved and doing a bit of a library makeover.

"So, it all worked out," Edward said, his arms folded behind his head as he lay in bed, watching Sarah brush her hair.

"*Jah*, I suppose so." Her voice was quiet.

"*Kumme*, sweet. You're still not fretting over the library, are you?"

"*Nee*. I was thinking about Carla and Shelley—the two women in the jail."

"Oh."

"They were so lonely and hurt. They had no men in their lives to talk with and no relationship with *Gott*."

"When I was away on the rigs, I met many men who were the same—lonely, searching. It was hard to watch. But you did something for them, Sarah. I saw it when they called good-bye to you. You gave them a moment of kindness, of sweetness, and that is what we are called to do—sometimes it's all we can do." He patted her side of the bed. "*Kumme*. Lie down and let me hold you."

She smiled at him and turned down the light, then went into his arms. A few minutes later, he whispered the words he'd been longing to say to her all day. "You don't need to ever do it again, Sarah."

"Do what?"

"Try to rescue me . . . take my place because you are afraid I might be hurt."

She was quiet for a few moments. "But Edward, I love you and I believe, somewhere deep inside, that you have already been hurt enough in life."

He kissed her tenderly. "I can manage, sweet. I promise."

That *nacht* he had another panic attack and awoke, gasping for breath, his heart pounding, and the last vestiges of some haunting dream still with him. Sarah put her hand on his arm and he patted her fingers. "I'm all right," he managed to say.

"Edward, you must face this thing inside that haunts you . . . whatever it is."

But I don't know what it is . . . I may never know. . . .

She seemed almost to be able to read his thoughts because she turned up the lights and brought out the heavy book she'd shown him once before. "Here. *Grossmuder* May's journal. There's a very brief entry in it about your grandfather passing and you being found at the Bear's Cave."

He took it and read swiftly.

"Maybe you should go talk with your *fater* about what happened that day. He may be able to help you and put an end to this anxiety," she suggested.

"*Jah.*" Edward frowned. "Though *Daed* has rarely spoken of his own *fater.*"

"Well, it's worth a try. I will pray for you." She stretched up to kiss him, and he found comfort in her touch.

Elias is sick, badly down with a fever. I tend to him . . . I do not want to. I want to pour the tea down his throat until he chokes, and who would be the wiser? But I would know. . . . *Gott* would know. I expect Elias will recover —he's too mean to do anything else.

May

His ankle feeling better, Edward saddled Sunny and rode over to his *daed*'s that morning. Priscilla and Hollie were still asleep and Joseph was already in the workshop. Edward's *fater* was enjoying an early morning cup of coffee alone.

"*Kumme* in, *sohn*. Why are you about so early?"

Edward sat down and accepted a cup of the steaming brew. "Well, *Daed*, I actually wanted to talk about your *daed*. I know I found him when he was dead and that I ended up at the Bear's Cave, but I don't remember anything in between. I was hoping you could help fill in the blanks."

"Why do you want to think on it?"

"I don't know. . . . Ever since I stopped drinking, it's been on my mind. I've started having what Sarah calls panic attacks, so if you can help me, I'd sure appreciate it."

"I'm sorry, *sohn*. I don't know any more about that day than you. . . . Truth is, I wasn't that close to my *fater*. Anyway, *Daed* was found dead in his cabin—we think by you first. Then you were lost for almost a day. We found you in the Bear's Cave in a kind of shock. . . ."

"Who found him after I did?"

"Solomon Kauffman."

"Well, that's no help. The man's memory is gone."

"I'm sorry, *sohn*."

Edward was quiet for a few moments; then he had to say what was in his heart. "*Daed*, did you know it was *Grossdaudi* who gave me my first drink—when I was eight?"

His *fater* hung his head. "*Nee* . . . I didn't know that."

"I don't mean to hurt you. I grew up responsible for doing my own drinking, but I started at first

238

because it helped me get over missing *Mamm* so much."

"*Ach*, I missed her, too, Edward, but I didn't know you hurt so much, and Mary was so young. I'm not making excuses . . ."

"I know, *Daed*. I just wanted to tell you . . . and, *Daed*, I love you."

His *fater*'s eyes filled with tears and the older man nodded. "And I love you, *sohn*. More than you know."

Chapter Twenty-Nine

The following Saturday, Bishop Umble came to the door of the cabin quite early. He had a fishing pole slung over his back and carried a beat-up green bait box.

"*Ach*," Sarah said. "Were you wanting Edward to go fishing?"

"*Nee*, I want to go fishing and I'd like you to go have a look at Martha. She's having some sort of—woman trouble. And, while you're down there, I've got a horse that seems colicky, and I was hoping Edward might take a look."

"All right," Sarah agreed with a smile. She saw the bishop off, hurriedly began to pack her bag with odds and ends, and waited for Edward, who seemed to be looking for something.

"Got it," he called at last from the bedroom.

They set off together on the cloudy morning, the trees blowing in a light misting rain that made the leaves shiny and pretty nonetheless.

When they reached the Umbles', Edward spoke casually. "I'll go in with you first. Say hello to Martha, then clear out of your way."

"All right."

Sarah opened the screen door, then the back kitchen door, then stopped dead in her tracks in absolute amazement as the bevy of women gathered there cried out "Surprise!" in happy unison.

Sarah's eyes swept the large kitchen, which was filled with tables and chairs and bright fabric of many colors. "What—is this?" she asked weakly.

"Well, as yer man calls it," Martha Umble bawled out, "it's a dressing, not a quilting—so go in the other room and get dressed."

Sarah looked down at the gray dress she was wearing in confusion. "But I . . ."

Martha waved a hand toward the bedroom. "Just go along and let yer smilin' man help ya."

So, Sarah threaded her way through the happy women gathered, pausing to kiss her *mamm* and Clara, and then entered the master bedroom with Edward behind her. He closed the door and leaned on it, looking at her expectantly in the light of day that came through the window.

"Well . . ." he drawled.

"Well, what?" she asked, still completely confused.

He started to whistle, then went to the closet to remove a royal blue bride's dress that appeared to be exactly her size. "Edward, what . . ."

"Do you remember the last time you saw this fabric?" he asked softly.

She flushed in spite of herself and he laughed softly. "I had to wash and press it, but I promise it's *gut* as new, and today you will wear it as the bride at your dressing."

"But I don't need more dresses," she protested.

He walked up to her and caught her gray sleeve between his long fingers. "You do and you will because it will please me to see my bride clothed in the colors she brings to the world . . . and to my life. Everything was gray before you, Sarah. Everything. And I want the whole world to know how it's changed. So, please, for me, accept these new dresses and never wear gray again. . . ." He bent and kissed her full on the lips, and she could only nod, speechless at his words.

"Now," he murmured huskily, "let's get you undressed."

Edward was more than proud to lead his blushing bride, clothed in royal blue, from the Umbles' master bedroom to the center of the kitchen and help her up onto a wooden chair. Once more, she stared down at him in confusion until he produced a yellow measuring tape from his pocket.

"What I was looking for at home, sweet," he murmured; then he raised his voice. "I thought a few measurements might help, as Martha had to make this dress by guessing, though she did an excellent job. You all don't mind, do you?" He winked over his shoulder and stretched out the tape across Sarah's waist, and she snatched it hastily from his playful hands. "Edward King," she hissed. "My mother is here."

Everyone laughed as he surrendered the tape to Martha, then stretched to kiss his bride good-bye. "Have a *gut* day, my love."

"You too," she whispered.

And then he went to gather his fishing gear and meet up with the other men of the community who were without their wives for the day.

Sarah merrily helped cut out pieces of bright blue and burgundy, pink, purple, and green, according to the proper patterns, while other friends ironed out any creases with the heavy old-fashioned irons heated on the stovetop.

Martha was everywhere at once and Sarah loved her for it. She heard her older friend giving sewing instructions to women who'd probably been making dresses since before Sarah was born. . . . "Now pin and sew the dress bodice front to the dress bodice back at the shoulders,

Mary Graber. And don't forget to measure, pin, and hem the sleeves to just the right length." Martha paused for a quick breath. "Anne Knepp, pin and sew pleats into the skirt front and back pieces and into the apron. And pin and sew darts into the cape back. And for pity's sake, pin and sew the cape front to the cape back at the shoulders."

Sarah giggled, which caused even Martha Umble's stern face to relax, and soon everyone was pressing and hand sewing, measuring and hemming. Sarah had to admit to herself that it was almost more fun than a quilting and that her husband had a creative mind. She hoped he was having a *gut* time with the other men and didn't have a chance to feel any panic.

Edward talked to Joe as they ambled along through the woods. It seemed the bishop had heard of a new fishing hole deep in the forest, past Jude and Mary Lyons's cabin, and he was headed for it today. Bear and Blackie had been mournfully left behind so that they wouldn't scare the fish, but Edward had to admit that he'd secretly grown to enjoy the presence of the little dog and missed him a bit.

He looked around for some familiar landmark and didn't see any but had the feeling he'd been in this part of the woods before. "I haven't been back here in a while, I guess," he said to Joe.

His *bruder* gave him a strange look. "*Gross-daudi*'s cabin's back here, or at least what's left of it."

"*Ach*," Edward muttered, feeling the now familiar symptoms of panic begin to rise up within him. But maybe Sarah was right . . . maybe if he saw the remnants of the cabin, he'd feel better somehow. He lifted his chin and drew a deep breath, and suddenly Solomon Kauffman was walking beside him.

Ben huffed to keep up, juggling fishing poles. "*Daed*'s fast, for all that his mind is what it is."

Edward had an impulsive idea. "That's all right, Ben. Why not let your *Daed* walk with me for a bit?"

"Well, I'd be glad of that," Ben said with relief, already dropping back.

Edward looked at Joe. "I'd like to talk with Solomon, if it's okay, Joseph."

"Hmm? Sure." Joe walked on ahead and Edward stepped close to the old man, who had an amazing stride for his age.

"Solomon?"

The old man squinted over at him. "Elijah King? You be dead, I thought."

Edward thought fast. "*Jah*, I be dead. Were you the one who found my body?"

"Sure as can be. Stretched out on yer bunk. There wuz nuthin' to be done for ya. Forgive

244

me, Elijah." The *auld* voice quavered and Edward swallowed.

"I forgive you, Solomon."

"You still runnin' 'shine, Elijah?"

"*Nee.*"

"Well, now, that's too bad. I could use a jar," Solomon confided.

So could I . . .

Sarah was amazed that, near lunchtime, ten new dresses and aprons had taken *gut* shape under the skillful fingers of the women, and she had never felt so blessed or indulged. It was while she was fitting close stitches along a delicate hemline that she noticed Esther Zook, Deborah's *mamm*, slip unnoticed in the front door.

Sarah felt a surge of gratitude; she hadn't really had a chance to talk with the dead girl's mother except to see her at church, and she got to her feet now to go to greet her personally.

"Esther," Sarah said softly, laying her hand on the shorter woman's arm. She could see that Esther had lost some weight, and that there were faint circles beneath her eyes.

"Didn't know whether to *kumme* or not, Sarah. I've been kind of blue."

Sarah put her arm around the older woman and drew her into the room. "*Sei se gut*, sit by me, Esther. And I promise to *kumme* see you next week about that blue feeling."

There were murmurs of greeting and tender words for Esther as she was welcomed at the table. Sarah knew her people were especially gentle with those who had suffered grief, even if there was a certain practical acceptance of death as coming from the Hand of *Gott*.

Soon, the tempo of work resumed, until Martha declared that it was time to eat, and all of the sewing work was carefully folded and laid aside and then everyone bustled to bring out their various dishes.

Sarah knew what to expect for lunch from a quilting but was amazed at the way each woman had outdone herself for the dressing; fried cornmeal mush, coffee soup, bacon and egg bake, ham salad spread and fresh bread, Amish noodles, homemade applesauce, cherry pie, and so much more that Sarah could barely find a way to taste every dish.

She thought about Edward as she ate and talked gently with the other women and hoped his day was going as wonderfully.

Edward hadn't seen his *grossdaudi*'s cabin after all because the bishop had veered off the track suddenly, heading deeper into the woods until the sound of the rushing creek began to override everything. He was grateful for the sound; it drowned out the beating of his heart, and even as he helped Solomon put on his waders, he was

246

glad to have something else to concentrate on and think about. Every part of his mind and body seemed to scream *I know this place . . . of course I do. . . .*

But then everyone was focused on finding the right spot along the creek that bubbled and gushed and gave way to secret deep holes where rainbow trout were likely to lie in the chill autumn waters. Ben had *kumme* to collect Solomon with a hearty word of thanks and Edward crossed the creek instinctively to a mossy bank, sitting down and dropping his line into a shadowy depth. When he felt a nibble, he tugged lightly, automatically, then brought up the first fish of the day. A rainbow—a good ten inches in length. There were cheers and good-natured groans, but as Edward studied the beautiful iridescent colors of the fish, something in him had to let it go. He found the hook in its mouth, worked it free, then let it slide back into the water, ignoring the protests from the other men.

He didn't care but dropped his line in again, sitting in a world far away until someone sat down beside him. He looked over to find the bishop's keen blue eyes upon him and almost groaned aloud.

"What?" he asked, verging on being testy.

"That was a fine fish you released."

Edward shrugged. "It was beautiful."

"*Jah*, and maybe you're not in the mood to take and kill today. . . . You know, your *grossdaudi* fished this spot a lot."

Edward's head snapped up. "What?"

"Mmm-hmm. Of course it's not far from where his cabin was, but he and I would *kumme* here—when he'd invite me, which was not often, mind."

"What was he like? I—I can't seem to remember clearly."

"*Ach.*" The bishop paused, as if considering. "He was a giant of a man. Drunk most of the time, frankly. He rarely came to church. Preferred to keep to himself. But he had a full belly laugh and you know, he always threw what fish he caught back in, too. Said they 'needed to grow a bit more,' no matter how big they were. I think he had some kindness in his heart, though he didn't want to show it."

Edward felt the urge to cry but didn't know why—he was looking for shades of a haunting ghost, signs of a man who seemed to have so affected his life, and he couldn't let the feeling go, like he'd let the fish go . . . *like I let the fish go. . . .*

The bishop clapped him on the shoulder, startling him. "Well, I've got to talk to the men here, Edward. I hope you'll draw near and listen."

"*Jah* . . . of course." But his heart was far away.

Sarah tiredly went home that *nacht* with the ten neatly folded dresses and new aprons carefully

248

wrapped in brown paper. It had been an amazing day, one that she would cherish for always.

She saw that there were no lamps glowing from the cabin and decided that Edward must have had an equally *gut* time fishing and eating. She let herself into the dark cabin, pleased to hear Blackie's happy yips.

"Hello," she greeted the dog, dumping her packages on the kitchen table, then jumped a mile when a deep voice answered her.

"Hello."

She put a hand to her throat. "Edward, you scared me."

"I scare myself sometimes."

She moved to turn up a lamp, finding him seated at the kitchen table, his elbows on the wood and his head in his hands.

"What's wrong?" She went to him and put an arm around his shoulders.

"I wanted to drink today, Sarah, badly. But I didn't."

"That's *gut* though, right?"

He sighed and pressed his head against her belly. "I don't know. I don't know who I am anymore. What I'm supposed to be doing. It seems I've lost myself in one afternoon."

She thought hard, stroking his overly long hair. "Well, what happened today exactly?"

He sighed aloud. "The bishop spoke at the water, talked about the Marcellus Shale thing.

Wanted to thank *Gott* that we were brought back into unity with one another. Though some had invested, it had all worked out all right. He made me seem like a hero for testing the faith of the community and then revitalizing it through *Derr Herr*. . . . Sarah, I'm no hero. I felt like a fraud and I—I found out some bits and pieces more about my grandfather. Nothing really good."

She drew a deep breath. "Do you know what you need?"

"What?" he asked listlessly.

"Bed and to be made love to."

He tilted his head back with a faint smile, looking up at her in the fall of the lantern light. "That does sound interesting."

"*Ach*," she murmured. "I can make it interesting."

"Good," he whispered. "Please do."

And she did.

Elias lingers on—days now of fever. He wastes away before my eyes, though I feed him the strongest broths I can make. I wish he would die. *Gott* forgive me—I pray for it. But he lingers . . . I will call for a doctor tomorrow, though the community would frown upon it. I must do something to help Elias—for honor's sake and for my marriage vows. . . .

May

Chapter Thirty

That Monday, Edward did feel rejuvenated by two nights of his wife's tender and passionate ministrations and got up with the intention of taking care of *Grossmuder* May's garden and tools.

Autumn was an important planning period on any farm, and even though it would be a small harvest, there was much to do and Sarah was more than happy to participate.

"But," she pointed out as they made their plans over breakfast, "I am not going to wear one of my new dresses to get all dirty in. Please may I wear gray?"

He laughed, feeling *gut* inside for the moment. "In this case, *jah*, I give my permission." And he kissed the pert tip of her nose.

They decided that the first order of business was to harvest the pumpkins, gourds, and squashes. *Grossmuder* May had harvested many of the seeds, Sarah knew, to create a bird-friendly garden in winter and she wanted to keep that tradition. But harvesting the many twining vegetables was no easy task. Edward had to lift the larger pumpkins, some easily weighing over seventy-five pounds, while Sarah used the red cart she found in the shed to carry others, with

Blackie happily trotting over vines alongside her.

For now, the pumpkins and strange-looking gourds would be stored in one of the smaller barns, but soon Sarah knew she'd have to spread out a tarp and gut the vegetables for their seeds, and then scrape out the valuable insides to be canned for the long winter. But that was for another day, and hopefully she could con Ernest and Clara into helping.

Next, she wandered far afield for an hour, collecting and saving seeds from different wildflowers to sow the following spring. She wanted to bolster her wildflower population as well as looking for different herbs she might use to dry.

Then she and Edward both began to plant for spring color to *kumme*—pushing spring bulbs deep underground; crocus, tulip, daffodil, lily, and hyacinth. The bulbs would burst right out of the mud after the snow melted with bright and happy colors.

Then there was the rather dull and dusty job of digging up the potatoes and turnips and sweet potatoes. Although there wasn't much of a harvest, Sarah hated the feel of the damp earth under her nails and often had to pause to blow on her fingers because they got so cold. Edward came along and kissed her fingertips, ignoring the dirt, and she had to laugh. She watched him walk away with love in her eyes as he went to winterize the tools in the barn.

She knew things must be sharpened and oiled for winter storage to prevent rust and damage before spring. She sighed tiredly as she got to her feet. The day was nearly done and she hadn't thought of supper yet. She decided quickly on pretzel soup and went into the cabin.

She washed her hands and then found the pretzel jar, shaking some out into a large bowl. Then she crushed the pretzels and got a mixture of butter, flour, milk, and water boiling on the stovetop. She added the crushed pretzels and a dash of salt and a pinch of pepper. It really was a great-tasting soup for a chilly day, and she had it nearly ready when Edward and Blackie came in.

"Mmm." Edward sniffed appreciatively. "Pretzel soup. I haven't had it in a long time. *Danki*, Sarah."

"*Ach*." She laughed low. "I'm sure you can think of another way to thank me later."

He smiled at her boldness and she knew that she would have her thanks.

Chapter Thirty-One

Word reached Ice Mountain that Coudersport was going to have a fall festival, and Sarah thought it would be a perfect time to go see if Miss Betty at the library needed any more help with the book shelves. When other *Amischers* had heard about the library, there were many volunteers who offered to both go to the festival and stop in to give a bit of help with the library. So, Bishop Umble arranged to rent a church bus, with Mr. Ellis to drive, and on a bright October morning, a whole group of folks from Ice Mountain set out for Coudersport, hoping for a day of fun and excitement.

As they drove into Coudersport, they saw that the usually quiet small town was absolutely bursting with people, buses, and cars. A bright banner proclaimed it the FESTIVAL OF FLAMING FOLIAGE, and indeed, the mountains were alive with reds, oranges, and cheerful yellows, as if *Gott* had taken a paintbrush to the trees Himself.

Edward swung Sarah down off the bus step, pleased to see her looking so lovely in a pale green dress and a crisp apron. "You're the most beautiful woman here," he whispered in her ear, and she merely shook her head, as if he'd muttered a bit of inanity. He smiled at her and she blushed; then he took her hand, and many of the folks from the bus began to follow them as they set off for the library.

When they got there, Edward was surprised to see that the squat building had a fresh coat of paint in light cream, and even the lion looked a bit more majestic with new color. He held the door for the ladies entering and then went in himself. The place smelled of new paint and fresh-cut wood. And, most surprising of all, was the woman who sat behind the desk. It was surely the same woman with her brown eyes, but now her hair was down and she wore a cheerful blouse and skirt. She smiled gaily when she saw Edward and Sarah and got up to greet them.

"Oh, I'm so glad you've come. I have to tell you that the day you—um—wrecked the library was the best day of my life."

"But why?" Sarah asked.

"Because, sweetheart, the community got together and redid the whole place. I've got sturdy wooden shelves, windows that open, volunteer readers, and new books! You have to come and see."

She led the group into the adult section, and Edward was amazed at the transformation. Many people were perusing high, stable wooden shelves, and many others sat at oaken tables, their heads bent over books.

"And," Miss Betty indicated in a proud whisper, "I've got a free table, where folks can come in to take or give books. It's worked out wonderfully."

Edward idly ran his hand over the free books and something caught his eye. It gave him an idea for Sarah's birthday, which was fast approaching. He turned then, in time to feel his wife slide her arm around his waist, and he felt the bump of her cast through her dress.

"Isn't it *wunderbaar*?" she whispered.

"Yep. But hey, why don't we go see if we can get that cast off while we're in town? I think it's about the right time, and the hospital's not that far a walk from the festival."

"I'd be only too glad to get it off," Sarah admitted. "It itches."

"Then let's walk up there now."

They said good-bye to the very different Miss Betty and her new library and started up the hill to the hospital, passing visiting marching bands getting into formation for the parade that was due to start in a few hours.

To Edward's surprise, halfway up, they met Joseph walking in the same direction. He had his arm slung around the shoulders of a tall *buwe*, Jay Smucker.

"Joe, what's going on?"

Joseph shook his head and muttered in an undertone, "Red Smucker was drunk this morning before Jay left. I think he may have broken one of the *buwe*'s ribs."

Edward frowned, glancing at Jay, who had his head down. Red Smucker was known on the mountain to be tough and mean . . . *but to beat your own* sohn. . . . Edward felt an unreasonable surge of anger course through him and promised himself that he'd have to go see Red when they got back to the mountain. . . . He was aware that Sarah was looking at him worriedly, so he smiled and patted her arm, but he didn't think she was fooled. Still, they arrived at the hospital and asked for Dr. McCully, who appeared only too glad to help both Jay and Sarah.

Joseph elected to stay behind with Jay for X-rays and treatment, and promised to meet up with them later, while Sarah held up a very thin arm, shrunken in musculature due to the cast. "I'm glad I've got my sleeve to cover the arm," she joked, rolling down the fabric as they walked away from the hospital.

"I'm sorry you had to have that cast at all."

"*Ach*, Edward, it's all right. So much *gut* has *kumme* from that *nacht*. The cast was simply a small blessing." She stretched up to kiss his cheek as someone in a group of passing *Englisch* youths made a wolf whistle sound and she pulled away, embarrassed.

"Don't worry, sweet." He laughed. "*Englischers*, for some strange reason, don't believe that we *Amisch* engage in PDA."

"PDA?" she asked hesitantly.

He snuggled her close. "Public displays of affection."

"*Ach* . . ." she murmured, then laughed. "Then why do some of us have fifteen children?"

"Now that, sweet, begs for a different response, and one that I cannot give here."

He delighted at the flush that stained her fair cheeks, then led her across the crowded street to where there were many craft stands set up.

"*Ach*, Edward, look at all these beautiful things. I hardly know where to begin!" Sarah said excitedly. "But, oh, is this boring for you?"

"*Nee.*" He shook his head. "I like to see you happy."

"*Danki*," she whispered. "And I like to get ideas for things to make to pretty up our cabin. I'm so glad Bishop Umble allows some decoration."

She passed over the beaded jewelry and the bracelets made from stone and wood. But she stopped at the alpaca fleece and felt its superb softness, wondering how many skeins she'd need to make a fine rug.

The woman at the booth was helpful and Edward laid out the money without a word. Sarah soon found that she needed to be more careful when she looked at things, for he was all too quick to buy them for her.

They passed dollhouse miniatures, soaps and lotions, tote bags, decorative flags, and a myriad of other items. Then they came to a booth of sterling silver and Sarah bit her lip once more as she fingered a baby's cup, finely crafted, tiny, and with a handle on either side. Edward took it gently from her hands and she turned to look up at him.

"Is it—I mean . . ." she floundered.

"Not *gut* to prepare?"

"Something like that."

"Sarah King, as *Gott* wills, I shall surely plant my seed in you. Buy the cup and may many little hands hold its handles."

Her eyes filled with tears and she gladly handed over the money and watched while the man carefully wrapped the silver. She took it back happily. "I'm finished shopping," she said then. "I have everything I could want."

That *nacht* Edward lifted the rough washcloth from the filled metal bathtub and watched Sarah's long bare legs as she stepped in with pleasure. She settled her rounded bottom into the steaming water and leaned back with a soft sigh of pleasure.

"Mmm, I'd have to agree," Edward said from where he knelt beside the tub, his blue shirt-sleeves rolled up to his elbows, the warm lantern light playing on the golden hairs of his forearms. "I love bathing you."

"Why?" she asked teasingly, her voice sleepy and relaxed.

"Because afterward, I get to carry you to bed and make love to you while you're still damp."

"Hmm . . . is that the only reason?"

He trailed the washcloth across her neck and down over her soft breasts. "*Nee*, it depends of course how many times I get to see that look of amazement in your eyes when you fall over the edge and into the sun . . . that's something, too."

"*Ach . . .*" she purred as his hand dipped lower. "I'd have to more than agree."

Later, when he'd exhausted both her body and her mind with pleasure, he slipped from the bed and hastily dressed in the dark. He hadn't forgotten his personal promise to have a talk with Red Smucker. . . .

Chapter Thirty-Two

Edward saw the lantern light in the Smucker cabin and then noticed Red himself, sitting at the kitchen table through the front window. Edward went up the steps and gave a light knock at the door. He didn't want to rouse Jay or his mother, and sure enough, Red came to answer.

"What?" The tall man belched in greeting.

"I'd like to talk with you. Outside." Edward turned, not waiting for a response, and stepped off the porch into the moonlit yard, a couple of yards from the *haus*.

Red came out after a few moments, clearly intoxicated and irritated, but Edward didn't care.

"So is your *buwe* asleep, Red?"

"What's it to you?"

"Well, my *bruder* had to take him to the hospital today for broken ribs. Thought you might like to know."

Red clenched his fists. "That whelp. I'll give him something to go whining about—"

"No, you won't," Edward said calmly.

"Huh?"

"I said you won't, because if you so much as lay a finger on that *buwe* or your wife again, because I assume you beat her as well, I'm going to do something about it."

Red threw back his head and laughed from his vantage point of being a foot taller than Edward. "You are, huh? Well, what would that be, King? Match me in a drinking contest? See which one of us can run our wife down faster with a horse? Tell me."

Edward had learned to avoid getting angry over digs when he'd worked on the rigs, and that forbearance stood him in good stead now. He merely shrugged. "I'm telling you the way it is, Red. Take it for what you want."

Fast as a serpent, Red reached out a brawny arm and grabbed Edward's throat. He began to squeeze, and Edward couldn't help but cough as he struggled for air. He clawed at Red's hand and was finally released with a shove that sent him gasping and reeling. "Now, git going, King. And don't tell me how to manage my family again."

"I'm—not—leaving," Edward managed. "You'll have—to—kill me."

"What?" Red asked, clearly perplexed.

Edward knew that Red was rotten, but he was

no murderer, so he said it again. "You'll have to kill me."

Sarah rolled over to feel for her husband's hand and found Blackie instead. She came awake with sudden intuition and slapped the pillow. "Blast him, Blackie! He tricked me!"

She got out of bed, deciding not to waste time putting on her dress but drawing on a pair of Edward's pants and a shirt instead, cinching one of his belts around her tiny waist. She ran out into the kitchen, pulled on a big overcoat and boots, then picked up a lantern. "I'm sorry, Blackie. You'll have to stay here." And then she was clomping through the woods in the direction of Red Smucker's *haus*.

Edward decided that Red might not be a murderer, but he might well *kumme* pretty close without much conscience. This was after Edward was fairly sure that his own ribs had been cracked, he'd been sent spinning against the trunk of a tree, and held upside-down by his still tender ankle.

"Why won't ya fight?" Red asked finally.

"Because—I'm—*Amisch*."

"*Ach, kumme* on. So am I, but the bishop's nowhere around, is he? I can't take to beating a helpless man."

"But that's what you do to Jay and your wife,"

Edward pointed out breathlessly, preparing for another blow. But, to his surprise, none was forthcoming. Instead, Red dropped him and sat down on a nearby stump.

Edward made an effort to get to his feet, then opted for crawling nearer the other man instead.

"Look, Red. This is what I'm going to do. If I hear that you beat your family again, I'm coming over and you're going to have to take it out on me. And I won't fight you."

Red looked down at him with bleak eyes in the moonlight. "When I drink, I forget myself."

"Well, try to stop the drinking."

"Ha! I can't. And you can't none either. You're foolin' yerself for that pretty wife of yours."

Edward shook his head. "*Nee*. I thought so maybe at first, too, but it's for me, Red. It's truly for me."

The other man dropped his head in his hands. "Well," he choked, "I ain't worth it."

Edward suppressed a groan and tapped him on the knee. "*Jah*, you are. You've got to believe that, Red. And if you believe it, your *sohn* will believe it, and your *grandsohn*, and you'll be the one, with *Gott*, who stops a whole generation of drinking maybe."

"Mebbe. I don't know. I gotta go in now and think on it. You sure you mean what you say about comin' around here if I . . ."

"Absolutely." *If I can survive . . .*

"All right." Red stepped over him and walked to the *haus*, lifting a hand in farewell while Edward tried to roll over to get to his feet again.

By the time he managed, he was looking up into the brightness of a single lantern, and he thought maybe Red had had the insight to *kumme* back; then he saw Sarah's long, unbound hair.

"Sarah—I . . ."

"I am so angry with you, Edward King, I cannot even speak."

It seemed the wrong time to point out to her that she was speaking as he lay helpless while she examined him by lantern light.

"Swollen eye, bruised jaw, sprained neck, dislocated shoulder, cracked ribs, bruised pelvis, sprained ankle; shall I go on?" Sarah asked, her anger not diminished by morning's light.

"*Nee*," he said miserably.

"And the worst of it is that you used a bath and sex to get me to sleep so you could go out and so nobly get beaten up."

He winced; even her voice seemed to hurt his head.

"Sarah, I . . ."

"*Ach, nee* . . . no pretty words. You are going to lie in this bed today and Martha Umble is going to be your nurse."

"Martha Umble?" He groaned.

"Yes, she's just what you deserve. I've got other work to do. There's some sort of flu going around, and *Daed*'s *kumme* down with it, so I promised *Mamm* I'd stop over." She handed him a mug of tea none too gently and he took it with a bruised hand.

"Sarah, I'm sorry."

"*Nee* . . . I will not listen. There's Martha at the door now." Sarah left the room, telling herself that it was exactly what he deserved after she and Joseph had had to leave their beds last *nacht* to get him home. *And for what? Did he honestly think Red Smucker was going to . . .*

She opened the door and stared at Red Smucker. "Uh . . . may I help you?"

"*Jah* . . . I didn't want you to be all upset with yer man because he took a beating last *nacht*. He did it for me and my family, and I've been up all *nacht* thinkin', and he made his point like. . . . I ain't gonna hit the *buwe* again, or my wife, just Edward, like he promised."

Sarah slowly crossed her arms and began to tap her foot. A wiser man would have withdrawn, but wisdom was not one of Red's strong suits. "Like he promised?" she asked.

"*Jah*. A mighty fine thing, too. Just wanted to let ya know. Might I have a word with him and . . ."

"No, Mr. Smucker, you may not," she said, slamming the door in the big man's chest. Then

265

she marched back into the bedroom. "You promised to let Red Smucker beat you up whenever he's drunk?" she demanded.

Edward spewed a mouthful of tea back into the mug and coughed abruptly. "Where did you hear that?"

"Did you promise?"

"Sarah, sweet, it's not like it sounds. . . ."

"Bah!" There was another knock at the door. "I'm telling you, if that is Red, he's going to wish he wasn't."

"Sarah?" Edward called in alarm. "Sarah?"

"Now what's all this hollerin' fer?" Martha Umble asked, coming into the bedroom with a grin. "I ain't yer pretty wife, but I knows how to keep a fella company. Ya want me ta tell you a story?"

Edward sighed and relaxed against the pillows. "*Nee*, Martha. *Danki*. I'm fine. Just fine."

Sarah entered her *auld* home, surprised to be met nearly at the door by Clara. "What's wrong? Is *Daed* bad off?" Sarah asked, glancing toward the closed master bedroom door.

"I think so. *Mamm* won't say. She made Samuel go to school and Ernest go over to the workshop like nothing much is wrong, but I've heard some dreadful bad coughing, Sarah."

Sarah took off her coat and lifted her bag, which held all kinds of herbs and teas for the flu. "All right, Clara. I'll go check and *kumme* let you know."

Sarah knocked lightly on her parents' door and then entered, closing it quickly behind her. The room smelled heavily of sickness, and she saw her *mamm* sitting in a chair next to the bed, seemingly half-asleep, while her *daed* lay on his right side, visibly working for breath. Then he gave a choked, raspy cough and Sarah froze, listening. She knew inside that this was a bad sickness and her heart began to pound as her *mamm* opened her eyes and silently mouthed her name.

Chapter Thirty-Three

Mahlon thought he could see his mother standing at the foot of his bed . . . *but she's been gone for nigh on twenty years now. . . . Am I dying, then?* He must have asked the question out loud because Sarah answered him—quietly and determined.

"No, *Daed*. Not today."

But then what about his mamm, *and there was Doc Shackelford, an* Englisch *doc who used to* kumme *around when he was a kid and give out vaccinations to all the* Amischers . . . *surely he must be dead now too. . . .*

"He's ghosting," Anne said mournfully.

"Seeing people who've gone ahead of him?" Sarah asked. *"Nee.* He'll be fine."

I'll be fine. . . . I'll be fine. . . . If only I could breathe right . . . used to be able to run a fifty-yard footrace and never hitch a breath, but now . . .

Then gentle hands insistently poured something awful-tasting down his throat and he was coughing and gagging, throwing up phlegm, until it seemed for a minute that things were easier, but then his lungs closed up again and he struggled for breath, turning his head from the inevitable spoon. . . .

"And I'll tell ya that being a bishop's wife ain't all it's cracked up to be. . . . Why, if you knew the way Joel left his socks and underwear layin' about . . ." Her voice droned on.

Edward nodded off now and then, longing for another mug of Sarah's tea but having no idea how long she'd be away. He felt bad now for frightening her, making her mad, and for worrying her when her *daed* had *kumme* down sick. He prayed Mahlon just had a touch of the flu because he knew it could be hard on older folks.

"Are you listenin'?" Martha's voice jolted him back to the moment.

"Jah," he said cautiously.

"Then what'd I say?" she demanded.

"Uh . . . underwear laying . . ."

"Humpf . . . well, and he also . . ."

Edward focused on her words, trying to ignore the pain in his body.

Sarah used the last of the ipecac and tried not to give in to despair. She saw the bluish color around her *fater*'s lips and wet her own mouth. Then she looked at her mother. "*Mamm*," she whispered finally, "I think you'd better send for Ernest and Samuel."

Her mother choked on a sob and fled the room, and Sarah concentrated on spooning more tea down her *daed*'s throat, her eyes blurring with tears.

Mahlon was surprised to see a big man who reminded him of Edward standing at the foot of the bed. He tried to peer closer, but the giant laughed and shook his mane of blond hair. "*Nee*, I ain't Edward. I'm his *grossdaudi*, Elijah King. I'm figuring you are too young to know me well."

"I'm—sorry . . ." He broke off, coughing, and Sarah rubbed his head.

"*Nee, Daed*. Nothing to be sorry for."

Mahlon nodded, trying to close his eyes when Elijah King boomed out again. "Listen. My time is short. When you *kumme* back, ask the *buwe*, Edward, this question. . . . How do you forgive yourself? If he can answer, he'll be free."

When I kumme *back? When I* kumme *back?*

Suddenly, Mahlon saw Sarah lying on his chest as if he'd floated just above his own body. He heard her words clear as day as she reached in her bag and slipped some herb or another beneath his tongue; then she began to pray. He remembered the dove when she was little, flying free against the sky, and he suddenly knew that freedom, and he knew she was no hex but someone who loved deeply, divinely, and she was wonderful.

He sat up on the bed and held her to him, drawing in a clear breath of air. She fell back and stared at him in wonder. He smiled, then laughed. *When I* kumme *back . . .*

"*Ach, Fater*," she cried. "Praise *Gott!*"

"*Jah*, indeed. And remind me the next time I see your Edward that I have a question to ask him."

Edward was half-asleep when he realized that Martha had gone and Sarah was back in her rightful place. She'd drawn up a chair close to the bed and he was troubled by the tiredness he saw in her eyes.

"Sarah, surely you haven't been so worried all day about a few bruises?"

She shook her head. "My *daed* almost died."

"What?" Edward was truly shocked.

She nodded. "Pneumonia. Deep in his lungs.

270

In fact, I thought we'd lost him, but then . . ." She paused thoughtfully, and he reached out and took her hand in his.

"You prayed for him, didn't you, Sarah? Like you did for my *fater*?"

He watched her gray eyes well with tears. "*Jah*, but I don't want you to find me strange or . . ."

He kissed her fingertips. "I find you wonderful and I know you're overwhelmed and tired. *Kumme* to bed, please, sweet, and I will hold your hand. No unruly sex tonight, I'm afraid."

She smiled a bit and he had to smile in return. "No longer angry with me?"

She shook her head. "*Nee*, but if Red Smucker ever *kummes* within two feet of you again, I will give him an herb that will keep him in the *outhaus* for two weeks at least."

Edward looked at her in awe. "You can do that?"

"You betcha."

Elias is dead. The *Englisch* doctor could do nothing—said I should have called sooner. Pneumonia of both lungs—far gone. Dear *Gott*, praise be and forgive me for my praise. I feel as though an evil has gone from this world and I cannot help but rejoice . . . but I must get away. This *haus* haunts me, and I think Elias is around each corner—waiting . . . though he be gone.

May

• • •

It took a full week of careful nursing to see Edward back on his feet, and even then, Sarah didn't want him to ride Sunny. But he cajoled her with a winning smile and murmured promises in her ear that made her shiver with desire, and then she gave in.

"But only," he said, tapping her nose lightly, "if you go with me. And you can carry Blackie to boot."

"*Ach*, Edward, I don't know. . . ."

"You told me you trust me."

"And I do; it's the horse I don't trust."

"I promise to keep you safe, sweet. *Kumme.* We can have a picnic high up in the fields."

Sarah smiled then, secretly wondering what else they might do all alone in the tall dried grasses, and went to pack a picnic lunch.

She filled the satchels with hard-boiled eggs, pickled beets, and sweet pickles, each in small containers. Then she made the egg salad Edward favored that held a touch of celery and a dash of spicy mustard. She made ham spread sandwiches and took the time to double boil sweet chocolate and half-dipped a plate of peanut butter cookies until each dripped and cooled with dark decadence. She put in napkins, plates and silverware, and a flexible jug of apple cider, then took the lot out to the barn, where Edward was preparing Sunny.

"Got everything?" he asked with a smile, taking

the saddlebags from her and slinging them over the saddle. "Now, I'm going to have you tuck your skirt into your—uh—bloomers—so that you don't startle Sunny with any flapping about."

"Edward, I can't ride like that. Somebody will see me."

"Nobody will see you. *Kumme* on, Sarah." He bent and kissed her once and hard.

"*Ach*, all right. But don't look."

"But I've seen . . . All right. I won't look." He turned away until she called that she was ready, then turned back to mount up. Then he reached down and pulled her up in front of him, holding her securely and the reins at the same time.

"I decided to leave Blackie in the *haus*," she explained. "I figured he might make Sunny nervous with his yipping."

"Well, we'll bring him next time," Edward promised, and they set out for the higher fields of the mountaintop.

Chapter Thirty-Four

The foliage was at its absolute peak and the reds were so rich they looked like a painting, especially where the colors were reflected in the creeks and lake, producing vibrant mirrored images. Occasionally, a still green leaf peeked out oddly under the masses of orange and yellow, but what was far more attractive to Edward was the lemony scent of Sarah's hair, drifting up to his nostrils and making him feel like she was part and parcel of nature's bounty itself. He also liked the slight bounce of her firm breasts against his arm where he held her safely upright against him, and the way her bottom nestled back to meet the juncture of his thighs each time Sunny moved.

By the time they'd decided on one of the high fields, with the tall red and brown grasses stretched out to the trees, Edward was feeling painfully aroused. *And she obviously can't tell because she's squirming like a kitten against me. . . .* He dismounted with some difficulty, then reached up and swung her down, letting her slide full against him as she hit the ground. She made a delicious *O* of surprise with her mouth, and he fell to kissing her with deft strokes of his tongue. She returned his enthusiasm with delightful skill and he managed to break away to ask the eager question. "May we have dessert first, sweet?"

"You mean peanut butter and chocolate?" she teased, running her small hands up and down his shirtfront.

"*Nee,*" he groaned, too far aroused for even wordplay. "Please, Sarah."

"*Jah,*" she whispered.

He quickly tied Sunny, then led Sarah some distance from the horse, walking until the grasses were waist high and it was as though they waded through an ocean of soft stalks. Then he turned to her and slowly pressed her to the ground, the grasses yielding to form a pliant bed beneath and around them.

He reached down and undid the jumble of skirts then pulled down her bloomers and found the warm skin beneath her shift, damp and ready for him. She reached up and helped him with capable hands, working at his pants while he leaned back and squinted into the sun. Then he was free and she guided him home, making small breathy sounds of pleasure that caused shivers to run down his back and wrapped ribs until he could restrain himself no longer and fully gave in to the pleasure he sought, and she soon joined him in mutual ecstasy.

A few moments later, he lifted his head to look down in wonder at her when she spoke softly.

"I think I've just conceived, Edward."

"What?"

She giggled, like a little girl with a precious secret. "I know it sounds silly, but I can feel it." She pressed his hand against her belly, the outside of her womb. "Can you feel it?"

He shook his head, bemused but smiling. "If you want me to, sweet."

"Some women can, you know. I've read it in *Grossmuder* May's journal. But anyway, I know it as sure as I know my own name."

Edward thought hard. "It's your body. I suppose anything is possible with *Gott*, and I pray that you are right."

She pulled his head down and kissed him until he felt a quickening in his blood. "*Ach*, Edward, we must *kumme* back to this spot to conceive all of our *kinner*."

At this juncture, he would have agreed to anything. So he nodded and smiled. "*Jah*, sweet. *Jah*."

Sarah had just laid out the little delicacies she'd packed for the picnic on the large blanket when she heard voices coming through the field. She looked over at Edward, who shrugged and stood up. He waved to someone, then put his hands on his hips, obviously waiting.

"Who is it?" she whispered.

"*Englisch* hikers. I'm afraid we'll have to share our lunch, sweet."

Sarah groaned faintly, wanting their privacy to continue but grateful that they hadn't been interrupted a few minutes earlier. She put her hand up to make sure her *kapp* was straight, then got up to greet the hikers.

There was a man and a woman, each carrying what to Sarah seemed like massively tall backpacks. But the two people were young and looked healthy and were obviously grateful for the invitation to lunch.

"I'm Sam and this is Dolores. We're doing the Appalachian Trail but kind of got lost a little bit looking for the Pennsylvania Grand Canyon."

"Well, you're not that far off," Edward assured them, then looked at their map and made a brief mark on it with a pencil Sam offered.

"Gee, thanks, and thanks for lunch. Everything looks great, Miss uh . . ."

"Sarah," she replied sweetly. "I'm Edward's wife. Are you two married?"

"No," Dolores answered. "Just living together for now."

"Oh . . ." Sarah said, feeling at a loss as she handed out plates and things.

Sam grinned. "You're Amish, right? Not Mennonite. You probably think living together isn't that great, but it works for us."

"We try not to judge," Edward offered.

"Well," Dolores said, smiling, "you two look awfully young to be married. May I ask how old you are?"

"Dolores," Sam hushed her, but Edward gave their ages with ease.

"Oh, these pickled beets are the best," Sam assured Sarah. "So, can you tell us how much of that TV show *Amish Cops* is actually real?"

Sarah gazed at him helplessly, but Edward laughed. "I used to work away on the Marcellus Shale gas rigs. I saw that show a few times— it's completely false. I had no idea people would go to such lengths to make up stuff about our people."

"Oh, the Amish are big now in English culture," Sam said. "Dolores even reads all those Amish romance books."

"Amish—romance?" Sarah asked faintly.

"Yes." Dolores colored a bit. "They're all perfectly clean, well, for the most part."

"Okay," Sarah said, not understanding as she got out the peanut butter cookies, which were received with lavish enthusiasm.

When everything had been eaten, the hikers hefted their packs once more, shook hands with Sarah and Edward, and headed back across the grass.

Sarah watched them go. "Strange," she murmured.

"Well," Edward said as he bent to nuzzle her neck, "we probably seem strange to them, too."

"*Nee*, I mean the clean Amish romance thing. . . . I've never known an *Amischer* to be dirty as a person."

Edward threw back his head and laughed, and she smacked him lightly in the chest. "What are you laughing about?"

He sobered quickly and cuddled her close. "I'm rejoicing in your innocence, sweet."

She pouted, then touched his sleeve. "Well, thanks to you, I'm not that innocent."

"And I wouldn't have it any other way."

Chapter Thirty-Five

Edward woke to the delicious smell of boiling pumpkin and sweet spices and realized that Sarah must have chosen this day to take on the piles of pumpkins and gourds in the small barn. He glanced out the window and saw that it was a clear day, but the wind blew, sending some fresh leaves in gentle swirls to the ground. He decided it was a *gut* time to slip away to Joe's to see how Sarah's birthday spice box was coming along.

He dressed hurriedly and went into the kitchen, only to find Ernest and Clara there, already helping their big sister. "I'm sorry I overslept," he said, moving to kiss Sarah on her temple. She nodded and smiled, clearly absorbed in her work.

"I'm going to run over to Joe's for a bit, if that's okay with you."

"Hmm? *Ach*, fine . . . but Edward, can you stop at Ben's and pick up some more cinnamon?" she asked, stirring a big pot of pumpkin cubes.

"All right, sweet."

He said good-bye to Ernest and Clara, then stepped out onto the porch, only to nearly slip on a large tarp spread there, filled with pumpkin guts. He shook his head as he navigated the stairs. . . . *When Sarah does something, she goes all out . . . and I am blessed in that.*

He started to whistle, going down the path, when he noticed Mahlon rather hanging around near the large oak at the foot of the hill. He called to his father-in-law, glad to see him up and around.

"Mahlon . . . how are you?"

"I be fine, *buwe*, thanks to our Sarah and the Hand of *Gott*."

Edward nodded. "I know. Sometimes I feel that I'm fine because of her."

But Edward sensed that there was something more the older man wanted to talk about, so he kept walking and Mahlon fell into step with him, finally giving a huge sigh like a big golden retriever.

"Edward, I've got a message for you, and ya probably will find it strange."

Edward smiled. "Okay. Go ahead."

Mahlon drew a deep breath. "It's from yer grandfather, Elijah King."

The smile slipped from Edward's face and he stopped dead still. "My grandfather? He's been dead since I was a child."

"I know, and I debated inside ta tell ya or not, but it feels right to say."

Edward swallowed. "Can you start at the beginning?"

Mahlon ran a hand under his hat, then looked

280

Edward square in the eye. "It's like this . . . I wuz dyin', I think, and I started to see folks who'd gone on before . . . my *mamm*, a doctor, folks like that. But then there came a man I didn't know but who looked like you—a big fella. He said his name was Elijah King, and ta tell you to answer this one question. . . ."

Edward waited impatiently while Mahlon took out a blue checkered hankie and ponderously blew his nose.

"And then?" Edward prompted.

"The question was—how do you forgive yourself? He said if ya could answer that, then you'd be free."

Edward puzzled over the words, then felt a familiar sinking sickness pulsing in his chest and knew he was having another panic attack. *Just great . . . I go two weeks without panic and then my dead grandfather, who gave me my first drink, shows up to make me miserable. . . .*

Mahlon must have sensed that Edward was feeling ill and shook his head. " 'Tis sorry I am to give you such words. Maybe they're foolishness, *sohn*, the ramblings of a fever dream— even though they sure felt real."

Edward reached out and patted the other man's sleeve, trying to pace his breathing. "It's all right. I appreciate that you gave me the message and I will think about it." *A lot. Like forever, and never come to an answer . . .*

Mahlon gave him a bone-crunching hug and they parted ways at Ben's store. Edward decided to go inside to seek some cinnamon and some advice.

Canning pumpkin was supposed to be relatively easy, but *Grossmuder* May had had a bumper crop and Sarah began to think that there would be no end to the pumpkins Edward kept hauling from the smaller barn.

They finally got some sort of system down. Clara sat outside on the tarp with a rubber apron on and cut the pumpkins in half from top to bottom. Then she'd scrape out the seeds and pulp, leaving the flesh clean. Then Ernest would bring the readied pumpkin into the *haus* and they'd slice it into one-inch-wide wedges and cut it into one-inch cubes. Then Sarah would boil it for two minutes, add spices, and transfer the whole thing into sterilized quart jars, pouring water from the pot over the cubes to cover them.

Then the entire routine had to be repeated again.

"I'm sure glad for your help," Sarah told Ernest and Clara while she stepped out of the steamy kitchen to catch a breath of cool air on the front porch.

"*Ach*, we love to help," Clara declared, and Ernest gave a mumbling assent.

"You don't know how nice it'll be to add my

own canning to *Grossmuder* May's in the root cellar. It feels like I'm really a *hausfrau* now or something." Sarah laughed.

"Because of pumpkin?" Ernest snorted.

But Sarah saw Clara lift her eyes to meet hers in gentle mutual understanding, and she was very glad she had a sister at that moment.

Edward entered Ben's store and completely forgot about the cinnamon. He walked the length of the place, going to the back where Ben worked his second job as a bootmaker. The jolly man was at it now, his large apron tied about his hulking frame as he carefully pounded on an upside-down boot set on a form.

"*Ach*, Edward . . . *gut* to see ya. You *kumme* wanting more dress material for your wife?" Ben teased.

"*Nee*." Edward helped himself to a black licorice whip from the jar on the counter. "I actually need some advice."

"Advice?" Ben looked pleased and put down his hammer. "Well, then, you've *kumme* to the right place, Edward. Tell me all about it."

"Well—" Edward drew a deep breath. "Do you believe in ghosts, Ben?"

"Ghosts? *Nee* . . . why, do you know one?" There was an expression of complete seriousness on Ben's face and Edward almost laughed, but then he remembered his own panic.

"*Nee*, I don't know one but I've had sort of a message from one and I . . ."

Ben picked up his hammer and started to pound. "Can't really stop to talk now, Edward. I'm sure everything will be all right. Perfectly fine."

Edward sighed, sucking on his licorice. Clearly Ben was of the superstitious sort, as many of the Mountain *Amisch* were, but Edward had never suspected it of the hulking store owner.

Edward waved good-bye and headed out, deciding he might as well check on the spice box as he'd intended.

Chapter Thirty-Six

Sarah was hot and tired when she heard Clara's squeal of dismay. Sarah ran outside to the porch and promptly slipped into the huge pile of pumpkin guts and felt the distinct urge to gag. *I'm pregnant . . . I know it.* Clara tried to help her up but ended up falling herself. Sarah looked up and saw Ernest gazing down at them with disgust.

"Clara, whatever is the problem?" Sarah asked, flinging stringy strands of pumpkin off her hands.

"It's Blackie. He's hiding—under there."

Clara pointed a sticky finger to the highest

mound of pumpkin innards. Sure enough, Sarah could see the little whiskery face peeking out with seeds plastered all over the dog's ears and nose. Sarah started to laugh and then Clara laughed, and finally Ernest gave in as he reached to dig the dog out.

"You want me to give him a bath, Sarah?" Ernest asked.

"*Nee*, not until we're done. I have the feeling he'll only get in it again."

"That is one *narrisch* dog," Ernest said, shaking his head.

"*Ach*, but so cute," Clara pronounced.

"All right, back to work." Sarah sighed. "Ernest, how many more pumpkins do we have in the barn? We should be getting to the end, right?"

Her *bruder* gave her a glum look. "I think we may have about sixty, Sarah. You'll be eating pumpkin from now until eternity."

Sarah drew a deep breath. It was not the *Amisch* way to waste anything, so she knew what she had to do; she just wished Edward would hurry home to make the work go a bit faster. . . .

Joseph tilted his dark head to one side and seemed to be thinking carefully. "How do you forgive yourself? Answer the question and then you'll be free . . . All right, it's a mystery. Let's tear it apart."

"You mean you're going to take it seriously?" Edward asked, half in disbelief, half glad.

"Sure . . . why not? *Gott* speaks to us in many ways. This may be how he's speaking to you. Sooo . . . How do you forgive yourself? You've got to ask yourself what you need to forgive yourself for, I guess. And then you get some kind of freedom for the answer. . . . Well, what kind of freedom do you need?"

Edward shrugged. "I'd like to be free of these feelings of panic I have every time talk of *Grossdaudi kummes* up. It's a miserable way to feel, and then I start anticipating the next attack, so it all becomes a vicious cycle."

"All right," Joe said. "Ask *Gott* to show you how to be free of those feelings. Maybe even free of *Grossdaudi* himself. I could pray with you right now, if you'd like."

Edward stared at the floor with its faint clutter of wood shavings and was immediately humbled by his *bruder*'s offer. "You know, Joe," he said throatily, "there was a time not too long ago when I might have laughed had you suggested praying together, but I—I've changed, and I'd appreciate it very much."

"*Gut* enough." Joe nodded. Then he began to pray. "Dear Heavenly *Fater*, You who made us all. We ask that You would bring comfort and wisdom to Edward, that he would have the discernment necessary to understand what true freedom is, and that it comes from You. In the name of *Derr Herr* . . ."

Edward stepped forward and gave his *bruder* a hug. It felt *gut* and true, and he felt cleaner inside than he had in a long while. "Thanks, Joe."

"No worries. Now let's take a look at Sarah's spice box."

Edward watched as Joe uncovered a round object on one of the workbenches. The circular cherry box shone with many coatings of lacquer, and Edward smiled in pleased surprise at the workmanship and fine grain of the wood.

"It's beautiful, Joe."

"Wait till you see inside." He carefully removed the lid, and inside were fourteen boxes, all fitted together and each carved from a different wood type.

"The *buwes* and I wanted to get creative, so you've got everything from oak to chestnut to pine in there and a lot of other woods in between. Each box is finished so that she can safely store whatever spice she likes without worrying about the smell of the wood bleeding over into the scent of the spice. I'm rather proud of the workmanship, and I think you gave us an idea for doing a few more of these for folks hereabouts."

Edward picked up each tiny box and felt its smoothness and the superb fit of the lid. Then he hugged his *bruder* again. "I love it, Joe, and I know Sarah will, too."

• • •

Edward hurried home, realizing how much time had passed while he'd gone seeking advice. He hadn't wanted to leave Sarah with all the work of canning and was glad when his own front porch came into sight. He carefully stepped around the laden tarp, only to jump out of his skin when the orangey mass started to move. Edward froze, staring down at the top of the pile, thinking he'd truly lost his mind.

Then Blackie poked his seed-covered head out and Edward laughed in relief. Sarah must have heard him because she came out of the door, none too clean herself. "Edward, did you bring the cinnamon?"

"Cinnamon . . . *ach*, Sarah. I'm sorry. I forgot. Do you want me to go back, sweet?"

"*Nee*," she sighed tiredly.

"Well, then, let me help. Where are Ernest and Clara?"

"I sent them home. They were pretty much exhausted."

"As are you, my love. I can see it in your face. Why not leave the rest of the pumpkins to feed the stock this winter?"

"Stock?" she asked.

"We need a milch cow or two, especially if— when the *kinner kumme*. So I thought I'd go to an auction sometime soon and bring us home a few gentle cows."

"*Ach.*" She looked incredibly relieved. "I would so love if the pumpkins remaining could feed the stock."

He laughed and pulled her close, pumpkin seeds and all. "And I would so love to help you clean up the kitchen and give you a bath. What do you say?"

She kissed him lingeringly in response.

That evening, Sarah took a lantern and made Edward tramp down to the pantry with her to look at the rows upon rows of quart jars of freshly canned pumpkin. "It's the first of our fruits," she explained when he didn't quite understand her fascination.

"*Ach* . . . you mean the first thing we put up that will last?"

"*Jah.*" Her voice lowered. "That and the *boppli* I'm carrying." She arched a brow at him, and he laughed.

"You're so sure?"

"I got sick to my stomach today when I slipped in the pumpkin guts, and I never get queasy over anything."

He pulled her close and ran a hand over her soft belly. "Hmm . . . then maybe we're in for a long nine months, sweet."

She shrugged, leaning into his hand. "Maybe. You'd better be prepared."

Chapter Thirty-Seven

The autumn days shortened and the leaves began to fall from the trees, creating a rich tapestry on the paths and hillsides, along with the bumpy fall of horse chestnuts and black walnuts. Sarah grew restless as her morning sickness increased, and though there was more than enough to do between her healing duties and preparing the cabin for winter, she always wanted to go for an afternoon walk, and Edward and Blackie were more than happy to oblige her.

This day, she set out determinedly, her small footsteps trailing through the leaves, until Edward asked idly where they were going.

"I'd like to walk back behind Jude and Mary's cabin, far back in those woods, and drink from the cold creek water."

Edward couldn't bring himself to say anything. *She wants to walk right past where my* Grossdaudi's *cabin was or is—whatever is left of it. . . . And she knows about the so-called message. . . . Could she know something more?* The thought left him cold and his hands began to sweat. Still, there was something to be said about facing your fears with the one you loved, so he let himself follow her through the woods.

They paused at Jude and Mary's cabin but no

one was home, and Edward felt his anxiety ratchet up a notch when he didn't get the anticipated reprieve from heading straight into the forest. But he walked grimly on, and even Blackie grew silent the deeper they went into the woods.

Suddenly, Sarah caught his hand. "*Ach*, Edward. I don't know why I felt the urge to *kumme* here today, but there is something restless in my spirit that longs for you to have this freedom my *fater* spoke of. . . . But I brought you here without asking and now it's too late. . . ."

He was about to ask why it was too late when they came upon the site of the abandoned cabin. Edward stopped still as the floodgates of his memories opened and he saw himself with his grandfather inside the dilapidated place. The once well-blocked chimney had lost many of its stones, and creeping moss and vines plunged through the hole in the roof where the beams had caved in. Surprising bits of color stood out, though: his grandfather's bowl and pitcher, unbroken, bone white with a blue pattern of flowers around the top, and the bright red of the bed quilt, clearly the home to mice and squirrels yet still whole in memory. Edward stepped closer, remembering the bed the last time he had seen it.

"How do you forgive yourself?" Sarah asked softly.

He spun around to face her, his face wet with

the tears that welled, unbidden, from his eye. "Tell me how to do it then," he cried. "Tell me how I'm supposed to forgive myself for what I did."

"What have you done?" she asked, and he stared at her as if she was mad.

"You know . . ." He gasped, reaching down to catch her arms in his. "Dear *Gott*, somehow you know."

She shook her head, her hair coming loose to fall from her *kapp* and cover his hands. "*Nee*, Edward, please . . . tell me. What have you done?"

And then she watched as he bent his head and sank to his knees in front of her, his sobs echoing against the stillness of the trees.

He was nine years old, visiting his grossdaudi *in his small cabin deep in the woods. The familiar still stood outside, almost blending with the fall leaves on the dipping tree limbs. But the fire was out . . . strange. He scampered to the door of the cabin and it gave easily beneath his sturdy hand. He entered, peering into the gloom of the unlit room. He saw his grandfather lying half-dressed on the pine frame bed. Blood trickled from the side of his bearded mouth and he clearly worked for breath. Edward felt the* auld *dark eyes lock with his, and his grandfather made a weak motion with one gnarled hand.*

"Geh . . . help."

Go get help . . . Edward turned and ran, banging out of the cabin door and tearing outside. His foot caught on the still, and suddenly the whole mysterious contraption collapsed into a heap on the ground, burning his legs with the remaining hot and pungent alcohol. Edward thought of the beating he was sure to receive for destroying his grandfather's prize possession and forgot about his need to get help. Instead, he took off for the auld deserted Bear's Cave . . . to wait, to hide. . . .

"Coward," he choked out at her feet. "I was a coward and I let him die."

Sarah dropped down in front of him and grasped his shoulders hard. "*Nee*, Edward, you were a child, a young child. And he was going to die anyway. There's nothing that could have been done for him. *Grossmuder* May's journal gives proof of that."

He shook his head. "How could something so small—a still—be the cost of my grandfather's life? How could I do it?"

"Edward," Sarah said firmly, "answer the question—the one he asked of you. How do you forgive yourself?"

Edward closed his eye and sank back on his legs. He felt himself shivering but knew it wasn't from the cold. He saw himself as a little *buwe*, almost ran past himself, governed by fear. Fear of

a beating. Fear of losing his grandfather's still —
not thinking that he might build another, and
then the truth—the terrible fear of losing his
grandfather like he'd lost his *mamm* . . . And the
abject loneliness of knowing that there was
no turning back from death and its brutal
finality . . . no matter how much a young boy
might beg of *Gott*.

Edward opened his eye and looked at his wife.
He realized that she was crying, too, tears for
him, for who he'd been. He drew a deep
shuddering breath. "You forgive yourself by
realizing that you're not the one in control; *Gott*
is . . . And even if He seems harsh or strange
sometimes, He acts with love in the end."

Sarah sniffed and nodded, reaching out to
take both of his hands in hers. "Edward, do you
still feel panicked?"

He searched within himself and realized he
didn't, that it seemed as if a large burden had
been rolled away and he was left feeling clean
and whole. He knew he wasn't likely to have a
panic attack again, but even if he did, he'd work
through it somehow with Sarah's help.

He got to his feet, then helped her up. They both
stood looking at the old cabin. "Do you want
Joseph to rebuild this place for you, Edward?"
she asked gently after a moment.

He shook his head. "*Nee*, but I would like you
to go with me to visit my grandfather's grave. I

think I'd like to plant a tree there in his memory."

She stroked his chest with soothing fingers. "That would be nice."

He bent and kissed the top of her head. "*Danki*, Sarah, for loving me enough to help me answer all of life's difficult questions—even the ones from long ago."

"I know you would do the same for me, my love."

And they stood in mutual faith and accord, a new day beginning in their hearts.

Chapter Thirty-Eight

Today I left my old life behind, may *Gott* have mercy on me. I'm going to the place called Ice Mountain, far from the brutal hands that held me. I realize that I am called to be a healer like Frau Zug, and I will do my best to find freedom both for myself and for the others whom I serve. . . . I have also *kumme* to the point and place where I can thank *Derr Herr* for my gone husband. . . . He taught me— brutally—to be strong. And I will survive and use my strength to serve *Gott* as well.

May

Sarah closed the journal with a relieved sigh and felt a kinship with *Grossmuder* May even though the older woman's life had been so very different from her own.

"Sarah?" She looked up as Edward poked his head into the bedroom. "It's time to go."

"I know. I guess I just don't like all the focus to be on me—even the dressing was hard."

He came in and pulled her gently from the bed. "It's your birthday, sweet, and you deserve to have a celebration."

She smiled at him, reaching up to touch his long blond hair. "I think our baby will have blond hair."

He smiled. "Are you going to tell everyone tonight?"

"*Jah.*" She gave him a shy look. "Unless you'd like to."

"I'd be glad to," he told her proudly. "But before we go, I have a surprise for you."

"What is it? I do love surprises."

He laughed, then went to his dresser and withdrew a large square package, neatly wrapped in blue paper with a small bow.

"*Ach,* what is it?" she asked.

"Isn't that the point?" he teased. "Open it."

She sat down on the bed and slowly undid the paper to reveal a large light green–covered book. She opened it only to find blank pages inside. She looked up at him in question and he sat down next to her.

"It's a journal—like *Grossmuder* May's, but for

you to write your adventures in healing. . . . I thought you'd like to leave your own story for our *kinner*."

She flung her arms around his neck and kissed him with exuberant enthusiasm. "*Ach*, Edward, it's so wonderful. I never would have thought of it for myself. . . . Thank you."

He reached in his shirt pocket and handed her a pen. "I'll leave you for a minute, shall I? So you can start your first entry?" He bent and kissed her head and walked out.

She listened to his footsteps recede, then bent over the first blank page.

Dear Journal . . .
 Sometimes the greatest loves in life start out as the most complicated, and this makes them all the more worthwhile. . . .

Sarah King

Epilogue

One year and nine months later

It was a warm sticky morning in mid-July on Ice Mountain. The ice in the mine was at its peak, even spilling out beneath the confines of the baseboards and sending chill air to the wild ferns that grew there and nowhere else. The meadowlarks called to one another in the trees near the King cabin and it smelled deliciously of the promise of rain.

Edward glanced at Sarah, where she lay on top of the quilts, a brief shift covering her rounded pregnant belly. Another child . . . he marveled, looking over to the crib where a delicious morsel of humanity slept for the moment.

Edward pulled on his pants and went to look down into the crib, only to find the wide gray eyes open and a welcoming smile on the *buwe*'s face. Very gently, Edward reached down and gathered his little *sohn* to him, rubbing at the thatch of blond hair that was beginning to cover the typical first year baldness and marveling once more at the two tiny pearls in the bottom of his mouth. "It's your birthday, sweet," Edward crooned.

"Dint," the baby said emphatically.

Edward interpreted. "Drink?"

"*Jah*. Dint."

Edward smiled and took the child out into the kitchen, situating him in his carved wooden highchair, a gift from *Oncle* Joe, and went to the sink for the silver cup that he and Sarah had bought at the fall festival oh so long ago. He poured a bit of grape juice inside, then handed it carefully to the baby, who took it with fair coordination and only had a little trickle down the folds of his neck and belly.

Edward just sat and admired his *sohn*, something he did quite a lot.

"Hello."

He turned to see Sarah standing in the doorway, looking incredibly beautiful. Her breasts strained with pregnancy against the batiste fabric and her belly did the same, while her long hair fell in sleepy disarray about her hips.

"Hello," he returned, feeling it was an inadequate way to greet such rare beauty.

"You know, you're really *gut* with him." She walked barefoot into the kitchen and laid her hand on her *sohn*'s head, then moved to bend and give Edward a sultry kiss that sent his blood racing.

"Don't kiss me like that," he tenderly admonished. "I wouldn't want to have my way with a very pregnant woman."

She leaned against him and he gently rubbed her belly, feeling the movement there. "Well," Sarah asked lightly, "are you ready for another delivery?"

Edward squeezed his eyes shut and shook his head. "Dear *Gott*, don't remind me. . . ."

Nine months to the day she'd told him she'd conceived in the tall grass of the field, she'd gone into labor, but she hadn't cared to share that point with him until it was too late to do anything but deliver the babe himself. He realized now that he should have been suspicious

—her quiet pacing, her frequent trips to the
outhaus, *and then wanting him out of the*
bedroom for minutes at a time. Finally, she'd
entered the kitchen with an excited, triumphant
glow to her face. "I'm at eight centimeters,"
she'd announced. He'd almost fallen off his
chair.

"What? How do you—what?"

"I checked myself," she said breezily. "We
should be at ten soon and ready to go."

"Where are we going?" he'd asked in
desperation, praying she'd made some womanly
plan he didn't know about. Right now, even
Martha Umble was looking pretty good. . . .

"Nowhere, silly. Everything's ready for you
and I'll tell you what to do." She'd wandered
back into the bedroom and he'd followed
frantically, glancing with horror at the sheets
she'd spread out on the bed and the little basin
of bits and pieces—nursing paraphernalia—
that he was not going to touch, no matter
what. . . .

But then she caught hold of his arm and
squeezed, a sound of abject pain wrung from
between her lips, and she looked at him. "Oh, I
have to push."

He snapped into motion, helping her to the
bed, rolling up his shirtsleeves . . . and then it was
all a wonderfully horrifying blur while she
shouted instructions and he mutely obeyed—

blood, fluid, tying, clipping, the whole thing like an orchestrated attack on his senses. And then that first cry and the realization that he had a sohn.

"It's a buwe, *" he said, marveling at the slippery body in his hands.*

"Wrap him up," Sarah said calmly, like she was asking for a Christmas package to go.

Edward marveled at her and then handed her her sohn, *carefully cocooned in a clean blanket. She unashamedly put the baby to her breast, guiding the little mouth and untucking the tiny lip until the nipple latch was just right. Edward started to cry and she reached one hand to touch his hair.*

"A sohn, *and you were wonderful, Sarah."*

"So were you," she said softly. "What shall we call him?"

Edward swiped at his eye. "I have an idea, but maybe you won't like it. . . ."

She smiled at him. "Elijah? Elijah Edward King? A chance for a new life . . . restoration. I think it's a fine name."

Edward nodded, not even surprised that she knew and understood. But then he drew a deep breath and caught her gaze. "But Sarah, I am never going to deliver another one of our children again."

"Well, whyever not?" She sounded surprised and he groaned. . . .

●●●

The rain came in the afternoon, just before Eli's birthday party was due to start. Joseph and Priscilla came with Hollie and their baby, John, whom they considered a red-haired wonder, like his mother. Sarah's whole extended family came as well as Edward's, pushing the little cabin to its limits but filling the walls with joy.

Edward caught Joseph's eye over a slice of red velvet cake. "I think we may need to build the cabin out a bit."

"*Jah.*" Joseph smiled. "Especially if you continue to produce *kinner* at the rate you're going."

"Will you do the plans?" Edward asked his big *bruder*, feeling so grateful that there was now a loving accord between them.

"I'll start tomorrow," Joe promised.

Edward gazed around the kitchen, drinking in the love of family and friends, babies and blessings, and the love of his heart, his wife, his joy. . . . This was freedom.

Center Point Large Print
600 Brooks Road / PO Box 1
Thorndike, ME 04986-0001 USA

(207) 568-3717

US & Canada:
1 800 929-9108
www.centerpointlargeprint.com